Michael Ralph Fredericks

LIGAI NDOLKAH
(WHITE COUGAR)

AUSTIN MACAULEY PUBLISHERS™

LONDON * CAMBRIDGE * NEW YORK * SHARJAH

A CIP catalogue record for this title is available from the British Library.

ISBN 9781398410312 (Paperback)
ISBN 9781398410329 (ePub e-book)

www.austinmacauley.com

First Published 2022
Austin Macauley Publishers Ltd®
1 Canada Square
Canary Wharf
London
E14 5AA

Foreword

This story has been with me for a long time. I wanted to write it because it seemed to me something I had experienced, almost as a former life. However, the astonishing thing was that the more I researched the details of what I envisaged, the more factual aspects of reality came to light.

Although this is a work of fiction, you will recognise certain things that seem familiar.

Ligai Ndolkah	White Cougar
Apache	Enemy
Ndee	Own people
Wickiup	Buffalo hide or brush covered wooden home
Tipi	Mobile buffalo hide home
Shis-Inday	People of the mountain forests
Mescalero	People of the mescal (agave)/one of the Apache tribes
Faraones	Pharaoh
Goshe	Dog
Bienvenidos	Welcome
San Vicente de la Ciénega	St. Vincent of the Marsh
Matrilineal	Society based on the female line
Mesilla/Las Cruces	A small town, village, pueblo
Muchacho	Comrade/friend
Chiricahua	One of the American Apache tribes

Chapter One

He awoke as usual, spluttering and gasping for breath, leaning over and shooting black sputum and some blood into the spittoon by his bed. Gradually, his wheezing and the heaving eased as he sat up. He took some more of the laudanum at his bed-side table and there was increasing relief as the drug took hold.

The sun was just appearing as the light brightened. He looked at the watery yellowish colouring over the hills as he opened the curtains. The sky was blue, that May morning in 1865. Today was to be his last day in England, leaving his West Derby home and setting off for the Americas.

John Lawson was 16. He had been diagnosed with consumption by the doctors. They could do nothing for him and had told his parents that the only hope was for him to seek out a dry climate. The North-West of England was hardly conducive to his health. Despite his problems, John was still quite tall, already nearly six feet tall. Although pale and pallid, quite skinny and not too much over nine stones or 130 pounds, he had high cheek bones, piercing blue eyes and reddish-blonde hair.

The large rambling house was typical of that owned by the landed gentry of the mid-19th Century. The grey brick resembled the landscape and the shadowy hills. The Lawson family had not made its money from the land. Their fortune was from the sea. The Lawson Line had traded the oceans for nearly two generations since the end of the Napoleonic Wars. John's father, George, was the head of the company which had been founded by John's late grandfather, William. George had seen the biggest growth to the business.

Despite the American Civil War, business with the United States had continued. There had been the collapse in the cotton and tobacco trades with the demise of the South. There was still corn, furs and American timber. Cotton and sugar were sourced from as far away as Egypt and the Caribbean. The exports from England were manufactured clothing, mainly cotton from the Lancashire mills, machine tools, arms, railway parts, including timbers, and last, but not least, emigrants, especially destitute Irish people seeking a change of fortune.

Things were slowly returning to some sort of normality. The war had ended in April. The President, Abraham Lincoln, had also been assassinated. Andrew Johnson had replaced him and seen through the final surrender. It was not the greatest period to be visiting. However, time was not on John's side.

The Lawsons were an unusual family of their day. William had been a great supporter of William Wilberforce and the anti-slavery movement of the 1830s. The business ethics were run as a social enterprise of today. Oh sure, the company had to be profitable and make money. It had not got involved with the Secession States or taken any moral posture. Some Liverpool companies had even made reparations to the South to keep trade and links going.

The people, who worked for William and now George, were very loyal. The owners treated this as a family concern and the employees felt they were part of the family. In what was a very dangerous occupation, workers knew they would be looked after and, in the event of anything more serious, so would their families. It meant that the ships had good crews, men who knew they could rely on one another and who had great trust. They all knew about John's plight. They liked him and admired his resolution to fight his illness and they were prepared to help him accordingly in whichever way they could.

Whatever else had happened to him, John had not neglected his education. Because of his illness, he tended to be sedentary to avoid setting off excessive breathing difficulties and that painful coughing. He was well-read. He had studied the family business, looked into the law, understood sailing and engineering and, in mixing with sailors at the port, had learned Spanish from their matelots when they docked. He had developed his art and his bedroom was full of his landscapes and seascapes. His eye for detail showed in the pictures of the old brigs, schooners, tri-masters and clippers. Recent pictures showed the more modern steam ships and packets that now traversed the Atlantic. His sense of colour showed in the shades of blue and grey hues of the sea and the greens and browns of the landscapes. He was also good at pictures of people; not portraits nor caricatures, but a likeness to features.

When he had been well enough, John had gone out with the hunt. He knew how to ride and he knew how to shoot. In fact, he was a good shot, decisive and accurate. He loved horses and dogs and had an affinity with both. It wasn't soft love. John showed he could be firm with animals but he also eschewed an understanding of the way they thought. In that way, they knew who was boss but they also knew that John was caring and would look after them.

So today was the day he was leaving this behind. He was setting sail on the SS 'Crosby', bound from Liverpool to New York in search of the last adventure or a possible cure. Both John and his family were totally realistic about what he was doing and why he was doing it. The family company had arranged things well in advance with the various American banks. John would be able to obtain bank drafts in several places to get whatever money he needed. It would be impossible for him to carry too much anyway and he'd need provisions and clothing throughout his journey.

John moved away from the windows and slowly over to the basin. He poured in the water from an ewer and had a good wash. The effort made him splutter and cough, again bringing that deep rasping of his throat which accompanied it. He dressed, wearing a wool sweater, slacks and boots. Lastly, he took his comb, brush and toothbrush, putting them into his trouser pocket. Without a glance back, John closed the bedroom door.

"Good morning, darling," said Ann.

"Morning, Mother," came the reply, as John gingerly made his way down the steps of the wooden staircase. "How are you this morning?" she said, as she laid her hand on his elbow. He looked at her soft brown eyes and he could see the slight puffiness and the tears she had shed through the night. He kissed her on the cheek. "Alright," he said. There was a lot to say on this last morning. Strangely, neither of them could summon up the words with both of them plucking up the courage to remain stoic and brave. George came bounding down the steps, a big man with a ginger beard, full of bonhomie and roaring "What a beautiful day!" But even he was somewhat more subdued than was his norm.

Mary, the maid, came in with a trolley with breakfasts for them all; fruit, eggs, bread and tea. The sun rays were like strobe lights fluttering through the curtains waving in the light breeze. The birds were singing in the garden outside the dining room as they sat down. Nobody said much. Nor did they eat much. It was too momentous an occasion and everyone was a little choked.

With the meal over, John departed the table, so he could clean up before the start of his journey. George went out to the stable to harness the trap to the horse for the journey to the docks. He brought it back to the front door. Giles, the butler, had collected all of John's gear. There was the roll bag, which was to be his main travelling luggage, but additionally, there was a trunk which would be left on the ship when it returned to Liverpool.

They had decided, beforehand, that Ann would say her goodbyes at the house. It was too painful for her to travel to the docks and, maybe, show her emotions in public. Even in those days, people would have understood but Ann wanted to shed her tears in private. George and John would handle that parting in a more stoic manner if she wasn't there.

The little party stood outside the house. Mary was hiding her tears as best as she could and gave John a hug and a kiss on the cheek. Giles shook his hand and each of them put one arm around the other's shoulder. Finally, John took his mother in his arms and squeezed her tightly.

"Don't fret, Mamma dear," he said. "I shall be alright. Just you wait and see." That was too much for Ann. She gave him a last kiss and turned and ran up the palatial steps back into the house. George gave Mary one of those knowing looks and she scurried after her mistress.

Giles stepped back as father and son climbed onto the trap. George lifted the brake and summoned the reins to move the horse forward. They trotted down the drive and onto the lane leading to the city.

"Well, at least you have a good day to sail," said George. "It should be calm and the weather seems set fair for you. Maybe, that's a good omen?"

"May be," murmured John in reply. "We'll see."

They said little else during the journey. Neither was of a mind to discuss trivia. "Have you remembered this or forgotten that?" The die was cast.

They arrived at the Albert Dock alongside the berth of their ship, the steam packet named the 'Crosby'. All of the company's ships were named after places in the locality of their Merseyside home.

Several of the men were hard at work on the last-minute preparation so that the ship could take advantage of the eleven o'clock tide. Many of them waved from the deck as George and John appeared. They were met by Captain Nathan Harrison and the Boatswain Joseph Young.

George was never slow on the uptake and sensed immediately that something was wrong. "Morning, Harrison, Young. Where's Adams?" James Adams was first mate and would traditionally have been expected to meet the boarding party.

"Morning, sir," responded Harrison, as he removed his cap. "We have a problem."

"Fill me in," said the owner.

"Several of our men were having their last drinks in the town, yesterday evening, before we set sail. They were set upon in the 'Black Goose' Tavern by a gang working for the Doughtys."

"So what happened?"

"In the race to escape, Jimmy tripped and he was hit over the head with a baton. We think he was shanghaied to a ship that sailed on the overnight tide and set for the Americas. It's a brig with green sails and doesn't have our legs. We believe it's called 'The Shamrock'."

"What are you saying?" George mused. He knew the answer already.

"I've spoken to the men already and they are of a like mind. Many of their crew are not true seamen. We can outstrip them in the next two to three days and get him back. You know we look after our own. Loyalty means everything to us and we know it does to you." Captain Harrison knew how to manage emotions. George was under no illusions either. He looked at John, standing alongside him, and spoke quietly, calmly. "Well!"

"No choice, Dad," said the young man. "You have bigger things to worry about than me and my health. With what awaits me, wherever I am, wherever I go, you know I will have to face dangers and risks. At least here, I have friends who will look after me. You know it's the right thing to do. There's no debate."

George felt his heart ache and his breast swell with pride at his son's words. He maintained a cool and calm demeanour, looking steadfastly at John, and then turned to Captain Harrison.

"It seems the decision's made. There's nothing further to say. Good voyage, captain." He was about to add, "Look after my lad" but thought better of it. They were all family of a sort and no one had to be singled out.

"Aye aye, sir," Harrison replied. He then added the answer to the question that hadn't been asked. "And I'll take the greatest of care of John."

The old man looked at his son. He shook his hand to say goodbye. Then, for once, the emotion took over and they embraced. The hands had unloaded everything for the voyage from the trap. John turned and walked up the gangplank followed by the captain and the boatswain. George also turned and then, without a glance back, climbed onto the trap and rode off back home.

The crew and the dockside labourers untied the hawsers, raised the walkways and the anchor. The Crosby was ready to depart and with a hoot, moved out easily into the Mersey. The ebb flow was beginning to gain pace and the ship gathered speed downstream.

John had walked up on the bridge and took once last glance back at the city, now disappearing rapidly behind them. He wondered if it would be the last time he would ever see it and immediately shut all morbid thoughts from his head. Instead, he took in the newly built feature of the Liver Building and the two symbols of home and welcome, the Liver Birds. He then turned away to watch the ship headed out, past the Wirral to the port, and into the Irish Sea.

The sea started to become choppier. There was more of a swell. The white horses were becoming more prevalent and John was feeling a little nauseous. He decided to leave the bridge and return to his cabin.

The men were working hard both above and below deck. There was a renewed vigour in the engine room as the stokers maintained the coal supplies into the furnace. Up top, the crew was checking all the ship's guns, forward, aft, starboard and larboard. All merchant ships were well-armed to deal with pirates, particularly if they had to trade in the Caribbean. This crew had a mission, a focus. It would take some luck to find 'The Shamrock', but they were all determined to give it their best shot. Jimmy Adams wasn't just the first mate. He was a friend. The decision for the chase had come from them. Nathan and Joseph had just concurred.

Chapter Two

Despite the prevailing south-westerly wind and the increasing swell as the Crosby neared the Atlantic, the ship made good headway. It also gave the crew good heart as they chased down the sailing ship. The steamship would be gaining rapidly in these conditions. Ships heading for the Americas followed regular shipping lanes. There was logic to this. If any vessel got into trouble, there was a better chance of rescue.

The usual trip to the United States was around five to seven days for a steamship and ten to twelve for a sailing vessel. They rounded Ireland just before nightfall and headed into the wind and the waves. Having got over his initial queasiness, John was feeling better and came up on deck to watch the sunset.

The crew was putting out the lights so that the ship could be seen. As the dusk set in, it became clear that there were other ships around them. Their specks of light sparkled through the spray.

Nathan Harrison approached. "Are you feeling better?" he asked. John replied that he was not quite as bad as he had felt earlier. The captain insisted he got some food and liquid inside his body and asked him to his cabin to join him for the evening meal.

Nathan had also asked Joseph to join them. They had lime juice and rum to drink. The meal was boiled beef, carrots and potatoes, followed by a spotted dick and custard pudding. Everyone on Lawson ships had the same fare. There were no special privileges for rank. Everyone mattered on the board. Illness or weakness put pressure on the rest of the crew. It wasn't altruism. It was plain common sense in maintaining the wellbeing and morale of everyone on board. Even if a family member travelled, there was no special dispensation, other than the usual decorum afforded to ladies. They were normally allowed to take over the captain's quarters and the captain went into the spare cabin.

Because of John's condition, neither Nathan nor Joseph smoked after the meal. The captain spoke.

"If my calculations are right, we should come across the Shamrock by around the middle of the day tomorrow. We are at least fifty percent faster and we gave them a twelve-hour start. Assuming we are headed along the same lanes and they do not suspect we are chasing them, we have a chance."

"Do we know where they are headed?" asked Joseph.

"We think it's one of the American ports rather than the West Indies," said Nathan. "However, if we are wrong, that's it. They could be miles away in any direction."

They sat quietly for a few minutes, wrapped up in their own thoughts.

"OK! Let's get down to business." Nathan was in captain's mode once again. "John, if you are up to it I want you to man the port gun. I am not expecting much resistance from the Shamrock. Many of them are pressed men and they won't want to fight a losing cause. You are a good shot and you'll be clear of any close contact. It makes sure I have every man in the crew available in case there is trouble."

"I'll not let you down," John replied.

"I know you won't." said the captain. He turned to the boatswain. "Joseph, I'll want you to lead the boarding party. You'll have to prepare the small arms out of the munitions chest and make sure every man is adequately supplied."

Nathan cleared the table. "This is the plan." He used the crockery and cutlery to demonstrate the detailed approach. John and Joseph listened intently. "I'll brief the men at morning call and, between us Joseph, we'll designate who does what and when. The rest is up to luck and the weather conditions at the time." He looked at his timepiece. "Right, gentlemen, it's time to check the watches. Let's hope I'm right and we don't overtake the Shamrock in the dark."

He turned to the bottle of rum and poured out a small tot for all three of them. He raised the toast. "Here's to success on the morrow."

"To success!" they responded.

While the captain and boatswain checked all was well with the crew and those on the watch, John went up onto the deck. They were still fighting the south-westerly winds but the ship ploughed on regardless. The sky was clear and the stars bright. John looked at Orion, following the line of the belt to point to the Plough and the alignment to the Pole Star. He then went below to try to sleep and to prepare for the morning.

The dawn broke with John in his usual state, waking, coughing and spluttering. After he had sat up for a while, the pain eased and there was less

12

phlegm. The ships' crew were hard at work, either maintaining the ship or getting ready for potential action. Joseph had them cleaning and oiling all the weaponry, priming the guns. The look-outs were posted. The young Midshipman, with his twenty-twenty vision, was in the crow's nest. They spotted several ships, but not the Shamrock, as yet.

One of the galley crew brought John his breakfast which was a porridge or gruel. "Better get summat inside you, Sir," he said.

John replied hoarsely in a gruff whisper. "Thank you!" He didn't feel like eating but he could see he needed to settle himself. "I'll try." The galley boy left him to it. A few minutes later, there was a knock on his door. Captain Harrison walked in.

"How are you this morning, John?"

"Rough," came the reply. John had managed a few mouthfuls of food. Then he forced himself upright. Though he was pale and ashen, he spoke with purpose. "I'll not let you, Jimmy, or the crew down. I am going to do my bit, whatever is needed."

Nathan looked at him intently. John matched his gaze with the blue eyes penetrating and striking deep from the soul. The captain spoke.

"You are a chip off the old block; like father, like son."

In spite of himself, John managed a smile.

"I'll get ready, Sir," he said. "I'm under your orders."

Nathan laughed. "OK, son, I'll leave you to it."

The weather remained fine and dry. The sun was warm. There was little cloud but the sea remained choppy. Several ships were sighted, but not the Shamrock. As the morning turned to afternoon, everyone became increasingly anxious. Were they on the right track? The crew was grim and becoming increasingly perturbed. They had readied themselves for the fight, the adrenalin was up and this was an anti-climax.

It was gone two when the look-out in the crow's nest spotted a sailing ship on the horizon. As they gained on it, it became clear that it was a brig with green sails. The closer the Crosby came, the more activity was seen aboard the sailing ship. They were heading into the wind and were soon to be overtaken. If they turned to run with the wind, they'd be heading straight towards the Crosby. There was nothing for it.

As the ships neared, the activity onboard the Shamrock turned to panic.

"Avast and heave to!" came the shout from Captain Harrison. He was using an improvised cone as a loud hailer.

"This is piracy," screamed Captain Sturridge. "You've got no right to board us or stop us on the high seas."

John sent a short burst of gunfire over the Shamrock and that ended any thought of resistance. There was no way the sailing ship had the firepower or the legs of the steamship.

The Crosby's crew threw over the lines with the grappling hooks attached. The Shamrock's crew were petrified and totally compliant in securing them. They rigged up the boatswain's chair between the ships and Joseph Young led his handpicked team across.

Captain Sturridge still looked belligerent but the colour had drained from his face. The crew stood silently in trepidation of what was going to happen next. One man had his head bandaged.

"Hello Jimmy," said Boatswain Young. "We came for you. How are you?"

"Still with a sore head," came the reply. "I thought you wanted to get rid of me so you could assume the first mate's role." Adams hadn't lost some semblance of humour.

Joseph laughed and the rest of his team cheered.

"OK! Who are the bastards responsible?"

James Adams responded. "Captain Sturridge and First Mate, Jackson," he said. "Jackson was the one who shanghaied me."

"You, men," Young ordered the Shamrock's crew. "Put them in irons."

"No!" was the counter command. Captain Harrison had made his way across. "I want them keel-hauled." His voice boomed across both ships.

The colour drained from the faces of Sturridge and Jackson. "You can't do that," hollered the captain of the Shamrock.

"Can't I?" queried Harrison. "Who's going to stop me?" He looked around. None of the Shamrock's crew dared to voice an objection. His own men looked shocked. Even John, still sitting with the gun, covering the action, was dazed by the turn of events.

"Tie them up," ordered Harrison. "Make sure their hands are behind their backs."

"Sir," said Adams, about to address his captain. The look of thunder, Nathan showed, silenced any further comment. This was a side of his character no one had seen before. Like his name, it was Old Testament justice and he was reaping vengeance.

"If anyone objects," snarled Harrison, "he can join them as well."

There was no more dissension.

The crew produced two sheets long enough to go around the stern of the Shamrock. Two crew members went aft, holding either end of the rope and lowered it over the rear of the brig. They then brought it forward about twenty feet before tightening it and fixing the two ends together.

Sturridge and Jackson were taken, struggling and tied close to each other on the long rope. The crew took the weight of the rope and pushed the men over the side of the ship without dropping them into the sea. Both men were screaming.

"Better save your breath," shouted Harrison. "You are going to need it."

The crew hauled on the line and the two men disappeared under the water and under the brig. They continued their steady pull until the two appeared, bloody with torn bodies, on the far side of the ship. They raised them up onto the deck.

Harrison had miscalculated. The keel was sharper than he had reckoned or there may have been more barnacles than anticipated. Perhaps he had misjudged the time the men could hold their breath. Both bodies were lifeless.

However, he remained calm. "We'll bury them at sea, right here. Now, this is the story. You hit a bad squall. The captain and first mate were lost overboard. If it hadn't been for the Crosby, you'd have been lost too. Few of you are seamen and know how to run this vessel. I'm giving you James Adams, whom you know, to skipper you to port as we tow you in for treasure trove. Now, if any man thinks those bastards didn't deserve what was coming to them, tell me now. Most of you have been press-ganged at one time or another. We'll have an end to it. In the meantime, we have to get to our destination and then home."

There wasn't a murmur. No love was lost for Sturridge, nor was it for Jackson.

The burials were arranged with haste. Both bodies were draped in linen. Harrison, ironically, led a small service, ending with the words, "I commend these bodies to the sea," and they were dropped over along with the line used for the punishment.

The towing lines were arranged and the Crosby crew, other than Adams, returned to their own ship via the chair, the last man taking the tow lines. These were attached to the bow of the Shamrock and the stern of the Crosby. The tow into New York began.

Later that day, Harrison had the luck that was to back up his story. The weather deteriorated and the ship hit a squall. It saved them washing the blood off the deck of the Shamrock as the rain and the sea cleaned everything. If God wasn't behind Nathan, maybe Poseidon was.

John was confined to his cabin, feeling very sick and had little opportunity to consider his thoughts on the events of the day. The crew on the Crosby was quiet. No one was speaking to the captain unless commanded. The usual banter and joviality was subdued. They didn't discuss the day's events, every man quiet within his thoughts. Was Harrison wrong in what he had done? Maybe he was and maybe he wasn't? Would they need to report the truth when they hit land and spoke to the authorities? Wasn't their loyalty to their skipper and one another more paramount? After all, didn't Sturridge and Jackson deserve everything that was coming to them? They hadn't considered the families of the men forced on board the Shamrock.

Similarly, the men remaining on board the Shamrock were also engaged in private musing. There was common respect for James Adams who was quickly proving to be a firm, decisive and fair leader. Those, who had been pressed into service like him, saw him alongside Harrison and the crew of the Crosby as a saviour. The other sailors had borne no love for the captain nor had they any for the first mate.

In the quiet confines of his own cabin, Nathan was having his own qualms. He had acted in righteous anger and haste. It was out of character but it was the act of a man driven beyond his tether. Jimmy wasn't the first crewman he had lost in nefarious activities. He was the most senior and he was a friend. Both were family men, held Christian values and loyalty was one of those mores.

Nathan perceived that the men, on both ships, for different reasons, would go along with the story that the two villains of the piece had been 'lost to the sea'. But, what would John think? After all, he was the owner's son. Would he lie to George or would he feel it his duty, to tell the truth? Would he be alive anyway? Nathan could hear him retching in the adjacent cabin. He then put the evil thought out of his head. He wanted no harm to come to the boy. He cursed himself for even considering the worst scenario.

John was suffering too much to give any thought to the day or to what he was going to do. He was sick from the pit of his stomach. His throat was sore. He was regularly heaving and gasping in turn. Maybe suicide was the answer to overcome the pain, nausea and disease. He was too single-minded and stubborn to really contemplate that course. John was a fighter.

Nobody slept properly that night, following the turmoil; the day's events and the choppy waves. The rising storm just seemed to pay homage to everything that had gone on.

The crew was still subdued the following day. Everyone went about their work in a methodical way. The tension was plain to see to anyone who had known this team previously.

John was late arising, having exhausted himself during the night. However, once he had had the usual short sleep before dawn and recovered from the early morning traumas. Once awake, John put some thought as to what he was going to do. He hadn't asked anyone. He hadn't spoken to the captain. He was, through everything that had happened, mature beyond his years. Like his father and grandfather before him, he was decisive. He was proud of both of them and what they had stood for. His mind sought out what they would have done in these circumstances.

He recalled a story he had heard about his grandfather. On one of his voyages, he had crossed swords with some slavers. In the confrontation that had followed, he had freed the slaves and executed the traders. This had never been officially recorded, for obvious reasons. Was what had happened here any different? Both incidents reeked of rough justice. Would his grandfather have approved of Captain Harrison's actions? Probably, he would have. Was there any point in punishing a good man who had probably gone too far? Would the crew back him and support him as Grandfather's men had supported him? John had no doubts about those on board the Crosby.

But what could be said about the Shamrock? Several of the men had been pressed and would be likely to go along with the story. The more regular crew was an unknown quantity.

John had made up his mind. He struggled up to the bridge. Nathan Harrison caught his weakened body and helped him to a seat. John was wheezing and gasping with the effort. He still managed to get out some words.

"Please, may I have a quiet word, captain?"

"Aye," said Harrison. He turned to Young. "Take over," he commanded. Then, more softly to John, "Let's go to my cabin. Do you need help?"

John nodded his agreement and support.

They made their way back in a gingerly fashion, Harrison occasionally having to hold John or stopping to allow him to regain breath. When he was seated, the captain brought him a glass of lime juice. John sipped it as he gradually gained composure and began to breathe a little easier. Nathan poured himself a stiff measure of rum, bigger than a normal tot. This did not go unnoticed by John, but he said nothing.

Both of them sat quietly as John recovered slowly.

Finally, he spoke.

"Nathan," he said, "I have put a lot of thought into what has happened on this voyage." It was the first time he had ever called Captain Harrison by his first name. "I think we should log the events, as you suggested."

The older man was relieved that he had John's backing but tried hard not to show any emotion. John sensed this but didn't press it. He continued.

"I am going to tell you a story about my grandfather. This must remain in confidence, even though the old man is dead. I wouldn't want his reputation to be tarnished in any way."

He related what he knew of the slavery story.

He then concluded.

"Sometimes, there is the law; sometimes there is justice. If we had handed Sturridge and Jackson over to the authorities, they would have had little more than a rap over the knuckles. I got to thinking how many families had been destroyed by their activities over the years. How many men had been snatched never to see their loved ones again? Even now, until we get word back from America, Jimmy's wife and children have no idea if he is alive or dead. At least now, we know those bastards cannot do this again."

Harrison responded.

"John, have you thought about the crews of the two ships? Can we rely on them to toe the line?"

Despite everything, even John had to smile at the irony of this metaphor.

"Our crew, on the Crosby, will back you to the hilt. I don't think Sturridge and Jackson had any support on the Shamrock. But, with your permission, captain, I'll take some soundings before we reach land."

"What are you proposing?"

"First of all, we both address our crew at a briefing today. I think we'll get a positive reaction. If so, we'll lower your boat and ferry across to the Shamrock and brief the crew there, after we've had a word with Jimmy."

Nathan sipped on his rum. "Are you up to it?" he asked. "I mean the boat crossing."

"At the moment, everything is an effort. I am determined to overcome all obstacles when things have to be done. That gives me strength and purpose."

"OK. Let me set it up."

"Good, that's agreed. But, remember, not a word about my grandfather. I wanted *you* to understand where I was coming from." He emphasised the 'you'.

The captain left John in the cabin and went up on deck to find Young and arrange the briefing. He filled the boatswain in on the bones of the conversation.

"I don't think you will have any worries on that score," said Joseph. "The crew having been sharing thoughts and I think you and John will be interested to know what they have to say."

The briefing was set for noon, eight bells, at the change of watch. The captain outlined the plan and the way they wished to record the log. John told the men of his thoughts, neglecting to add his grandfather's story. The men listened quietly but intently. They were intrigued by how this boy was fast becoming a man and the maturity of his thought.

"Lastly," said John, "if any man feels that he cannot go along with us, we will have to report the truth to both the American and the British authorities. Have you any questions?"

One of the oldest members of the crew was Jeremiah Jones, a leading seaman. He stepped forward and removed his cap.

"Permission to speak, captain and young sir," he said.

"Go on Jones," was the response.

"I have worked with the Lawson Line for many a year. The old man has always been good to me and my family. Captain Harrison has been the best captain under whom I have sailed. As you know, I am a highly religious man. I am troubled and so were several of the rest of the crew. So I prayed to God. Overnight, he told me that I had to make my own judgment. He also reminded me that vengeance lay with him. I don't know whether we did right or wrong, good or bad. All I know is that my conscience will not allow me to bring a good man down. It is not up to man to decide if you should be hanged for what you did. I will pray for you captain and pray for us for supporting you. I hope God will look kindly on your soul, and on ours, when it comes to judgment day."

He stepped back into the line and replaced his cap.

There was a pregnant pause, what seemed an everlasting silence. Suddenly, this was broken by a spontaneous cheer. The crew had made it clear that it was unanimously behind the captain.

"Thank you, Jones," said Harrison. "I won't forget your loyalty to me." He turned to John then back to the men. "Now we'll have to see what those on board the Shamrock say. If they cannot follow your lead, we will have to tell the truth and I shall have to face the consequences."

"We can always chuck the dissenters overboard," shouted one of lads. There was a little laughter at this thought. Harrison smiled but waved the idea away.

"They are good men as well," he said.

The crew was dismissed and the men sent back to their duties.

Using semaphore flags, Young signalled Adams that they wanted to meet at four bells, two o'clock, and requested the crew of the Shamrock was assembled then. Adams concurred and confirmed his reply. John asked the captain if they could take Jones as one of the rowers of his launch when they went across to the Shamrock.

"I think his speech is worth its weight in gold."

Harrison agreed.

The sea was a little calmer as they lowered the launch and they crossed to the Shamrock. They tied up to the brig and a rope ladder was lowered. John had difficulty climbing it but Adams had lowered a harness to help him. He stumbled rather breathlessly on board feeling sick and with his lungs on fire.

The meeting went better than they had dared hope. The crew of the Shamrock had never taken to their captain and first mate. They had ruled by fear and punishment. It was immediately obvious by the way the sailors greeted the boarding party. The atmosphere was much more relaxed. They had taken to Jimmy Adams. In a very short time, he had proved to be a likeable character, honest and disciplined. He had the trait of never asking others to do anything he wasn't prepared to do himself. Despite his injuries, he had shown that when he was only known to be one of the men. He hadn't complained. He saw no point. He was a pragmatist and that had settled the nerves of the less experienced men around him.

The discussions took place in a slightly different way to that on the Crosby. By the time John came to speak, he had recovered his composure. His voice was still weak but there was no doubting the steel and intent he held.

"Finally," he said, "before we ask you to speak, I must point out the consequences of whatever we decide. If you agree to support our version of events, there is no going back. Every man, on both ships, must stick to it. If there is any dissension, for whatever reason, religious or otherwise, we will just have to stick to the truth. If anyone changes his story later, we may all be tried for murder, piracy and mutiny." He turned and looked at Nathan. "Obviously, the main blame lies with Captain Harrison. My family will probably lose the business. So, men, we need to know what you think. I promise you, no one will come to harm if you are not with us. It's over to you."

The Shamrock's crew had elected a spokesman.

"Thank you, sir, for what you have said. We, the lads, are in total agreement. We hated both Captain Sturridge and First Mate Jackson. Frankly, we think they got what they deserved. If it hadn't been Captain Harrison and the crew of the Crosby, it would have been someone else. To be honest, we are all relieved at the outcome. So, the answer is yes. We are all agreed on the story."

In the time-honoured agreement over a contract, he spat on his hand and offered to Captain Harrison. Nathan was taken by surprise but then he smiled and responded in kind. The cheer that went up was more of relief. It was heard on the Crosby and the tension eased.

James Adams suggested a ration of rum for all on board the Shamrock. Joshua Young had decided the same onboard the Crosby.

There was no going back now.

Both crews were happier for the rest of the voyage. The weather also reflected this as the winds relented, the swell subsided and the passage became smoother.

John started to feel a little better. He was getting used to the rolling and pitching. His phlegm was not as black as it had been. The sea air and the greater warmth of the sun appeared to be doing him good.

Nine days out, the Crosby towed the Shamrock into the Hudson Estuary. They headed for the berths at the southern end of Manhattan Island to unload their respective cargoes.

Nathan Harrison filed his report to the Harbour Master's Office. Although there were telegraph facilities available, the earlier attempts to create the link across the Atlantic had failed. The only way to get messages back to England was by letter and ship.

So that's how it stood. Nathan Harrison sent a detailed report back to the Doughty Line in Liverpool docks. John took responsibility to do the same for the Lawson Line, to back up the captain's report.

They then arranged with the harbour master to send the mail on the next ship bound for England.

The New York police had their own problems with the gangs, immigrants and the aftermath of the war. They had still not re-established themselves from the riots of recent years. Events on a foreign ship, out at sea, were unnecessary distractions. After a few cursory enquiries, they accepted the reports and the eye witness corroboration. The file was closed.

John had learned a salient lesson over the voyage. He wasn't aware of it at the time. However, it was to prove to be crucial for him in the not-too-distant future.

Chapter Three

The two ships started to be unloaded the next day. John and Captain Harrison had to deal with the paperwork, the police, the merchants and the agents for the Doughty Line. This included the salvage claim to be paid to the Lawson Line for 'saving' the Shamrock, its crew and its cargo. Both Nathan and John managed to do this without a flicker of emotion. The agents quibbled but could not put up much of an objection.

The dealings with their own agents and chandlers were more straightforward and amicable. John was relieved to be back on dry land and feeling less queasy. His coughing and breathing were still not good and, at times, still painful. However, the sea journey appeared to have reduced the blackness of his sputum and he took that as a good sign. It was now the end of May and the hot humidity of a New York summer had not arrived. The late spring weather was much more conducive to his health; warm and dry. The blossom on the trees in the old squares of South Manhattan was still in full bloom.

In contrast, John couldn't help noticing the anomalies of the city. It was thriving and bustling with the trade picking up rapidly after the war. However, there were signs of the aftermath. The merchants and traders showed signs of affluence and dressed accordingly, especially in the finance areas of downtown Manhattan and the developing Wall Street district. In contrast, there were the beggars; broken men from the war, some with lost limbs, poor immigrants, many from Ireland, some from more eastern European origins, several being German. Lastly, there were the newly emancipated black Americans, released from slavery but with no work and little education, fodder for the Union army in the drive west.

Lawson used the National City Bank on the East River for their dealings in New York. John and Nathan went with the agents to sort out all the various transactions and to introduce themselves to the staff and management. John also had to plan his on-going journey. He didn't want to carry vast amounts of money with him for obvious reasons.

The telegraph system and bank transfers had been developed through the eastern states. It was spreading fast into the west and had reached as far as Santa Fe. The New Mexico Territory was not yet part of the United States. Many of the people who had drifted there were Southern sympathisers. Both United States and Confederate dollars were still in use, but the latter was losing value very rapidly. The famous 'impregnable' Bank of Santa Fe was well established as a stronghold within a fairly lawless area. This was where John was heading; the dry South-West. The National City Bank was able to telegraph Santa Fe in advance, letting them know of John's plans allowing him to pick up finances.

In case he needed money along the way, other banks along his route were also alerted, the first of these being the Buffalo Savings Bank.

The kind of bi-lateral trade, that had been a feature of the pre-war years, had not quite been re-established. The war had only just ended. The cotton belt was only now getting back on its feet and the economics had changed. Families had lost their lands and their slaves in the South. Despite sharecropping schemes, many of the former workers were too poor to take these up. Cotton had been a mainstay of the trade and it would take at least a year to build substantial crops again. That was why, despite being in a northern city, many New York people had sympathy with the South.

The agents, working with the Lawson Line, had thought outside the box. The Crosby was to deliver a combination of Pennsylvania coal and American lightweight manufactured clothing to Kingston, Jamaica. From there, it was to pick up a cargo of sugar and fresh fruits for the return to Liverpool.

Having concluded all the negotiations and meetings, John and Nathan returned to the ship. The unloading was virtually complete. Captain Harrison organised the watches with the men so that they could have some shore leave in turn. They were given part of their wages in dollars and briefed on the dangers. No one needed to be told twice after what had happened to Jimmy Adams in Liverpool.

The Doughty crew had returned, reluctantly, to the Shamrock. Their fate and their return to England were in the hand of their agents. Jimmy had been asked to skipper it. He had declined for two reasons. Firstly, he had no love for the Doughty family, especially in view of what had happened to him. Secondly, he did not wish to cross the Atlantic in a sailing ship manned by 'landlubbers'. The

Crosby could not take them back. James Adams was far happier returning to his role as a first mate, now that he had been cleared by a local doctor.

The next day was scheduled to be John's last day in New York. The Crosby was now being reloaded and prepared for its trip to the Caribbean. John carried the bare essentials, for the first part of his journey, in his roll bag. As a precaution, he wore a money bag around his waist, under his outer clothing, so that he had two lots of money about his person. The stops, along the way, would allow him to pick up more and buy necessities as his circumstances changed.

The crew was all there to see him depart. Even some of these hardened seafarers had tears in their eyes. The first mate, Jimmy Adams, gave John a bear hug and thanked him for his part in the rescue. In a short space of time, they had been through a lot. It had created a bond of respect, care for one another. They were a team; no, even more, they were a family.

The railhead for the Erie Railroad was on the opposite side of the Hudson. From the South Manhattan docks, John had to follow the west coast of Manhattan Island round to the ferry terminal. Sailings were frequent and the journey relatively short. John went to the office and paid for the ticket for his trip.

The weather was fine and warm. The river crossing was smooth. John spent the first part taking in the receding view of Manhattan. The bustle of construction was clear with many buildings being erected. John turned to watch the shoreline of the New Jersey coast. Again, the hustle and bustle of Jersey City was apparent. The main reason was that this was a conduit, the transportation hub and corridor which led to the west. As the ferry docked, John disembarked and made his way to the station.

The railhead was called the Pavonia Terminal. It was an unusual-looking building for which John couldn't determine a pedigree. Was it Gothic or was it Colonial? Either way, it had already gained a reputation for having a ghost. John was highly amused when he learned of this. He wondered what people might have said or thought about many of the buildings back in England, especially the mills.

The early part of the train journey was north to north-westerly up the Hudson valley. As the train entered the forests of upper New York State, it started to edge more westerly. The forests were thick and in full leaf, seemingly never-ending. Although the trains did not have the height of comfort, John was able to relax more and sit up. This helped to ease his breathing and reduce the pain. His coughing became more infrequent and the black, infected sputum declined.

He looked with interest at his fellow passengers in the carriage. There was a smartly dressed, if flamboyant, man in a suit and waistcoat; vest if you're American. He was only about five feet six inches but dapper with it. His boots were also fancy with a stylised pattern. They were highly polished. He had a case that turned out to have samples of whisky which he was peddling west. He was a drummer.

Another traveller was an attractive, New England, lady who was journeying to meet her husband, a cavalry officer who had been posted west. Her outfit showed her class and wealth. Her bearing was patrician, like a Roman Sufeta. It was as if royalty oozed from every pore.

The fourth person was a German engineer and railroad surveyor who was going west to develop the trans-continental links. He was slightly portly, about five feet eight inches and with a receding forehead.

Conversation between them was intermittent. The lady was the quietest. The engineer and the drummer discussed the samples and engaged in a little 'testing'. All of them were intrigued by why John was in America.

He told them of his illness and what the doctors had advised. He related the journey so far in matter-of-fact terms. The sea chase and the keelhauling were omitted which, ironically, made the story of the voyage seem quite uneventful.

The four of them went to lunch and shared some conversation. The lady ate sparsely; a light omelette. The drummer and engineer both had steaks; John had some poultry, not sure whether it was chicken, turkey, or some small game bird. The vegetables were fried potatoes and beans. John was reminded once again of the anomaly that was America at this time; the rich contrasting with the poor, the affluence and poverty, the hope for the future, and the hardship of the immediate aftermath of the war.

They returned to the carriage. John was not feeling too well again. He tried to hide it but the lady had noticed. Her demeanour had changed. She had been polite but hadn't really taken to the drummer and engineer. She felt more motherly towards John and was concerned for his welfare. She propped him up on his seat so that he could rest in a more upright position. John managed a fitful sleep which allowed his body to relax, relieving the pain and the constriction of his chest.

He awoke, just as dusk was settling and as the train pulled into Buffalo on the shores of Lake Erie. After they had checked he was alright, John said his farewells to the others and set out to find accommodation for the night. He was advised, at the station, to go to Mrs Rowbotham. She ran a guest house near the ferry port.

Mrs Rowbotham greeted John at the door and welcomed him in. She was a buxom lady with tied back hair who ran her household like a kindly, domestic goddess. She saw, at once, how pale John was. John booked in for the night, telling her his intention was to catch the ferry, next day and travel to Chicago that way. This was a more pleasant method of travel to hit the west.

John explained from where he had come and the purpose of his journey. The landlady's pragmatic instincts took over and Mrs Rowbotham returned to the practical issues.

"Now John," she said, "I imagine you will need some laundry doing. If you give me your dirty clothes and the ones you are wearing, I'll let you have my husband's dressing gown tonight and get everything clean for you by the time you leave. You can then have a bath as well. Now, do you want anything to eat tonight?"

"Thank you," said John. "I don't need anything to eat, just some water. But I will accept your kind offer of a bath and some clean clothes."

Mrs Rowbotham was as good as her word. She prepared John's bath and carried the water from the fire to fill the tub. She gave John the dressing gown and, after he had undressed and slipped into it, took his clothes to be washed.

John wondered why her husband hadn't done the heavy-duty work but he didn't ask. He slipped into the tub with satisfaction at the feel of the warm, cleansing water. Mrs Rowbotham had supplied him with towels, soap and a scrubbing brush. He took advantage of the opportunity to clean his hair thoroughly, a luxury that had been difficult on board the ship.

He went to his room and quickly fell into an exhausted sleep, the bath having relaxed his body and his breathing. Next morning, he woke as usual with the coughing and spluttering. However, it was not so painful.

He happened to be the only guest. Mrs Rowbotham had prepared him an American breakfast; waffles and syrup, crispy bacon and eggs, and coffee. She had washed and dried his clothes overnight and they were neatly folded for him to pack into his bag. The kitchen was large with a wood burner oven and room for a wooden table and chairs. There was a large Welsh dresser, on which the crockery was stacked and wooden cupboards and drawers for food, pots, pans, utensils and cutlery.

Mrs Rowbotham sat with John while he ate. He told her more about his journey and what he was doing. In turn, she told him about herself. Her husband had been a local shopkeeper who had gone to war, part of the Union army. He was reported missing at a battle, more of a skirmish as she could make out, at a place called Pickers Hill. It had been a bloody affair. She didn't know if anyone had survived from either side. Apparently, the site hadn't been discovered for some days and the corpses were in a bad state. The soldiers who found them said they had been mutilated by wild animals, possibly bears or wolves, and the stench was awful. They collected them and burned what was left of them in a pyre. So, there was nothing for her; nobody, no ashes and none of the belongings he had taken with him. She had sold the shop, as she couldn't run everything on her own, and resorted to the guest house to make a living. Her eyes had welled up in telling John this story.

John reached across and touched her arm. She smiled her thanks.

"You have your own troubles, young man. You don't have to be burdened with tales of an old woman like me."

"Don't be daft. I wondered why you were doing everything. I am just sorry I am not physically able to help you as much as I'd like to. And, by the way," John laughed, "you are not old. My mother would have a fit if she heard you say that."

"That's kind of you to say that. Having guests keeps me sane and gives me a purpose in life. Not everyone is as nice as you but, in the main, they're not bad."

John looked around the room again. "Have you any memorabilia?" he asked.

"Apart from the odd few clothes, like that dressing gown, I have very little. I cannot even show you a picture."

They both went silent, for a few minutes, in their own thoughts.

Eventually, John said, "I'd better go, buy a ticket on the 'Paddleboat' and get down to the boat landing."

Mrs Rowbotham only wanted a dollar for John's bed and breakfast. But, as she had done so much more for him, he insisted she took two.

"Thank you, young man. I hope you regain your health and find wealth and happiness as well."

John gave her a kiss on the cheek as they parted. Mrs Rowbotham blushed, a little, but she was secretly pleased.

John said, "I hope we'll meet again, in lot happier circumstances."

"Yes. I hope so too. Good luck and God go with you."

John stepped out into the bright morning light. The sun reflected brilliantly off the whitewashed walls of the house. Although there was warmth in the rays, the wind off Lake Erie kept the temperature down. John's first port of call was at the Buffalo Savings Bank at the junction of Main and Erie Streets. He introduced himself and asked permission to use the bank's telegraph to mail a message to the family's agents in New York. That way, he'd be able to send progress reports to them and, indirectly to his father and mother back in Liverpool, whenever a ship could take the post. He was still at the bank when the acknowledgment came through from the agents, wishing him well on his onward journey.

His following stop was at the wharf office to buy a ticket to Chicago on the next ferry. The journey was much more leisurely and comfortable than the train service. It was the 'posh' way to travel west and the facilities onboard the paddle steamer were much more conducive than the rail carriages. The $10 ticket covered accommodation, meals and travel as well as a personal cabin for the five-day trip. With a more arduous trek in front of him, it made sense for John to take it leisurely while he could.

The sailing was at noon with lunch at one o'clock, once the boat was underway. John hadn't particularly enjoyed the sea crossing but, he hoped, conditions on the lakes would be less volatile than on the ocean.

Once he was on board and settled in his cabin, John set out to explore the boat and see what it held. The top deck was for relaxation, weather permitting, with chairs in which to sit and view the passing shoreline. The second desk was the dining area and the galley with an open area all around the boat. Again, depending on conditions, one could dine alfresco.

Deck three caught John by surprise. It was a saloon, night club and casino with all the games; roulette, baccarat, dice, card tables for poker and croupiers. Even though the boat had not yet departed, sessions were already underway and people gambling. It didn't take John long to study the odds and to note the best chance of winning; the last person on the dealer's right i.e. last person to play, when you could size up the bets still left in play against him. John wasn't a gambler and didn't want to attract attention by being flash.

The lower decks were passenger and crew quarters, stores and, of course, the engine room.

John decided to keep himself to himself during the voyage. The more rest he could have the better it would be. He spent his time between sleeping, resting in the cabin, and going up to the next deck for his meals in the restaurant and, when it was nice, studying the passing landscape as the boat hugged the lakes' shores. Much of it was forested, sprinkled with the odd settlement and the occasional stopping port. The journey took them west along Lake Erie, north through Lake Huron and then west and south through Lake Michigan.

It gave him a lot of time to think. Some of that was put to good purpose. He was able to plan what he was going to do and what he would need to buy for the days ahead. However, some of his thoughts were introspective, reflective on what he had been through and in trepidation on what was to come.

He had experienced an awful lot in his sixteen years already. In many cases, this exceeded what most people entertain in a lifetime. He wasn't fully grown, not yet an adult, but he had matured beyond his years. He had had to make decisions that should not have been expected of a teenager. The thoughts turned him gloomy. However, John was not depressive and he shook himself out of his melancholy. He was a fighter. His illness was not going to beat him. He was going to beat it. That's why he was on this journey. He had to believe in that and make it happen.

The difference was that for the first time, he was on his own. So far, he had had family and friends, the crew of the Crosby, all of whom had looked out for him. Just recently, it had been some strangers, the lady on the train and Mrs Rowbotham, both of whom had shown considerable kindness and care. Was he always going to be so lucky?

John wondered about his parents. Would they know, by this time, how far he had got? Would they have been able to respond to the New York agents so they could send him a telegraph update? He could visualise his mother in tears mixed with relief.

John started to list what he was going to need and concentrated on being positive. By the time the voyage was over, he had determined everything and was well prepared.

The weather was distinctly warmer by the time the boat docked at Chicago. On disembarking, John wasted no time in taking himself to the train station and buying a ticket on the final rail leg.

The Atchison and St Joseph Railroad connected Chicago to the furthest western points to be reached by train. It was part of the more famous Chicago, Burlington and Quincy Railroad. The train passed along the southwestern shores of Lake Michigan before crossing the plains to the south. It stopped along the way at the townships of Peoria, Springfield and Quincy. The last sections were the two separate spurs to St Paul, further north, and St Joseph, further south. Both of the places were strange crossovers between eastern cities and western frontier towns, having vestiges of all the contrasting elements. There were plush hotels and stores, the railheads, wooden shacks, cattle stocks, pens and corrals, and the dirt streets. The people reflected the same diversity, the smartly dressed and suited business community, the prim and proper ladies, the storekeepers, gunsmiths, cowboys, horse traders, skinners, saloons, madams and showgirls. The law was reasonably well established and practised.

John's destination was St Joseph. A day's ride to the south led to the two great arteries into the west. For the first part, they were the same. Then the Oregon Trail split off to the North West and the Santa Fe Trail continued southwest.

The engine pulled right up to the end of the line and the final buffers at St Joseph. John left the train and booked into the local hotel.

"Good evening," said the clerk at the counter. He was very polite.

John had been about to say "Howdy" and was slightly taken aback. "Good evening," he responded.

The clerk smiled, in a slightly amused away, at John's accent. He dropped the upper crust tones and relapsed into his mid-western Missouri drawl. "Hey, you're a 'limey' aren't you?"

"Could be," said John, in a droll kind of way. He smiled back and said, "I'm from Liverpool."

"Well, welcome to Missouri." It sounded more like misery and that tickled John. "How can I be of service to you?" The polite tone returned.

"I'd like to book a room, get a bath and have something to eat and drink please."

"OK. Will you register, please? How long will you be staying?"

"I'm not sure. Can I leave it open-ended and give you notice when I'm leaving?"

"That will be OK, sir. However, I will require a $2 deposit to start."

John paid over the two dollars and signed the book.

The clerk handed him the key and showed him to his room. He explained the meal times and directions to the dining room and the bathroom.

"There is a Chinese washhouse where they'll clean your clothes overnight," he said.

"Thanks," said John. "I'll have a bath now and come down for a meal afterward."

"See you later then," said the clerk, as he returned to his desk.

Chapter Four

The next morning, John awoke with less coughing, spluttering and sputum than ever. The warmer, drier, Mid-West climate was suiting him. He rose early and, after breakfast, went downtown to the Bank of St Joseph. It was unmissable as the largest building in the town, almost like a big sprawling warehouse of more than two storeys.

His credit had come through and he was able to raise whatever funds he needed for the next leg of the journey. This was to be a very different experience from what he had encountered before.

John was delighted to have two telegraphs waiting for him. The agents in New York had facilitated the monies and wished him well. Better still, they had forwarded the first news he had had from his family and given a précis of the letter sent to him. His mother and father had received the letter he sent by ship from New York. They were delighted with his progress and heartened by the improvement in his health. His father also told him of the new attempt to build the telegraph link to England. This had failed ten years previously. It had been successfully resurrected and there were high hopes it would be completed by the end of 1865.

The bank didn't have a separate telegraph facility and John sent his replies from the official office.

"Thank you for all the news and arrangements. My health is improving. The next leg is from St Joseph to Santa Fe. I'm organising all I need. You may not hear from me for two months."

That last was a chilling thought. It was realistic. John had about 900 miles to travel and it wouldn't be at speed. His next stop was the large general store to sort out provisions. He needed advice about the conditions and the clothing required. Some of the things he had listed out on the boat already; others were unknown to him or had slipped his mind. For example, tent, bedroll, cooking and eating utensils, rough shirts, jeans, hat, boots, socks and underwear were obvious.

He had to prepare for the summer storms in New Mexico; a slicker would be essential. He hadn't thought about 'chaps' to protect his legs from chaffing while constantly in the saddle. He was advised to get a sombrero rather than a Stetson or bowler, the last of which was more prevalent at the time. The deeper sombrero was a better shade and also doubled as a watering basin for himself and to water a horse. That led to water canteens. The neckerchief was another essential extra protection for the neck from the sun and the mouth and face from sandstorms.

All of these were arranged and left with the storekeeper. There may still be things to add and he couldn't carry everything anyway. The following port of call was a little more exciting and alarming at the same time. It was the gunsmiths.

The store was a veritable Aladdin's cave of weapons. The Civil War had left the legacy of a vast array of firearms. Some of these were better than others and John had done his homework even back in England. One of the contributing factors as to why the South had lost the war was the rifles. As with most of the guns in England, the Confederate Army had only been able to obtain single-shot breech loaders. The Union troops had repeater rifles and so had the advantage in front on battles. Underlying this was the economic advantage held by the North, industry, commerce, money and numbers of people.

There was a shooting gallery out the back of the shop and John took advantage to test out the various offerings. The best three rifles were the Henry, the Spencer and the Springfield. (The early Winchesters had a reputation for sticking and jamming.) After testing and sighting the rifles, John elected to purchase the Spencer with its seven shots repeater. It was slightly heavy but it was reliable and accurate.

There were dozens of handguns on display. Eventually, after testing them, John alighted on the Navy Colt. This was a six-shot repeater with a longer barrel than most revolvers. This made it more accurate over a greater distance.

The gunsmith was amazed at John's knowledge and decisiveness in choosing his weapons. Having picked them, John was equally as fastidious in purchasing the important ancillaries; the scabbard for the Spencer, the gun belt and deeper holster for the Navy Colt, ammunition, and the cleaning and oiling tool kit to keep both weapons in perfect working order. It was almost as if he were a professional gunfighter.

John paid for everything and asked the storekeeper to keep them for him while he got everything together for his trip. The gunsmith was only too pleased to help him. In their short meeting, he had taken a great liking to John and admired him for his bravery and maturity in such a young man.

John's next thoughts were for food; that for himself and that for the horses he had still to buy. He ascertained where both could be obtained and told the stores and grain and feed merchants he'd be back. However, he did buy a bag of carrots.

Down the street were the corral, horse traders and blacksmiths. There were many types of horses available. Once again, John was single-minded in what he required. He had considered buying a wagon and horses and dismissed them as impractical for his journey. Two strong horses were a much better bet; one for him to ride, one to carry everything else.

He was wandering through the livery stables when there was a snort to his right. He turned to see a large horse, red eyed and bristling. Instinctively, he knew it had been badly treated, for whatever reason, and didn't like people.

"You can't trust that one," said a voice behind him.

"Why not?" asked John.

"He's a bad 'un."

John was not to be put off. He noticed there was another large horse in the adjacent stall.

Both of them were American Percherons, jet black in colour. The first was a stallion, seventeen hands high. The second was a mare, slightly smaller at about sixteen and a half hands. John knew about the English Percherons which were plough horses back home. Both breeds were strong and tough, working horses that could plod through the day. They would never be fast, like other smaller American ponies, but they had the stamina and resilience for a long trip.

To the dealer's amazement, John opened the door to the stallion. It snorted. John produced a carrot and offered it to the horse but did not move forward. It resisted, at first, then lowering its head, moved towards him and snatched the vegetable, stepping back quickly.

"Why is he like that?" asked John.

"I dunno," came the reply. "We've had to hit him to keep him in line."

John didn't respond. He couldn't believe that these big gentle beasts could ever behave in that way unless they had been abused. Instead, he asked about the history.

"We got 'em from a homesteader who died. I've also 'gotta' tell 'yer' there's a catch. There's a dog, a mongrel, that's really attached to both these animals and they'll have to be sold together."

John hadn't considered taking a dog on a long trip. Unless it fended for itself, it would be difficult to carry the extra rations. But the advantage could be an additional companion and possibly, a guard. He didn't let on to what he was thinking. The trader was not going to easily be able to sell the horses and John was determined to drive a hard bargain.

John went into the adjoining stall to see the mare. She was immediately more approachable and took to her carrot straight away. John stroked her nose and she responded. He could see she was about three years old and her teeth were in good order. When he examined her hooves, he noted that she needed re-shoeing. She hadn't been groomed too well.

John went back to the stallion. Having seen how John had been with the mare, he was less threatening and took a second carrot with alacrity. He allowed John to stroke him and his eyes were now less wild. John examined him. Like the mare, he was about three years old and his teeth were also fine. There was some bruising around his rump, testimony to the unnecessary beating. His grooming was worse than the mare's, reflecting the fear the men had shown in addressing this horse. Once again, he needed to be properly shod.

"Let's see the dog," he said. "I want to see what he is like with the horses."

The man went to fetch him. At first, the animal appeared timid. As soon as he saw the horses, his tail began to wag furiously. John wondered how he'd cope with a long journey and what state of health he was in. The dog sensed that John was different. John was sorry he couldn't offer him anything. However, the animal came to him, sniffed at his hand and wagged his tail. He was not in brilliant condition but did not appear to be diseased or suffering from mange.

"Let's negotiate a price?" said John.

They haggled for a while. At one point the trader expostulated "Who the hell do you think you are?"

John replied, "The buyer." This unexpected riposte caught the man by surprise and, momentarily, he was lost for words.

John continued. "For that price, I want all three animals properly cleaned and groomed. Both horses are to be properly shod. I also want a good saddle, stirrups, bridles and rope."

"I suppose, lad, you'll be wanting a free year's supply of feed as well."

John didn't respond. All he said was "have we a deal?"

"OK!"

"Can you have those animals ready for the morning? Oh, I want them fed and watered as well."

The trader was about to explode but thought better of it. He begrudgingly shook John's hand and took John's money for the deal.

John gave the two horses the rest of the carrots and departed.

He returned to the grain merchant to order supplies for the horses for the following day. Finally, he visited the general store to order his own food and that for the dog. This included tinned food, bags of flour, beans, coffee, extra supplies of carrots, potatoes, beef jerky, salt and sugar.

Back at the hotel, John suddenly realised how tired he had become. He spoke to the desk clerk.

"Thanks for saving me the room. I'll be leaving in the morning after breakfast."

"That's fine. Can I wish you the best on behalf of myself and the hotel? Are you travelling with anyone else?"

"No," said John. "I had thought about it and the possible dangers. I don't want to be a burden to anyone else. It might also be safer not to be in a party. I'll draw less attention to myself and not be seen as a threat to other people."

"I hope you're right."

John went back to his room, settled on the bed and dropped into a fitful sleep. He was, at the same time, exhausted and exhilarated, expectant and anxious.

He awoke about two or three hours later, coughing and spluttering. The town was quietening down as dusk was about to fall. John cleaned himself up and went down to the dining room. He had a steak, beans and fried potatoes, followed by an apple pie. John suddenly realised he hadn't eaten so well or so much in a long time. He was pleased that he had the appetite and took that as a good omen.

It took him ages to settle down that night. His sleep was broken on several occasions.

He was up and ready soon after dawn. It seemed to be a good idea to start the day with a hearty breakfast which included corn flapjacks, eggs and bacon. He picked up his belongings from the room, settled the hotel bill and walked to the livery stables.

The horses had been fed, watered, groomed and shoed. John took nothing for granted and checked them thoroughly, much to the annoyance of the trader.

"Do you have names for them?" John asked.

"Nah," came the blunt and terse reply.

John put the blanket and saddle over the stallion, talking to him all the time and letting him rummage for the carrot in his vest pocket. "Now then, boy," he said, "I've decided to call you 'Raven'. That's the biggest blackbird I know." Turning to the mare, he said, "And you, will be 'Midnight'." As he mounted Raven and led Midnight out by her bridle, the dog appeared. "You'll just have to be 'dog' until I can think of a better name."

John picked up all the provisions from the merchants and from the stores, loaded them up on Midnight and the party set off out of town. They created an interest and some amusement, a lad riding a huge horse, leading another laden one and having a mongrel trotting alongside.

Then suddenly, they were on the trail, the town was behind them and John was on his way.

Chapter Five

The first day was relatively uneventful. John soon knew what saddle soreness was and was grateful he had been persuaded to buy the chaps. Raven was proving to be quite docile now that he was being treated well and Midnight plodded along contentedly without any fuss. Dog was proving something of a problem. Out on the trail, he was quite excitable, racing off in front of them and racing back, doing three times the distance he needed. By the middle of the afternoon, he had tired himself and needed to be carried across John's saddle. John just hoped, as the days went on, he'd learn and settle down to a sensible pace.

The trail was well worn and well-marked through the farmland, ranches and scrub. The wind whipped up some of the light soil into fine dust and this was irritating to both John and the horses. The bandanna across his face gave some relief.

Late in the afternoon, John rode into the small town of Independence. This was to be his last chance to stay in a hotel and sleep in a bed for some time. He took advantage to stable the horses for the night and arrange for Dog to remain with them. It was a strange sensation, walking, after having been in the saddle all day. His appearance caused some amusement and ribaldry, especially when he went into the saloon to get a drink. Who was this young dude, wearing a sombrero, riding and leading two strange horses and trailing a dog? John took the ribbing in good spirit and didn't react. It wasn't anything other than good-natured. The laughter increased when John said he couldn't drink whiskey or beer. People listened when he explained what he was doing and why he was here. The banter became lighter in tone and there was a genuine air of respect shown to John. Townsfolk and cowboys wished him well and good luck on his travels. Plenty of advice was given. John listened, took it in his stride but didn't commit. He was single-minded and determined and he would do things his own way.

The hotel facilities were pretty basic. The bath was a tub filled with ewers of hot water, supplied from the oven fires. Nevertheless, that gave John's aching limbs some relief and he was grateful to wash the dust off himself. The evening meal was a basic meat stew and potatoes but it was wholesome enough.

The next day was more interesting. Although St Joseph had been the railhead, Independence was the true starting point for those travelling west. It was the centre from which the wagon trains began. Consequently, John was to see more travellers along the route.

Everyone had to traverse the Missouri River and it could not be forded. There was only one nearby crossing. That was Todd's Ferry Landing. John was surprised at how fast the river was flowing. He joined fellow travellers waiting for the ferry. They were frontiersmen in their own right; cowboys, trappers and mule skinners.

Because of the treacherous nature of the river, the crossing was made on a rack and pinion craft, secured by ropes and pulleys to either bank and hauled across by hand. The pressures of the flow could cause some instability. Some of the animals were nervous about stepping on board. John kept Raven and Midnight calm by offering each one a carrot as he led them on. Dog trotted aboard as if this was another adventure for him and he didn't have a care in the world.

Most of John's fellow travellers were going west rather than south west. Once they had crossed the river, they would all follow it upstream to the confluence of the Kansas and Missouri Rivers, forcing them south west to Gardner. This was where the Santa Fe and Oregon Trails split apart. They didn't travel together as they rode at different speeds; the cowboys on their ponies were the quickest; the mule skinners with their wagons, the slowest. Once across the Missouri, John went on his way, alone. Dog was settling down to the pace of the horses, only racing off if he saw the odd gopher. So far, he hadn't caught anything.

This was the start of the Great Plains and the vast grasslands of the Mid-West. At that time of the year, it was already becoming very dry. This was the land of the various Plains Indians who had roamed the prairies and the surrounding hills. This was where they hunted and lived; later in his journey, John would enter the territory of the bison.

Gardner was nothing more than a supply stopover, not much more than a couple of shacks for stores. John camped out for the first time, unloading Midnight, cleaning down, feeding and watering the animals. He collected brush and fallen wood. He built a fire to do his own cooking, using fat and flour to make some flapjacks to eat with his jerky and heated up, tinned beans. It wasn't brilliant fare but it was sustaining. John vowed to get better as a cook.

The night fell rapidly and the darkness revealed a fantastic sight of the heavens and the multitude of stars. The temperature dropped rapidly and John was pleased to wrap up warmly and get into his bedroll. Dog took the hint to come and lay down beside him. John found this reassuring. He had a bodyguard, an early warning alarm system. He woke, shivering a little, just before dawn. There was soon enough light to reset the fire. John boiled some water for cleaning purposes. Luckily, at his age, he didn't need to shave every day. He had awakened with little coughing and retching and he took this to be a good sign.

The sun's rays soon warmed the atmosphere. John fed and watered the horses and let them graze on the sparse grass. Both horses nuzzled up to him and made John feel even better. He then set about making his own breakfast pushing the eager Dog away as he was getting impatient for some food too. Using his knife, John opened a can for him and a can of beans for himself. He also fried up some bacon and made some coffee with the rest of the boiling water. The breakfast was already better than the previous night's meal.

John cleaned up the utensils, the campsite and the fire. He loaded up Midnight, saddled Raven and gave both horses another carrot from the sack. He brushed and groomed both horses down and checked their hooves. He then set off to the south west following the rough track.

The days and nights were similar, except when John was able to stay at different staging points. They also allowed him to replenish some of his supplies, especially the feed for the horses, carrots where he could get them, tins for himself and Dog. The following two nights were at the McGee Harris and Havana Stage Stations.

The following few nights were out in the open. John made Council Grove prior to crossing the Neosho River. The next nights were the watering holes at Diamond Spring and Lost Spring. Two more days' travel took him to the Cottonwood Crossing and the Little Arkansas Crossing, both of which were fordable rivers.

John was now in the country where, 'the buffalo roam'. The next stop was Fort Zarah and the 'city' of Walnut Creek. It was full of cavalry and mule skinners and the start of the 'real' 'Wild West' and 'Indian Country'. They all thought that John was mad in what he was doing. No gory tales and Native

American phobias were going to dissuade him from his mission. In the end, they gave up and allowed the 'insane' Englishman to continue.

It was two days ride to the next fort. The half-way point was Pawnee Ridge but he saw no one. The following day, he spied a herd of bison in the distance but no sign of any hunters, Indians or Mule Skinners. The sight and huge numbers were mind-boggling. John realised the power these animals could bring in a stampede. He mused about porpoises and dolphins racing alongside ships at sea. As night approached, John arrived at Fort Laramie. He got the same reaction he had received at Fort Zarah. There was no animosity, maybe even a hint of admiration.

The following day was to take John back into civilisation; well if you can call it that. He was headed for Fort Dodge and then Dodge City. John took advantage of this to have a day's rest in the town and to see if he could catch up on the communications to and from his family and the agents.

Dodge was relatively quiet during the day. If John thought he would get a peaceful night and the best opportunity of a good night's sleep in a comfortable bed, he was sadly mistaken. He was able to stable the horses and get them checked over. Dog was OK staying with them. All three animals appeared glad of a rest day.

The noise that night permeated John's hotel room. The windows had to remain open. It was now too hot to do otherwise. The airless room would have been stifling. However, John was able to have a proper bath and a decent shave and these revived him.

John put on a clean shirt and went out for a meal. The restaurant was a rowdy dive with several cowboys, soldiers, townsfolk, gamblers, mule skinners and drifters. John had deliberately avoided all provocation by leaving his guns back at the hotel. His appearance, still pale, and his garb, suggested he was a tenderfoot. When it was clear that he wasn't going to rise to the bait, his detractors soon became bored.

John had to experience the saloon. The raucous noise and the honky-tonk of the piano, bursting through the swinging doors, were like the sirens luring sailors onto the rocks. The room was crowded; gambling tables, men at the bar milling with the hostesses.

John was accosted, almost the moment he entered.

"Buy me a drink," said this voice, as she grabbed his elbow. This young pale boy looked like a good catch and was pretty handsome compared to the majority of men in the saloon.

"I don't drink," said John, slightly embarrassed and horrified at the same time. He looked at the woman and gently eased his arm away. It was difficult to put an age on her. Her mousey hair, heavy make-up and shadows under the eyes meant she was a well-worn eighteen or into her thirties.

"P*** off," she hissed. "You nancy-boy!"

For a moment, it looked like one or two of the men were taking umbrage at John. He moved to the bar and the woman alighted on another potential punter.

John ordered lemonade. Both this and his Scouse accent created some mirth. But, John got into conversation with the men around him and the mood quickly lightened. Once John explained his illness and why he was there, the natural bonhomie and comradeship of the pioneering Westerners surfaced. He was able to elicit their sympathy and best wishes.

Suddenly, there was a crash from the other side of the room. A chair was hurled back and a table disintegrated as two men grappled and two others jumped aside. Cards, money, glasses, bottles and drink scattered across the floor. As the two men scrambled up, one of them reached for his gun. But someone was even quicker. An onlooker grabbed the butt from him and slammed it across the side of his head, knocking him cold.

"Calm it fellows," said a deep, reassuring voice. He was one of the Town Marshals. "Tell us what happened?" he asked the other guys at the table. He bent down and fished two aces out of the fallen man's sleeve.

"I guess you've sussed it," said one of the men at the table. "Thanks for stepping in and being so fast about it. You probably saved at least one of us."

"All part of the job," he drawled. He turned to the bartender. "What's the cost of the damage?"

"About five bucks should do it."

As they cleaned up, swept the floor and retrieved the cash, the Marshal asked how much of the pot belonged to the man he had felled. As it appeared that the pot had been won by one of the other players, the Marshall reached into the man's inside pocket and found his wallet. He peeled out five bills which he passed to the bartender.

He turned to the crowd around. "OK, fellows. The law will take it from here. You are witnesses. This man has paid for the damage. He has another ten dollars which will be the fine for breaching the peace and causing an affray. Luke," he called to one of the other deputies, "help me get this piece of sh*t out of here and to the jailhouse. We can release him in the morning when he's sobered up. He'll know he's no longer welcome in Dodge."

The pianist recommenced and everyone settled down once again.

"Well, young 'fella'," said the man alongside John, "is that the first piece of Western action you've seen?"

"Kind of," John replied. He smiled almost bemusedly. "Worse things happen at sea, you know!" He didn't say anymore and his companion didn't really understand that English expression. It wasn't entirely facetious. John had seen worse things at sea.

The noise increased as the night wore on. It was all in good, boisterous fun and spirits soared; physically and metaphorically. John was feeling very tired, excused himself and walked back to his hotel. It was still noisy within his room, even with the windows closed, and it was too hot not to leave them open.

He decided to stay an extra day, get himself and his clothes cleaned and get some fresh supplies. He crashed onto the bed and, despite the din and the clamminess, he soon fell asleep.

He woke in the early hours, in a sweat; coughing and hurting, not feeling as well as he had been recently. John needed the laudanum to ease his chest and lungs. It felt like a setback. Eventually, he got back to a fitful sleep.

When John awoke, it was already light. There was the hustle and bustle of trade replacing the noises of yesterday night. Horses and wagons were on the move, people on the sidewalks. He was not as bad as he had been earlier. His breathing was easier once again.

John got dressed and, taking a spare set of clothes, headed for the barbers. He asked for a shave and a bath. That helped him to relax. He changed clothes and found a Chinese laundry to wash the trail from the grubby garments he had taken off. He told the Chinese lady, he'd pick them up the next morning and gave her his thanks. The next stop was a brief visit to a general store. To his delight, he was able to buy a sack of carrots for the horses. He also found a bone for Dog. John put these on a holding account to be paid for with all the other things he'd need for the journey.

He took some of the carrots and the bone and went to the livery stables. The horses welcomed the vegetables with alacrity; Dog jumped up at him, wagging his tail like mad, grabbed the bone and ran off to a private corner, laying and protectively covering his booty. John asked the blacksmith if he could leave the animals with him for another day and was told that was fine. He felt the extra rest would be helpful to them as well as to him.

There were no further messages for John at the telegraph office. He let the agents in New York know of his progress and reaffirmed his plans to continue to Santa Fe. From there, he went to the Dodge City Bank, presented his credentials and withdrew enough money to cover his purchases.

Once John had been back to the store, he replenished his food for the journey. In particular, to be safe, he needed more canteens of water as he was to follow the 'dry' route. He arranged to pick them up the next morning. John relaxed for the rest of the day as best as he could. He had a meal and went to bed early. It proved difficult to sleep, but eventually, John settled into the 'land of nod'.

The next morning, having picked up the animals and the supplies, bills settled, laundry collected, John set off down the Cimarron route. He had been forewarned that this was an arid journey. Distance and times were crucial to ensure that water was found every day. It was also more dangerous in that these were the Great Plains across which Comanche and Kiowa bands roamed. The Comanche, in particular, were like toll keepers, sometimes demanding payment from people travelling across 'their' lands.

The road was hot, flat, dirty and dusty. The winds swept up the gritty earth. The vegetation was coarse and sparse. The ride was a boring plod. Even Dog was not his effervescent self, just trotting calmly alongside the two horses.

They saw no one for four days as John kept to his timetable; the first night at Lower Springs, the second at Middle Spring, the third at Upper Spring and the fourth at Cold Spring. John had now crossed from Kansas into the Oklahoma Panhandle. The country was becoming more rolling. The weather remained unrelentingly hot and dry. Progress was steady and slow.

Raven raised his head and snorted. Midnight blew a low reply and Dog took close order. There was movement on the rises to John's left. Suddenly they appeared. Six young Comanche braves swept down on their ponies, whooping and hollering, forming a moving circle around John and his animals. For some reason, John was not afraid. He leaned forward to quieten Raven, stroking his head and halting his progress. He did what he thought would be most unexpected and dismounted.

One of the braves rode up fast and close to John, whipping off his sombrero in one swift and deft move. He rode off in celebration, wearing his prize and crowing to the cheers of his companions. John remained calm. He walked over to Midnight and removed a bag of carrots. Dog stayed close on his heels. He gave each horse a carrot and signalled with the bag to the Comanche, holding a carrot in the other hand. Everyone rode down rapidly and every pony took a vegetable on the run. John had reasoned, and hoped, these were young men, out for some fun in what was otherwise a boring, humdrum life. They were no different to the gangs in the docks and slums of Liverpool. They might be dangerous, especially if provoked. They enjoyed scaring people, oblivious to the danger to themselves and other travellers when people could reach for their guns ever so easily. John's reactions had taken the tension out of the meeting. Had he spoiled the fun? No! He had intrigued them.

The lead rider walked his horse up to John and dismounted next to him. The other five followed suit.

"Do you speak English?" John asked. Seeing a lack of comprehension, he tried, "Habla Espagnol?" There was still no response. John walked over to a piece of rough scrub and broke off a stalk. He then drew some figures in the dirt on the ground. The first set was an outline of the British Isles and America, showing wavy lines and a simply drawn boat upon them. He pointed to England, then motioned the up and down of the waves and pointed to himself and back to the boat. He then drew a train and then a horse to show his journey to date. He drew a bed, showing himself lying on it and marked England again. He held his mouth and chest and coughed lightly. He showed the journey across America to where they were now. He then drew the sun and pointing to it, tapping his chest, showed why he was there.

The braves were fascinated. They jabbered amongst themselves and looked at John with some awe and admiration. There seemed to be some agreement between them. The one who had taken John's sombrero returned to his pony and came back with what appeared to be a decorated wooden lance. The figure on the lance resembled a snake. The brave walked over to Raven, who baulked a little. The Comanche motioned John over. While he held the horse, the brave affixed the lance to his saddle and tied a braid to it. John was a little perplexed.

The brave returned his sombrero to John's head, taking his stalk and made his own drawing in the dirt. It showed an attack on a wagon train. The next picture was of a wagon with the lance sticking up at the front. This was allowed to pass. John nodded in understanding and grasped the brave by his wrist. The Comanche responded likewise. It wasn't that John had paid a toll. He had given them something and, in their code, this required a reciprocal gesture. It was a sign of safe passage and was to be respected. John looked at the rest of the band and walked over to Midnight. He picked out six sticks of jerky and gave one to every brave. Their eyes lit up at this unexpected gesture and they ate them with alacrity.

One of the braves motioned a bottle and pretended to drink. John laughed and pointed to his chest and cough. He pretended to drink from an imaginary bottle and collapsed on the floor. The Comanche laughed in turn and understanding. John had no alcohol and they were somewhat disappointed.

They rode along the trail with John for a while, shooting around on their ponies, showing off and playing horsemanship skills. They were good; riding backwards, handstands on the backs of the horses, pretending to shoot rifles under the bellies of their animals, running behind them holding their tails before remounting them. Then suddenly, as quickly as they had arrived, they were away and soon out of sight.

To the west, it was starting to show higher land and that night John reached the station at McNee's Crossing on the North Canadian River. To the east and north, from where he had come, was Oklahoma; to the south and east was Texas; to the west, Colorado and the foothills to the Rocky Mountains. John's continuing journey was to the southwest and New Mexico Territory. Technically, he was no longer to be in the United States of America. That was for the future.

The men at the crossing were surprised to see John. A lone rider, coming this far, unprotected and vulnerable, had made an unheard-of journey for a tenderfoot. They corralled, watered and fed the horses, amused and admiring at the same time. They noted the Comanche lance attached to the saddle, with the snake-shaped sign engraved upon it. Dog was fed and given a juicy cattle bone to gnaw. He went into the corner of the main shack, closely protecting his prize.

"Well young fellow, what brings you out here?"

They listened, intently, while John told them of his adventures over a meal of pork and beans.

"I came here from England, Liverpool to be exact. My family owns a shipping line. Some time ago, I was diagnosed with consumption, and that it was incurable. The doctors suggested that my only hope was to travel to a hot, dry climate to dry out my lungs. With our links with America and our knowledge of the climate here, New Mexico Territory seemed to be a good bet. Yes, I was scared."

John hesitated for a moment and continued.

"I am scared. I knew there were dangers. The war has just finished. The west is untamed. There are outlaws. There are Indians. There are thieves and vagabonds."

The men grinned at this quaint English description and John smiled in response.

"The alternatives were hardly brilliant. This is my 'last chance saloon'."

John was pleased with his American analogy and his audience laughed.

"Most people are nice and want to help. That's the beauty of the west. You know. Homesteaders help one another through the harsh winters. You guys! You welcomed me today as an unexpected visitor and looked after me tonight. There are too many prejudices upfront before people know the truth. That is borne of fear of the unknown, something that is close to my heart. Every step out here smacks of that. But, I resolve it. I judge everyone when I meet them. I don't pre-judge."

He took a sip of water and cleared his throat. It was all a bit emotional.

"Earlier today, I met a band of Comanche."

The listeners stiffened, intrigued.

"How many, where there?"

"Six young boys; braves about my age, about ten or twelve miles back up the trail. They were lads out for some fun. They love it when people show fear of them. That's something they enjoy and it creates dangerous responses which can easily lead to bloodshed. It's no different to some of the gangs back in Liverpool or New York. They are young lads who do not fully appreciate the consequences of their actions. I was scared of their antics, but I quickly realised they meant me no harm. They felt obliged to return a gift. I had fed their ponies; they gave me the short lance and told me it was a sign of protection. I felt really honoured."

The wranglers reflected on John's words.

"So, how long have you been travelling?"

"It's about two months now. My next stop is Santa Fe where I can telegraph back about how I am doing. From there, who knows, but I am going further south-west into the even drier, desert climate."

The others looked on admiringly.

"Well son," said one of the older men in the team. "I don't think any of us who have done anything like you at your age." He turned his grizzled and grey looks to the rest of the team. They mumbled and nodded their assent in agreement.

"Let's drink to your success."

"I can't join you," said John, "other than with water."

"We'll toast to that," was the reply.

It was the end of June. The night was beautiful and clear and John was fascinated by the myriad of stars he could see. The sounds of the scrub and semi-desert edge of the plains were in abundance. John heard the bark of a coyote and the banshee cry of a screech owl. Dog was prone beside him, outside on the station's porch. He was still too intent on his bone to take much notice of the night's noises.

John suddenly realised how tired he was. He went back inside, rolled out his bedding and flopped down exhaustedly. He was asleep in moments despite Dog's annoying slobbering and cracking on his beloved bone.

To his shame, John was last to wake the next morning. The men at the station were already at work, tending to the horses, cleaning out the station and maintaining the ferry. This was all pre-breakfast.

Everyone was back into a hearty meal of eggs, bacon, grits and beans. The men gave John detailed advice on getting to Santa Fe, warning him of the dangers and emphasizing the need to take on as much water as he could at every opportunity. They made note of Comancheros but hoped that the short lance would go in John's favour. These roaming bands of rogue traders were unlikely to risk upsetting their key customers.

John listened intently. He made notes and map drawings to relate to the landmarks on the trail. The advice given showed him ideas on which plants and animals could be eaten, how to cook them, how to find water in the desert and how to get liquid sustenance from cacti.

By the time he departed, John's head was full of this increased knowledge. He was ferried across the North Canadian, leaving Oklahoma and entering New Mexico. This was the vast land that had been bought by the United States of America as part of the Gadsen Purchase of 1862. It was not a state but a territory that included what is the state of Arizona today. All of that was part of the grand plan to integrate the United States of America from east to west coasts and, in the South, from Texas to California.

The prairie land had changed more into scrub. The land was more rugged and increasingly dry. The vegetation was sparser with sage and cottonwood replacing much of the grass. There were even more hills and the distant mountain ranges to the west were becoming more prominent.

The plod continued. John camped that night at Rabbit Ear Creek. The next night was Pound Mound. The day after that was important as the next major water stop, Rock Crossing and the Canadian River. Four days out from McNee's Crossing, John realised the difference history had made to this land. He hit the small town of La Junta. It was still predominantly Hispanic and Spanish, or perhaps Mexican. Spanish was still the premier language. John aroused a morbid curiosity, especially because of the horses. Few had seen beasts like them in this part of the country. However, there was no animosity.

"Ole, gringo," he was greeted. Despite the sombrero, there was no hiding his white, Northern European features.

"Howdy," replied John.

"Habla usted Espagnol?"

"Un pauco. Por favor, hablamos Inglese?"

"OK," came the reply, "we'll speak English." It sounded like "weel speaker de inglesh." John wondered if his accent sounded as alien to the Hispanics.

He dismounted outside the cantina and tied the horses to the hitching rail. There was a water trough from which they could drink. John noticed there were some fresh lemons behind the bar and caused some amusement by asking if the barista could make him a fresh, cold, lemonade drink.

He found that he could sleep in a barn at the back and stable the horses and Dog with him. The food at the cantina took on a distinctly Latin flavour with Mexican beans, corn, chillies, tortillas, tacos and rice. However, it was good, wholesome and very tasty. John welcomed the change to his boring, bland diet which he had endured on the trail.

John was quizzed about his journey by the local people. It brought the usual responses; some thinking he was totally mad, others believing he was very brave. But, at least he had won their grudging respect.

That night, John spent his time cleaning up the animals. Dog was not keen on his bath but, after a few growls, he gave in. He looked very skinny when his hair was dampened. John grinned and gave Dog a bone in compensation. In contrast, the horses loved the brushing down they received.

John turned his attention to his weapons. The dirt and the dust of the desert surroundings were not conducive. He stripped, cleaned and oiled the mechanisms, checked the ammunition and reloaded the Spencer and the colt.

Next morning, John topped up his water and feed for the animals. He departed La Junta.

A small group of people, he had met the night before, saw John depart.

"Via con Dios, Senor," they called.

"Gracias," John replied. "God go with you too."

The desert was unremitting and the mountains to the west were looming ever larger. The journey was quiet, boring and uneventful. John spent the night at San Miguel del Vado. The following night he had reached Pecos Running. He was suddenly at the southern end of the Rocky Mountains and into the Glorieta Pass.

And then, there it was; Santa Fe; the end of the trail; a sprawling, bustling city, full of noise and activity. It was a meeting place for all types of people from all walks of life. It was a hotchpotch, a kaleidoscope, a cacophony of sounds and different accents.

John had made it. He couldn't describe the mix of feelings. There was a relief, joy at achieving his goal and anticipation of being able to communicate with those back home. It was the chance to let everyone know he had arrived. He thought about them all back home and how they would react to hearing from him. He visualised the joy and exhilaration his mother and the girls would feel; the pride his father would hold deep within his chest. He was tired, sore from the journey, heat drained, but he could hardly wait to send his news. He felt alive and he wanted his family to rejoice with him.

He rode down into the town.

Chapter Six

Coming from a port like Liverpool, John had been used to meeting people from several parts of the world. However, even he was amazed at the cosmopolitan nature of Santa Fe. He had expected the mix of white and black Americans and Mexicans. The numbers took in various Indian tribes, Chinese, others from Central America and all sorts of Europeans.

The town was dirty and dusty but was developing rapidly. All signs of building were apparent. The architecture of the town reflected the diversity of the populace. To put it bluntly, it was higgledy-piggledy. Town planning wasn't a feature of the Americas in 1865.

John calmed his inner exuberance and let the practicalities take over. His first task was to find livery stables for the horses and hopefully Dog. There was a blacksmith and ostler who agreed to care for all three animals. John took his personal belongings and headed to find a hotel. It was getting later in the afternoon. He was tired, dirty and dishevelled. Communications and messages could wait until the morning.

"Bienvenidos!" was the greeting from the clerk. He was a short, dark-skinned, stubbly bearded and round-faced man. He looked up and realised that the man under the sombrero was not Hispanic. "Welcome to Santa Fe, Senor." The smile was beaming and generous.

"Buenas tardes," said John. "Good evening." They both laughed.

"I am exhausted," said John. "May I have a room for a few nights, please?"

"Of course," was the reply. "Senor, you look like you could do with a good meal and a drink as well. I can recommend our dining room if you like good Mexican food."

"That sounds good. Can I have a bath and shave first, change into some clean clothes and get my dirty laundry sorted?"

"Si, senor. Of course. I can arrange that all for you. We have the barber attached to us and a Chinese laundry."

"Thank you. Gracias."

John signed the book and paid for five days stay. He needed to relax and sort out what he was going to do next. There was no haste.

The clerk took the book and read out his name. "Yon Lausanne" is what it sounded like. "My name is Antonio Hernandez." They shook hands.

Antonio noticed, despite John's journey, his time in the sun and his exposure to the elements, he was still pale.

"Are you OK?" he asked.

John explained about his illness and why he was in New Mexico. He told Antonio that, although he had improved considerably, his coughing and soreness had reduced significantly. Neither had disappeared. There was still some occasional blood in his sputum.

"There is a Sanitorium to the southwest. It is about twelve days' ride, desert and scrub before you come to mountains and forests. They have found silver there and it's being mined. But, it's got fabulous waters and the dryness is supposed to cure," Antonio hesitated. He couldn't think of the word in English. "Chew something, it sounds like!"

John looked puzzled. Then it came to him. "Tuberculosis?"

"Si Senor, of course."

"Tell me more."

"There's not much to tell. It's a pueblo, a small sanctuary run by priests."

"Would they help a gringo?"

Antonio looked hurt. "Senor, they care for everyone, no matter. They are religious men."

John felt humbled. "Abrigado. Apologies."

"That's OK, John. I'll tell you more details tomorrow."

They sorted out John's domestics; bath, shave, haircut, laundry and clean clothes to wear. He felt like a new man. The chilli, tortillas and corn were really appetising, as was the refreshingly sweet orange juice.

John went to his room and crashed out.

The next day was hot and dry as usual. John woke in his normal way but the coughing and soreness were much reduced. He washed, dressed and went down for a tortilla breakfast. After he had eaten, he went to the desk. Antonio was on duty.

"Buenas Dias, Senor. Good morning. Did you sleep well?"

"Very well," said John. "Like a log," he added. Antonio looked puzzled by the odd English expression, until suddenly, he had worked it out and roared with laughter.

"Where is the Bank of Santa Fe?" John asked.

Antonio feigned hurt. "Senor! Did you not see the most magnifico, magnificent, building, standing above all others in the centre of the town?"

"No," said John, "I was very tired when I arrived and didn't notice much."

"If you turn left out of the hotel, it's two blocks down. You'll see what I mean. It's a fort. They have a manned guard around the clock. It has the reputation of being impregnable." Antonio had some difficulty with that word but he had got the gist over. He was obviously very proud and in awe of the bank.

"And where can I find a good doctor?"

"Dr Ramos has his surgery on the way to the bank. He is at the end of this block."

"Thank you. I'll see you later. Adios!"

"Hasta proxima, Senor! See you soon."

John's first visit was to the livery stables to see the horses and Dog. The blacksmith told him that the horses needed re-shoeing and John gave him the go-ahead. He then went back, past the hotel to the doctor. Doctor Ramos was out on a visit but John was able to make an appointment to see him later that day. He then walked down to the bank.

It was everything that Antonio had said. It really was a citadel with big iron doors at the entrance. The armed guard was very visible. John was checked for weapons before he could enter. He had left them at the hotel.

Inside the bank, it appeared like a foyer of a grand hotel. There was a curve of grilled windows behind which the tellers sat. Overhead was a candle chandelier that could be lit if ever needed in the dark. Locked doors at either end of the curve led to the bank's vaults and the manager's office. It was an impressive aspect. The décor was a mix of Spanish and American features. It was a slightly incongruous combination.

John went up to one of the tellers and introduced himself.

"Oh, Senor Lawson, we have been expecting you. Senor Gonzalez, the manager, would like to meet with you."

John hadn't expected such hospitality and as nice a welcome. The agents had done a great job in preparing the way for his journey and easing any difficulties.

"If you can wait a few minutes, Senor Gonzalez will be free. In the meantime, we have some messages for you. If you'd like to sit here in comfort, I'll bring you a drink."

"Thank you," said John. "I can only drink coffee. May I have that please?"

The teller left him and went out the back. John went to sit on the settee by a low table in the main hall. A couple of minutes later, the teller returned through one of the doors bringing John a coffee and some telegraph messages.

One of the messages was from his parents. They were pleased and relieved with his progress and his plans. This had been forwarded by the New York agents. They hoped they would soon hear from him after his arrival. The other messages were from the agents, confirming financial arrangements and facilitating John's needs.

A large, dark-haired, moustachioed man appeared through one of the doors. Senor Julio Gonzales was smartly dressed. His dark, Latin-style suit, waistcoat (vest), and silk shirt were impeccable. Despite the temperature, he conveyed an aura of coolness. He greeted John warmly.

"Welcome to Santa Fe, Senor Lawson. We have been anticipating your arrival. First of all, come through to my office and we can talk in private. How are you feeling?"

As they walked through, John replied. "I am better than I was in England and I seem to be getting better day by day, thank you."

"That's very good. Would you like another cup of coffee?"

John noticed a flask of water and two glasses. "No thank you. I should like some water. It is very hot."

Julio poured them both a glass. "Now, young man, how can we be of service to you?"

"I just need to top up my finances and rest awhile. I have an appointment to see the doctor this afternoon and hopefully, he can give me a better examination."

"Is that Doctor Ramos?"

"Yes."

"He is very good and very honest. His English is impeccable."

"So is your English, excellent, Senor Gonzales. It puts my Spanish to shame."

Julio smiled. "In my job, in a place like Santa Fe, you have to be good enough to converse with all types of people."

John responded. "Antonio, at the hotel, suggested it might be best to go to San Vicente de la Cienega. I gather they have a successful sanatorium for curing tuberculosis. Maybe, they can help with consumption. Have you a sister bank in San Vicente de la Cienega?"

"I have heard of the sanatorium but I suggest that Doctor Ramos can give you the best advice. San Vicente de la Cienega is growing fast because of the mining activities and more and more prospectors coming into the area. Yes, we have contact with them, but there is no bank. It is a small pueblo or town."

"Thank you," said John. "May I ask one other favour of you please? Please can I use your telegraph facilities to get messages back to our agents in New York? They will be able to contact my family."

"That's no problem. You'll also be pleased to know that they have resurrected the trans-Atlantic telegraph cable and, hopefully, we'll have contact with England at the end of this year."

"That is good news. It is frustrating not to have more direct contact."

"Mas bueno! Very good! I'll set you up with my assistant. He can help you with the telegraphs and any finance you require."

They shook hands and Julio introduced John to his assistant, Enrique. He was a smaller, slimmer man, shaven but with dark stubble, a few years older than John. He was simply and smartly dressed in a white shirt and dark trousers. They left Julio's office and went into a customer services area.

John gave Enrique his financial requirements. While Enrique went off to finalise the details, John wrote the messages he wanted to send.

The first was to his family. "I am tired but as well as can be expected. My coughing and soreness have decreased. The dryness appears to be helping. I am staying in Santa Fe for a few days and seeing a doctor later today. There appears to be a sanatorium in San Vicente de la Cienega that specialises in TB. It means Saint Vincent of the Marsh. I may look to go there if that is the advice. I'll let you know what the doctor says. Thank you for all your love and best wishes. Love, John."

The second message was to the New York agents. It asked them to forward the first message to his parents, outlined his immediate plans and thanked them for all the support they had given him to date.

Enrique returned. "Here is your money, Senor. Now, would you like me to send your messages?"

"Yes, please. If you can send them to our agents in New York, they'll do the rest."

"How long are you staying in Santa Fe?"

"I reckon it will be a few days. I need a rest. The horses need to recuperate and to be re-shod. I am also seeing Doctor Ramos to get his opinion. It also gives us time to get some replies to the messages, although it's unlikely it will be long enough for a response from England."

Enrique nodded. "I understand. When you are ready, come back and see me or Senor Gonzales. We'll be happy to help."

"Thanks again," said John. "You have been very helpful, already."

John left the bank and returned to the hotel. The heat was getting to him and he collapsed onto the bed. He managed to doze until it was time, post siesta, to visit Doctor Ramos.

Fernando Ramos was a tall, dark, swarthy man. He was aged around fifty, John guessed. John sat down. His English was perfect.

"What can I do for you young man?"

John told the doctor of his background, his journey and why he was in Santa Fe. Fernando took everything in quietly, made the odd note on the pad on his desk, but didn't once interrupt.

When John had finished, he stood up. He came round behind John and started to examine him, tapping various parts of his shoulders, back, ribs, chest and throat. He listened intently, occasionally asking John to cough, noting where it caused some discomfort or hurt.

The binaural stethoscope had been commercially perfected by George Cammann of New York in 1852. He had written a treatise on its use and originated the commercial use of his design. Doctor Ramos had studied the paper and owned a model. He proceeded to show his expertise in examining John in greater detail.

Fernando returned to his desk. "Just relax for now." He made a few more notes. "OK, can you lie down on the bed over there, please?"

John settled on the bed. Doctor Ramos examined his reflexes and checking him lying on his back, either side and on his front. He took his time and was very thorough. John noted that, on the wall, the doctor had certificates from Madrid and Houston. This, plus the way he was examining him, gave John increased confidence that he was in good hands.

"Right! You can go and sit down again. Just keep calm." Fernando went back to his desk.

"From what you have said, it appears you have improved. I don't know how poorly you were in England. You are not clear and there is still some pleurisy or fluid in your lungs. The fact, you are coughing up less blood, is an excellent sign. So is the strength you have shown in your harrowing journey. You say, would it be good for you to visit the sanatorium in San Vicente de la Cienega? There are similarities but also differences in tuberculosis and consumption. There is something about silver that appears to help patients and the mineral is found in abundance down in the southwest."

He checked himself and smiled. "Did I say mineral? Should I have said metal? No matter! You realise that the distance is still another five to six hundred miles away. New Mexico is huge."

"I travelled nearly twice that to get here from St Joseph. If you think it's the right thing for me to do, I am sure I can make it. I am here for a few days so my animals and I have time to rest."

"I'll write up my findings. If you see me again, just before you leave, I'll let you have an updated check and give you all the data to show to the friars. The one thing, on which I must counsel you, is the weather. We get many more storms down here at this time of year, often late afternoon following the extreme heat of the day. They can be very frightening and quite dangerous if you are exposed in the open."

"Thank you for the warning." John hadn't realised how lucky he had been with the weather to date. "The main thing is not to make camp in an arroyo."

They both laughed at John's descriptive use of the Spanish word for which there isn't a true English equivalent.

"You must also be aware that you will be travelling through the 'Badlands'. There is a lack of water until you reach the higher grounds and the river forest areas. There are many renegade people; Mexican, Indian and White. They are cutthroats, thieves, vagabonds and murderers. If you thought the Santa Fe trail was dangerous, it is even more fraught where you are going."

John was quiet for a moment. He then spoke most forcibly and resolutely. "Doctor, I had nothing to lose in coming here from England. I am playing the odds. I feel better. The climate suits me more. This is healthier for me than England ever was. Yes, I have been lucky. Maybe I'll continue to be fortunate. But, I cannot really give up at this stage. My best hope is to go on and face whatever awaits me."

Doctor Ramos stood up and put his hand on John's shoulder. He resorted to Spanish for a moment. "Va con Dios. God go with you."

"He has been so far," said John.

They shook hands and John returned to his hotel. By coincidence, following Doctor Ramos' words, the skies were darkening and the humidity increasing. For the first time in the South-West, John found breathing difficult.

He had just made it back to the hotel when the storm broke. The rain was incandescent and the dirty, dusty street turned into a torrent of a muddy river. As fast as it had come, the rain ceased. The evening sun reappeared and the mud soon returned to dust. The humidity was reducing and there was more freshness abounding. John found his breathing eased and the ambient temperature became more pleasant. It was a lovely evening. John watched the sunset, brilliant red in the west. He washed and went down for dinner.

The next day, when he had eaten breakfast, Antonio called him over to the desk. Enrique had brought over a message from the bank. The New York agents had sent their reply to his missives of the previous day. They promised to forward written versions, by ship, to his family back in Liverpool.

John thanked Antonio. He visited the blacksmith to see the horses and Dog and then went to the bank to thank Enrique in person. As the heat of the day increased, he took himself back to the hotel and mused over his plans. He decided he would relax for another two days and then make the step forward on the next leg of his journey; the long trip to the sanatorium and San Vicente de la Cienega.

Over the next two days, John went about getting everything together as he had done way back in St Joseph. In particular, he made sure he had even more water than before. The direction he was going was not as well-trodden as the Santa Fe Trail had been. The water hole locations were not as well mapped. The dry desert and scrub areas might be the end of him if he couldn't find enough to drink, both for him and for the animals. He now had the experience gained over the last month. He thought that he knew what to expect.

It was now getting into late July. There was more heat; there were also more storms. The first rule was to never camp in a valley, wadi, or arroyo. The beauty of the sombrero and the slicker was that water just ran off them. The wearer remained dry underneath.

Dr Ramos was as good as his word. He had prepared a dossier for John to carry with him. It was written in perfect English and included day-to-day advice. He had also topped up his supply of laudanum, just in case. John thanked him profusely. Fernando brushed that aside.

"Senor John," he said, "I want to hear that you have got better and that you will come back and see us in Santa Fe when you are fully fit and well."

By the day of his departure, John had completed his purchases and plans. He left Santa Fe with mixed feelings, anticipation and exhilaration, fear and trepidation. The animals were pleased to be out of their confines. Dog was especially excited to be back on the road and John had to try to convince him not to race as when they had left St. Joseph.

The route was not particularly well marked and travelled. John had brought a compass with him from the ship and checked it regularly. The rolling, badlands, scrub, and desert were relentless. The heat wasn't letting up. Every day, it required a considerable effort of will to drive on; wash, feed the animals, cook, eat, clear up, de-camp, saddle up and load, ride, find water, if possible, and camp for the night. It was draining but John was determined. It was lonely with no one else on the trail. He saw the occasional animal; desert rat, sidewinder and a coyote. Seeing him, the horses and Dog, the coyote kept his distance. Dog was too hot or too well fed to chase the rat.

It was the seventh day out from Santa Fe when John's destiny took a distinctive turn. It was around noon when John was coming up a rise. Suddenly, Raven raised his head, his nostrils bristling and his body tensed up. Out of the corner of his eye, John saw Midnight react likewise. Dog went very quiet and into crouch mode. All three animals remained silent. John could see or hear nothing. Quietly, he drew the Spencer from its scabbard, checked the loading and readied it to fire. He laid it diagonally across his lap between his body and the pommel of the saddle.

As he came slowly to the top of the rise, he saw them in the gulch on the other side. A young man, an American Indian, he thought, was tied to a cottonwood tree. He had obviously been beaten and looked dirty and bloodied. But, he was still alive. He didn't look much older than John. He was not as tall but he was slim with jet black hair. Three other men were there. They looked Mexican, dressed as vaqueros, all with sombreros and gun belts, full of ammunition, crossing from each shoulder to the opposite waist. All three of them were holding and waving bottles. If not drunk, they were inebriated. Despite this, and John's sombrero, they knew John was white.

"Hey, Gringo, venez aqui."

John's adrenalin soared. He was frightened. He was in trouble. He knew it. Despite his inner panic, he sized up the situation. The three men were apart. The one nearest to him was the one who had greeted him. The second was with their three horses. The third was furthest away, next to the young captive.

Somehow, John kept his nerve. "No, gracias," he replied.

The man who had spoken had been smiling, with his face, mouth and teeth. His eyes were dark and studying John intently. It was then that John noted a change in demeanour. The man had been looking at him and his gaze seemed to darken. John realised he had seen the Comanche lance. It might have been the safeguard for him to date; now it was a threat. The other two men had sensed the change.

There was nothing for it. John swung the Spencer and fired at the nearest man as his three adversaries went for their guns. The boom startled Raven so much that he jolted John in the saddle. Even in falling, he had reset the Spencer and fired again. As he did, he felt the burn and searing pain on the side of his forehead.

John hit the ground with a thud and then everything went blank.

Chapter Seven

It was pitch black. When John awoke, he had a thumping headache. He seemed to hurt from the top of his head all the way down to the soles of his feet. His breathing was easier than when he had laid down before. There was an unusual smell. It was acrid and sweet at the same time. There was something sticky spread over his chest. He ran his finger over it and held it up to his nose. The strength of the odour hit him and caused him to cough. That wasn't as sore as it had been before but the rest of his body ached with the effort.

There was somebody in the place with him. A hand smoothed something cool and damp across his forehead. It was small but firm; a woman or a girl. Was he alive or dead? Were the Muslims right? Had he gone to heaven as a hero and was this his promised virgin?

His eyes started to become accustomed to the dark and he could make out a female shape. He closed his eyes again. When he reopened them, he sensed she was laughing at him.

"Shhh!" she said, as she mopped his brow. She said something else that was totally incomprehensible. He lay back and tried to relax. Her presence was soothing and he felt safe.

A million questions were going through his mind. How did he get there? Where was he? Who was this female? What had happened to the Mexicans and the young Indian? He was totally and utterly confused. Was it a dream?

His brain was hurting. His head was throbbing. The firm, cooling hands were calming him and they were easing his mind. He was beginning to enjoy the touch even more and the presence of what he sensed was a young lady. He wondered if, in all the strange cacophony of smells, one of them was hers.

Suddenly, he was hit by a shaft of bright light and a blast of heat. He was blinded for a moment. Then the brightness was gone. A third person was with them, a man. He spoke quietly and the girl replied. It was not a language that he understood, had heard before or bore any similarity to ones he might know. The tone implied that they were talking about him. Both appeared to be pleased with his progress and there was a comforting feel emanating from their dialogue. All through this, the girl continued to massage John and keep him cool. She raised his head slightly and put a cup or bowl to his lips. The drink was bitter but not unpleasant. He drank it in sips. There was a strong taste of various herbs. John could not detect their distinctive flavours. The girl laid his head back. He felt sleepy once again and dozed off into a world of hazy dreams.

The next time he awoke, it was getting cooler. It was late afternoon, not far off dusk. The girl was still there and tendering him. This time, when the light broke the darkness, it was less intense and things became clearer. The opening was a flap and John was lying on a bed of animal skins within a tipi. Like a tent, this was a mobile home made up of buffalo skins.

The person, who had entered the tipi, was the young man who had been held by the Mexicans. He still carried the bruises around his face and discoloured shading around his dark brown eyes. However, he now appeared to be fit and well. He smiled when he saw John had recognised him. He was quite a handsome lad, with an aquiline nose, unusual, as John was to find out later, for these Indians. They were Mescalero Apaches or *'Ndee',* as they preferred to be called. Apache is the word for an enemy; Ndee means one's own people.

John was now able to turn his attention to the girl. He gasped at his first proper sighting. Most Mescalero had rounded faces, pockmarked and ravaged by the effects of smallpox and other illnesses. They also tended to have flat, spreading noses. Like the young man, the girl was slim. She was strikingly beautiful, deep, dark brown eyes, long black hair, a sharp, straight nose and high cheekbones. It struck John that she was the young man's sister and in her early to middle teens. She even appeared to blush as John prolonged his gaze upon her.

Both the boy and the girl were dressed in deerskin clothing. John was undressed to his undergarments. He looked around and saw that many of his belongings were alongside him in the tipi. The clothes were laid out neatly and had obviously been cleaned. There was no sign of any blood. His guns and belt were alongside. The questions were racing through John's mind again.

"Who are you? Where am I? How did I get here?"

The Mescalero showed no emotion, nor did they answer. It was clear they did not speak English.

"Habla usted Espagnol?" John tried again.

"Si, un pauco," came the response.

Through a semblance of Spanish, English, Mescalero, hand signals and drawings, John slowly began to put together what had happened.

"What are your names? I am John Lawson." John pointed to himself.

The young man pointed to himself. "Paco Faraones," he said. The girl in turn said, "Linda Faraones." She pronounced her first name as 'leen-da'.

"Wife?" asked John. "Mujer?"

They laughed. John's first instinct had been right. They were brother and sister. He spoke to the girl but wasn't sure she understood.

"You have the right name. Linda means pretty in Spanish."

John turned again to Paco. "Where are the animals?" He put his hands to his ears pointing all the fingers up. The other two laughed.

"Bono," he said. He then added, "Goshe."

John was puzzled until Paco said, "Woof."

"Dog," said John. Not having named him properly, John thought Goshe would be a good name. It does mean dog in the Mescalero language.

Paco left the tipi but quickly returned with Dog. As soon as he saw John his tail wagged violently. He jumped on to John, licking his face. Linda grabbed him off and Dog growled. She gave Paco an angry glance.

"No, Goshe," John called. Paco took the dog away from Linda and put him outside the tipi. Linda motioned him to stay out as well. She got John to lie back and take it easy once again.

The story began to take place over several days. John was taking time to recuperate. He couldn't be loaded with too much too soon. In a strange way, Raven had indirectly saved his life. When he had shot the first Mexican, Raven and Midnight had both been startled. By throwing him sideways, the bullet from the second Mexican had just glanced John's temple. Even his falling did not cause John to miss his second shot. Both of the Mexicans were dead.

The three men holding Paco had been drinking. The one nearest to him did not realise the young Indian had loosened his bonds. While the focus of attention had been on John and the third Mexican was drawing his revolver, Paco jumped him, surprised him, grabbed the knife from the sheath on his belt and plunged through his left ribs and into his heart.

John was out cold. He had cracked his head badly and had a hairline fracture of the skull. It would have been dangerous to move him but there was no choice. They were in the middle of nowhere. Luckily, the horses hadn't scattered. Despite his own injuries, Paco was able to round them up. He used the saddles off of the Mexican horses to make a stretcher bed for John. He attached this to two poles cut from the cottonwood and tied them to the back of Raven and Midnight. He tied the Mexican horses and his own pony in a string using one of the dead men's ropes. He took all the guns, ammunition and clothing from them, but he didn't bury or burn the bodies. The animals of the desert had to be fed as well and they deserved a treat.

He then had to return to the village, the temporary summer residence for his band. He rode Raven, Midnight alongside and the trails of the other hoses behind. Raven did not object or protest to his new rider. Maybe he had understood the importance of the task.

The Mescalero, like many of the native Americans, did not live in tribes. They had formed bands, normally around fifty people, usually derived from a wider family or close grouping. This band spent their summer in a valley that was a tributary of the River Gila. John was not to know it at the time, but the village was about three days ride north of the pueblo at San Vicente de la Ciénega, his original destination. Today, this is in the area of Silver City.

If you were looking for Shangri-La or the Garden of Eden, you could do far worse than coming to this beautiful wilderness. The desert and scrub had given way to mountainous terrain, up to five thousand feet above the valleys, and nearly eleven thousand feet up, further north in the Mogollon Mountain Range. This semicircle provided a barrier to protect the land from the worst excesses of arctic winds in winter. The climate is described as 'four gentle seasons', rarely with heavy winter snow, but with temperatures up to one hundred degrees 'F', thirty-eight degrees 'C', in June or July. The population was sparse, mainly bands of Apache, some Mescalero, but largely Chihuahua. They migrated further north and into the river pastures for Summer, but returned into the more temperate desert climes for the winter. They were fiercely protective of their lands and inspired awe and fear amongst those venturing into them.

The forest was lush. Depending on the height, there were Spruce Fir, Douglas Fir, Quaking Aspen, Ponderosa Pine, Pinyon-Jupiter woodland and desert vegetation in the drier areas between rivers. Nearer the rivers, various species abounded; Arizona Sycamore, Walnut, Maple, Gambel Oak, Ash, Cottonwood, Alder and Willow. The land was the transition between the Chihuahuan Desert and the Rocky Mountains.

The main predatory animals were the Cougar, Bobcat, Mexican Wolf, American Black Bear, Grey Fox and White-nosed Coati. The animals, on which

65

they would prey, were Mule Deer, White-tailed Deer, Pronghorn, Elk, Rocky Mountain Bighorn Sheep and Wild Mustang. There were also many American Beaver. Birds of prey were Common Black Hawk, Zone-tailed Hawk, Goshawk, Mexican Spotted Owl, Osprey and American Bald Eagle. Ground birds included Wild Turkey and Dusky Grouse. American Dippers were found throughout the many streams. The most common reptiles were the Arizona Coral Snake and the Gila Monster. Other snakes were the Black-tailed Rattlesnake, Rock Rattlesnake and the Sonora Mountain King Snake. The fish were Gila, Brown and Rainbow Trout, Catfish and Freshwater Bass.

The Mescalero were not quite as nomadic as other Apache tribes. They had lived on the borders of New Mexico and Mexico for centuries. At first, they had welcomed newcomers such as the Hispanic Mexicans and Americans. The early days were trading between the various communities. Then, as certain peoples tried to exert control, disputes arose. Raids took place and an open enmity ensued. There was no love lost between the Mescalero and Mexican populace.

The reason for the more stationary nature of the Mescalero, compared to other Apache, was that they were more agricultural. Certainly, they were very good hunters and riders. However, they were named Mescalero after their economy based on the Mescal.

The Mescal plant is from the Agavaceae family. It grows to around one and a half to two and a half feet tall, depending on the variety. It has thick, green or grey-green, strong leaves that come to a point with a dark green or brown needle and a blooming spike. It is perennial, but it dies when it flowers, once in ten to twenty-five years. For this reason, it has the alternative name of the century plant. It is very hardy, can survive, in the short-term, down to eighteen degrees of frost, but conserves water when temperatures reach three figures. It propagates from tendrils, cuttings or seeds. It is a native of the desert climes of New Mexico Territory, the states of New Mexico and Arizona of today.

Mescalero society was and is complex. It is matrilineal, that is, based on the female line of the family. Men take on responsibility for their wife's family on marriage. This extends to polygamy, to protect widows amongst sisters and cousins when necessary. Women did take part in what is generally regarded as male roles. There were renowned, Mescalero, female warriors and hunters. Generally, though, women did more of the agricultural and the domestic chores.

The Mescal has a tremendous number of uses in food and drink. The heart is rich in saccharine and sweet, nutritious, but fibrous when baked. If ground alone, and/or mixed with cereal or sweet corn flour, it makes types of bread. It can be used to thicken stews and soups or as a porridge. Certain varieties of the plant produce a bean that can also be cooked. The young flower stalk can be eaten raw or cooked but is especially delicious when baked. Tender young leaves are best roasted. Sap, from old flowering stems, is used as syrup. Nectar from the new flowering stems makes an even sweeter syrup. Most of all, the sap can be bored from the base of the flowering stem to be turned into a very, potent, alcoholic drink called Mescal. It is still used in other drinks such as tequila and pulque. The liquid is medicinal. It is a diuretic, a purgative and a cleanser.

The saponins, in the leaves, can be extracted as soap, by simmering them into a mush. The leaves can be shredded to make very strong and fine fibres, thread, fabric, string, rope and paper. The thorns, on the ends of the leaves, make excellent pins and needles. The dried flowering stems are used as excellent thatching material in the permanent residence, the Wickiup, the winter wood built and buffalo hided home. The same material acts as a razor strop. The final, flowering spurt and spike make good lances.

There was no waste in this society. Harder materials, like animal bones and remains, were shaped into implements such as cups and ornaments or used to make glue. Fishbones were used in the making of weapons. What the Mescalero needed from the outside world, like metal instruments such as knives, they obtained through trade. Their most precious commodity was the horse.

John was finding this out all the time talking to Linda and Paco. He was frustrated at his immobility and anxious to let his family know what had happened to him and where he was. For now, it was impractical.

As his strength returned, he found out more. The mother of Linda and Paco was Maria Elena Sanchez. She had been snatched, as a nine-year-old girl, when a Mescalero raiding party had attacked a Spanish Mexican travelling convoy. Her parents were killed. Indeed, she was the only Spanish survivor of the attack. She was integrated into the Mescalero society. When she had achieved her second year of puberty, she was courted, in the Mescalero way, by the son of the man who had led the warring party. His name was Mangas Faraones. Faraones is the equivalent of the Egyptian word Pharaoh.

This explained why the children had more striking looks than the average Mescalero. Maria Elena's looks had been transferred to both Paco and Linda, particularly noticeable in their noses. Mescalero society is highly respectful to women. It is not a male-dominated hierarchy. The women play a great part in decision-making and the cohesion of the band.

Mangas had brought his horse to her wickiup. If she were to accept his proposal, she had to feed, water and brush the animal, return it and tether it to his abode. It was not considered appropriate to do that within twenty-four hours. Equally, three days was regarded as unacceptable. Maria Elena was then fifteen; Mangas seventeen. She accepted. They had gone through the extensive and beautiful ritual that is a Mescalero wedding.

Today, in their mid to late-thirties, their family was the prominent one in the band. Both had come to see John in his bed and thanked him for saving Paco. There was little emotion or expression shown. Apart from some broken Spanish with Maria Elena, John had difficulty communicating with them. He managed to portray his thanks for Paco saving him, in turn, and for Linda caring for him in the healing process.

At one point, Linda also told him that, before they knew his name, Paco had called him 'Ligai Ndolkah'. He had described how he had come quietly, over the rise and sprung like a big cat upon his prey. As John started to pick up the Mescalero language he learned what it meant; 'White Cougar'. He was very proud to be compared to that magnificent, strong, brave and graceful animal at the top of the food chain.

The Summer camp was along the plain of one of the rivers flowing into the Gila system. Corn and mescal were cultivated. The Mescalero were renowned horsemen and they kept, traded and broke ponies. Further upstream from the camp were canyons, some of them box, that were the home to wild horses which were occasionally captured. Meat and skins were sourced from local hunting and fish were taken from the river. There was pasture for the horses and hay was gathered in for the winter.

In disbanding the winter camp, a hunting party would travel to the plains to try to bring back some buffalo.

This was the most dangerous for the Mescalero coming into conflict with other native tribes, Mexicans and mule skinners. The journeys were becoming less productive with the excessive ravaging of the buffalo.

As the Summer grew into the Autumn, John became stronger. He was no longer bringing up any blood. His coughing had reduced considerably and the phlegm appeared to be infected no longer. He was frustrated that he couldn't travel and get messages back to his family. He became able to ride locally in the beautiful river valleys, canyons and surrounding hills. Linda went with him on most occasions. Despite her size, Linda had taken to Midnight and she had taken to the girl. Linda was an adept horsewoman. Occasionally Paco took him on a local hunting trip. The extra guns and ammunition taken from the dead Mexicans proved a boon. The people had more meat and were better fed than ever before.

All this time, John was gleaning more about the Mescalero ways. As he picked up the language, he was accepted into the group meetings and discussions. He didn't say much to start. This was a massive learning curve. However, the Mescalero were also keen to tap his knowledge of the wider world. They were intrigued by his journey and what had brought him to New Mexico. They were trying to understand what made white people tick. They were puzzled about the black Americans, a high proportion being the cavalry troopers they had encountered. John explained about the Civil War, slavery and emancipation. It hadn't all been good as ex-slaves became destitute when gaining their freedom. The only outlet was the cavalry and fighting the Indians as America swept west. As John was still recovering, the Mescalero were pleased to use him to teach the children in the band. This helped him to assimilate the language more quickly, especially as they were not backward in laughing at his pronunciation.

The one thing that John was not absorbing was custom. He had been a little puzzled as to why Maria Elena kept her distance. Although the Mescalero did not have a leader as such, Mangas was regarded as the senior and perhaps the most important. He was becoming closer to John acting as a father figure and mentor. The older man was truly grateful for him having saved his only son. The reason that Maria Elena was more distant was not that she didn't like John. It was the obvious opposite. Mother-in-laws are not supposed to be close to their daughters' husbands in Mescalero society.

Linda was of age and had not been close to any brave. Her time with John had brought her close to him. The group could see it happening. Mangas and Maria Elena could see it. Paco was delighted and Linda was happy to care for John and be in his company. They could laugh together, enjoy the rides together and gather the herbs and mosses she needed for her medication and treatments. It was only John who was oblivious to their relationship. So, it was up to the female to use her wiles.

It was late summer, getting into September, when they rode up the valley onto one of the mountain trails. The weather was still fine but there were hints of the chills to come. The colours were magnificent in the sages and brushes, the rich hues of the pines and spruces and the shades created by the sun getting ever lower in the sky. They had stopped to have a rest, let the horses graze, and have some food and drink for themselves. Goshe ran around, sniffing everything of interest.

John dismounted from Raven and walked over to Linda and Midnight. As she dismounted, Linda appeared to stumble and John caught her in his arms. Linda threw her arms around his neck her feet not yet touching the ground, and she kissed him passionately. John was surprised, embarrassed and delighted, all at the same time. She felt him respond. He was looking closely into her eyes. They were shining with a fire. He didn't know what to say.

Linda realised that. "Shh," she said, and put her finger over his mouth. They kissed some more and walked together hand in hand. Suddenly, neither felt like eating nor drinking. They kept looking at one another, smiling, kissing, walking some more and repeating those sweet, tender moments.

They finally sat down and had the food and drink they had brought with them.

"Where do we go from here?" asked John. "I didn't dare show my feelings for you in case I got it wrong. There might have been another man."

Linda laughed. "Have you seen anyone else in my life? For someone as clever as you, you are not so perceptive at times."

"You have helped me recover. I really did think I was dead when I first saw you. You were my reward in heaven; so beautiful, so wonderful, so thrilling. But, how can I stay?"

"You may be white, but you saved Paco. You are an accepted Mescalero. Everyone likes you and trusts you. My family loves you. But you also know that the Mescalero are not emotional people who are used to showing their feelings. I have inherited the Spanish side of me and that allows me to express my hopes and desires more fully. I didn't just care for you. I do love you."

"But, if I cannot stay, I go back, then what?"

"Do you want me to come with you?" This time, the dark, brown eyes were shiny with tears.

John wiped the wetness away, kissed both her eyes gently, took her in his arms and replied softly. "Yes, of course. But you also know, I wouldn't want to take you away from your family."

"It's the future that counts, not the past. It's our future. You and I haven't had the chance to decide what that is yet. When you came here, you did not think you had a future. Now your health is better, you have regained hope. You have a life.

You have found love. As long as you stay well, and the dry climate and the herbs and medicines we have, do appear to be doing the job, are you going to risk returning to England?"

"That could be foolhardy," John said. "However, I am desperate to let everyone know what has happened to me. They must be worried and they must fear the worst."

"Yes, I understand. We had the same fears for Paco when he didn't return. We will soon be going south into the desert for the winter. Along the way, we will find time to break off from the main party and travel to a town. My mother has some Spanish outfits I can wear. We'll look like a normal white and Hispanic couple if we dress properly. We might even be able to do some trading for the band. You can teach me to shoot and get me my own weapons."

"You bloodthirsty witch," John laughed.

Linda hit him playfully and they kissed again. "I am a better fighter than you think," she said. "Mescalero women have to be able to look after themselves. You've been warned!"

John fell back, feigning shock and horror, clutching his chest as though he had been attacked. "I have been shot; no stabbed; no poisoned," he gasped. "You are my dangerous woman aargh!" He fell back and lay prone and still. Linda jumped on him and they grappled in mock combat, which soon turned into a passionate kiss.

John felt her beautiful and small firm breasts pressed up against him. His heart was pounding. Linda felt his hard penis pressed through his jeans against her.

John released his grip. "I want you so much," he whispered, "but we'll do this properly, according to tradition."

Linda was both pleased and disappointed at the same time. She had been equally excited. "Thank you, I love you even more for that," she said. She gave him a big hug and a quick, sweet kiss. "We'd better get back."

They packed everything, mounted the horses, called Goshe over and headed down to the river valley and the summer camp.

"As my gift to you," John said, "I want you to have Midnight. You are so good together and I think she is your horse already."

"That is such a wonderful gift. I am so happy. Thank you! Thank you! Thank you!" Linda leaned forward and patted the head of her new horse.

John laughed. "I have an ulterior motive. When I bring my horse to your tipi, you won't have the excuse that you have to look after two animals."

Linda responded in kind. "What makes you think I am going to accept you?" John could see the devilment in her eyes. She was toying with him and he thought it best to keep quiet.

When they got back to the camp, all seemed normal. It was Maria Elena who sensed the change in her daughter, but she said nothing. Nobody else realised anything. Well, maybe they did but the true Mescalero would not let on.

However, next morning, everyone knew. John had arisen early, had fed and watered Raven and then tethered him to Linda's tipi. If the rest of the camp was delighted or despairing, the people didn't show it. The Mescalero went about their daily duties in the normal way. Paco took John on a hunting trip, bringing him a spare pony. He said nothing and his face betrayed no emotion. John was beginning to understand more and more about the Mescalero and their sang-froid. Paco concentrated on the stalking and the chase as they brought back some deer for the band.

It was late in the afternoon when they returned. John was perturbed to see Raven was still tethered to Linda's tipi. Paco made him concentrate on the task in hand, cutting up the deer, skinning, producing strips for jerky, separating haunches of meat and offal, separating bones, skulls and hooves for jellies, tools and glue. It had been a tiring day and, when he had finished, John collapsed into his tipi and was quickly asleep.

When he awoke next morning, everything had changed. Raven was back, tied to his tipi. He had been beautifully washed and groomed. He had been well fed and watered and looked in the peak of health. Linda had accepted him. As John saw other members of the camp, they did not appear to be treating him differently. There were no congratulations, not a smile nor even a glance. However, John sensed they were pleased. He now felt among the Ndee. He was part of them. He was also confused. Was it right to go and see Linda now? Was there some other protocol? He was longing to see her, caress her, kiss her and hold her tightly. As he was trying to decide, Paco came to find him.

Paco did allow himself a smile. "Well my brother," he said, "you are now to be my brother-in-law. We have a lot to do."

John was now totally perplexed. He stammered "Wh…hh.at?"

Paco laughed out loud to see John this way. "You have got to get ready," he said. "Come, you have to see my father. We do not wait on the ceremony. We have to make you fit for my sister."

John was aghast and this made Paco laugh even more.

"Look, we have got to do this properly. This is our way. I will guide you through it and what I don't know, my father will fill you in. It is lucky that we got the harvest and the hunts in before we move to our winter home. The women are caring for Linda. She knows what to expect and," he laughed again, "you don't."

In a strange way, John felt like he was more scared than he had ever been. It was similar to an initiation ceremony like the old Hellfire Club or the Freemasons back in England. Paco was amused at his obvious distress and this was proving even more intimidating.

He did sugar the pill somewhat. "I can tell you that everyone is delighted. We were all willing for this to happen. You are very much a part of our family." He meant this in the wider sense of the band rather than the immediate blood family. There isn't an exact translation for the Mescalero word.

They entered Mangas' tipi. The older man remained calm and enigmatic. There was no show of emotion. He motioned both of the younger men to sit.

"John," he said, "you do not know our ways and so, as Linda's father, it falls to me to explain it all to you. It is the custom for the betrothed couple to spend time apart up to the wedding ceremony. This is supposed to cement their love for one another and prove their fidelity. We have three days to dress you and we have a tribal, family, wedding coat. We need to lengthen it as you are taller than both me and Paco. In fact, you are taller than any Mescalero I have known. But, we will do it."

John was still in shock at the speed of events. Mangas continued.

"Linda will be prepared in the traditional way by the women of our family. They are well versed and we can leave all of that up to them. In three days' time, we will be ready too. We all meet up and we have several days of ceremony. You will see one another but you are not supposed to touch or show any intimacy. There will be music, dancing, feasting and the wedding ceremony. We will have built you and Linda a separate tipi outside of the village. At some point, the two of you will disappear and, before we have to break camp for the winter, you will have time together on your own."

John nodded his understanding.

Mangas became more serious.

"I must tell you the responsibilities of a Mescalero man. We ideally espouse monogamy in our society. Divorce is possible but very rare. The man is there for the female's side of the family. As Maria Elena is a one-off, I did not have any issues on this score. It is unlikely that you will have as Maria Elena and I have only one daughter. It is a sad reflection of our history and times that our men have been killed in battle or murdered. I am always in your debt for Paco."

He glanced across at his son who nodded agreement. "Neither of us could have wanted for more from you. We know you will look after Linda. We know she has chosen well."

John mumbled his thanks. He felt very humbled at the words of his future father-in-law. He then brightened and turned to Mangas.

"I came here not knowing what was to become of me. No one, not least me, expected me to beat consumption. I was going into a different world; a strange world; a violent world. There was always the risk of death and danger but that was nothing new. Now, things have changed. I think I am cured. You see I am stronger. I no longer cough up any blood and it does not hurt me to cough. Linda's cures and Mescalero medicine has completed what the better weather had improved. I love your daughter." Turning to Paco, he said, "I love your sister. I love your people. You have all cared for me in your way. Most of all, you accepted me into your band and made me a part of you. Linda and I are under no illusions. Things will be difficult. The whites, like me, are coming. Oh yes, there have only been a few so far. But, they will come. Next year, there will be more; the year after, more still. The other Indian Nations and tribes have seen it already. There were treaties with them, their *Ndee*, now their *Apache*."

Mangas and Paco listened quietly, absorbing what John was saying. They noted his true understanding of their words for *own people* and *enemy*.

John carried on. "The five, so-called, civilised tribes were betrayed. The Mescalero have been betrayed by whites, Mexicans and other Indians. This land, New Mexico, was bought by the American government, from Mexico, three years ago. It was called the Gadsden Purchase. You don't understand that concept. I admire you and the other American Indians for that. You believe that land is for everyone like air and water."

John hesitated for a moment before continuing. "We, the white men, have a concept of ownership. I am white. I also hope, you believe, I am truly Mescalero.

I don't know if Maria Elena would understand this better with her Spanish roots. If she does, and you cannot listen to me, listen to her."

John motioned across to a buckskin bottle. Mangas nodded and they all took a drink of water before John spoke again.

"Linda and I have discussed the future and what it holds. We will be together in whichever way we can. We want to be Mescalero. We may even be Spanish, Mexican, American or English. We will not be apart and we will look after each other, whatever it takes, wherever we are."

John then smiled. "I am glad you only have the one daughter. I don't think I could cope with two or more, no matter your tradition. One Linda is ample enough for me." Did Mangas and Paco raise a smile in their eyes; probably?

The next three days, the men were busy. They readied and lengthened the groom's coat. The bridal Wickiup was prepared with all the necessities; food, water and furnishings. True to the custom, they didn't see the women. They looked after themselves and made sure they cared for the animals. Goshe was racing around making a nuisance of himself frequently, looking for stroking and play from John. It was all part of animals sensing that change was afoot, needing to be reassured.

The wedding coat was magnificent. It was made of white buckskin. The buttons were beautifully carved tips of horn, attached to the garment with fibres of mescal thread. There were no buttonholes on the other side. Instead, there were fibre loops. Throughout, there were coloured threads, depicting the animals of the forest and desert, all of which the Mescalero knew well. It was wonderfully intricate and the pictures were vivid. The hues were stunning.

The preparation for the woman was even more elaborate. The Mescalero were not really religious but they were highly spiritual. Linda had to be made pure in everyone's eyes. During the pre-wedding period, her eyebrows were plucked. She was to wear no make-up and to be presented to her husband in a ghostly, apparitional form. Her hair would be brushed and straight. The dress reflected the four colours representing the four directions, north, east, south and west. To the Mescalero, these were red, white, gold and blue. The different shades were made from the tinctures of the earth, plants and animal extracts. It was necessary for them all to be represented on her outfit so that she would prosper for the future. Like the man's coat, there were intricate patterns on the dress based on the flora rather than the fauna.

One of the things, that the women of a village do, is weaving. A bridal casket is made from mescal fibres and presented to the bride at her wedding. This contains all the presents from the band for both the wife and the husband. Again, this is decorated in an ornate fashion with the flora, fauna and four colour depictions to bring the couple good fortune. The casket was secretly taken to the wedding tipi as a welcome surprise for Linda and John.

The food and drink were being prepared for the feasting. Everyone was involved. On the day everything began, the men brought John fully regaled. The women did the same with Linda. It was the first time they had seen each other for days, in fact, before the time John had tied Raven to Linda's tipi.

When John saw Linda, he gasped. Her face, without the eyebrows, looked severe. She was still beautiful. Her head was bowed and she maintained a demure look, not glancing at John directly. At that stage, the bride and groom were not allowed to meet. The village was there for the feast. Eating and drinking began for everybody. As the day wore into night, the festivities became noisier. There was singing and dancing involving the men, the women and the children.

At last, the betrothed couple were allowed to be together. The wedding ceremony took place with the whole village casting their blessings on the young couple, dancing around them and showering them with flowers and petals.

After that, the partying really continued. Weddings had been known to last for days. Usually, with the connivance of the elders of the village, the married couple slip away at some point. In this case, it being the end of the summer and the group having to move before the winter set in, everyone was aware of giving the newly married couple the time for a 'honeymoon'. During that time, the rest of the village would prepare for departure, travelling to their winter home in the south-eastern desert.

Everyone understood that the party would be foreshortened. In the early hours of the morning, John and Linda disappeared, leaving the village to go to the specially prepared tipi.

Chapter Eight

Once they had got away from the village, they were running hand in hand. They stopped and kissed passionately. John lifted Linda's smaller frame, swinging her around. They continued running to the tipi, collapsing into it, breathless, but still clasped together, giggling, laughing and kissing in between gasping for air.

The tipi had been beautifully prepared. The bed had been laid out on a straw base. It was covered with soft skins and decorated with herbs scattered all over the top. It smelt erotic, sweet and sensuous. They crashed on to it, kicked off their footwear, his boots and her moccasins. They scrambled inside the skins and started to undress one another. It was too frantic and they slowed to a more easy-paced seduction. John had calmed enough to remove Linda's top clothes more gently. He started to stroke her beautiful firm breasts and felt her nipples stiffen. He bent over and sucked them gently. Linda was undressing him and she found his penis. He was so pent up that he had to stop her stroking it before he came. They finished removing each other's clothing and lay holding each other, totally naked. Their kisses led to more stroking. John kissed Linda's nipples again and lowered his hand to play with her vagina. She was already responding and moist. She pulled him over on her, his penis hard and erect. She pulled it into her and John drove it forcefully, filled with so much excitement. It was the consequence of them both being virgins. Linda cried out with the pain of a first entry and John came immediately.

They separated and Linda was crying. John held her close and she snuggled in his arms, still sobbing.

John stroked her hair. "Oh, I'm so sorry, my love. What is it? What did I do wrong?"

"It's not your fault," Linda responded. She kissed him gently and he wiped away her tears. "It was the first time for both of us. You broke into me. My mother and the other women prepared me. They said it is better once you're over.

The next time, it won't happen again." She even raised a smile and teased him. "You'll be better too," she said, running her finger on his now, limp, manhood.

Feeling his chagrin, she put her tongue in his ear and whispered, "I love you."

John relaxed and kissed her back, gently caressing her face and drinking away the wetness of her tears. "I worshipped you from the moment I first set eyes on you. I wanted you so much. I didn't know if it was the right thing to try to win you. You were, and you are, my beautiful goddess, my angel and the only girl I have ever loved or wanted."

"I know," she said. She giggled. "You don't know what you said in your sleep, when you were recovering, after Paco brought you to us. Some of the things you said were very endearing. Your imagination in your delirium was quite vivid. Maybe, one day, I'll tell you the things you said you'd like to do to me."

She laughed and kissed him as she sensed his embarrassment. She was now hurting less and the soreness had abated.

"John, I knew you loved me. Your thoughts were so tender and loving. You wanted to do things with me, not to me. It wasn't one-sided. I knew you would be my man. I wouldn't belong to you; you wouldn't belong to me. We would be partners. That is also the Mescalero way."

"I'd have been your slave, if that was to only way to be with you," John said.

"You never needed to do that. I have a man who is now strong. You are caring and gentle. You are also brave and you stand up for whatever is right. You will look after me and I will look after you. Because of who we are, we may be able to succeed as Mescalero, Hispanic or white."

They kissed and snuggled up to each other again. Linda smelt so fresh and fragrant with the herbal deodorants and mescal soap mixes she used. They were tired and dozed off, entwined in one another's arms.

It was still dark when they woke up. More exactly, John was still in a world of dreams, lying on his side. Linda was behind him, one hand stroking his hair. Her other arm was around his waist, with her hand playing with his penis and gently squeezing his testicles. He moaned with quiet pleasure and arousal. Linda caressed the tip of his penis in a very gentle and loving fashion. John turned and kissed her passionately. He moved on to playing with her breasts, sucking her nipples and kissing several parts of her body. Linda climbed on to him in reverse. She offered her vagina to be tasted and licked while she sucked his penis. He was surprised at how sweet she was and the delight that gave him. At the same time, she was tantalising him with the expertise she was showing with her mouth and tongue.

"No more! No more!" murmured John. "You're making me come."

For a moment, the daredevil in Linda wanted to continue. Instead, she came off John and turned, sitting astride him. She lowered herself onto his hardened member, filling her vagina while she came forward onto his chest. He was not yet recovered or as impatient as earlier. Their lovemaking, kissing and cuddling were still passionate. This time, they were more controlled and, apart from a little soreness, Linda wasn't hurting. They moved in unison, Linda squeezing John between her legs, as she rode him. John was desperately trying to control his desire to release too quickly. They came together as Linda achieved a climax. They stayed entwined, only separating after they had both subsided. They were wet, sticky and happy. They kissed again and fell to sleep wrapped together.

The next few days went in a whirl. They had the horses and Goshe with them and had to look after them. They sorted the gifts and their own food and drink. They went riding into the forest and mountainside, picnicking and making love in the warm sunlight. Both of them were learning more about one another's bodies and what turned them on. The first time that Linda reached an orgasm was a surprise to her. She was holding on to a tree, bending forward while John entered her 'doggy-fashion'. The extra penetration and John's improving control were the triggers. John had the beautiful pain of being tightly squeezed and pumped out between Linda's thigh movements. Her wonderful laugh and wet kisses were stupendous as they came apart and John subsided so rapidly.

"Oh, my poor baby," she giggled. "Can you not keep up with 'Mamma'?" Linda really loved teasing John and rousing his embarrassment. However, she always did it in a loving way. Her touches were tender, she held him close, pressed her body against him and left him in no doubt that she was his woman and he was her man. In turn, John was always taking her hand, stroking her hair, helping her to wash and having her wash him. They were tempted to make love, on one occasion, in a stream. The mountain water was still too cold and it didn't help their ardour. Drying one another off and holding their bodies close together for warmth, produced the desired effect and a very sweet, loving seduction. They were wrapped in a blanket on the ground. They were in the spoon position and John entered Linda, softly and firmly, kissing her neck and arms, playing with her breasts and nipples, occasionally drifting his lower hand to arouse her vagina and clitoris. All the time he was thrusting and withdrawing 'baby', into and out of Linda gently. Linda began moaning. For the first time, she climaxed and then she reached an orgasm, before he came. John continued and, when he erupted, she sensed a mini-climax. They didn't speak. There were no apologies. They had reached the stage in which their love was for one another. They accepted whatever occurred and enjoyed the level it achieved. If they achieved a loving congress that reached the heights, they rejoiced in that. They also enjoyed everything that was good but not perfect. The beautiful thing was that they still wanted one another even when they had finished the physical act. On this occasion, with her having subsided first, Linda did not tease John about his limpness. She lay in her cocoon with the protection of his body cradling her, his arms holding her and his hands caressing her. That was bliss. They lay contentedly and drifted off to sleep.

This sojourn, in their lives, was not to last. On the fifth morning, since their wedding, they heard horses approaching the tipi. Paco had arrived with five ponies, one of which he was riding, the other four he was leading. He dismounted and came to see them.

Paco had a great smile when he permitted himself to indulge in it.

"The band is now ready to move," he said. "My father has asked if you would do us a favour. We have a wagon and we would like to use it to haul all the heavier equipment. Could you use his four ponies to ride and carry your belongings? In turn, may we use Raven and Midnight to haul the wagon?"

Turning to John, he said, "You'll notice that one of the ponies, a stallion, is bigger than the others. I thought you might ride that."

John was reluctant to see Raven go. The large Pinto, he was offered, was about fifteen hands high and big enough for him. It was a beautiful animal.

"How do you feel about that?" John asked Linda. He saw from her face, she was equally reluctant not to have Midnight.

"I suppose that will be OK." John thought he heard a quiver in her voice. "Go on, Paco, take them."

"We haven't named them yet. Perhaps you would like to do that for us." He handed the string over to John. John tied them to the tipi and then helped Paco get Raven and Midnight. Both of them had become used to him since they had pulled John's stretcher under his guidance. John and Linda gave their respective Percherons a loving stroke.

Then, Paco was gone, riding his pony and trailing Raven and Midnight.

They were very quiet. John looked at Linda and took her in his arms. Her eyes were moist. He hugged her and kissed the wetness away.

"It's sensible," he said. "It's why I bought them in the first place. They are very powerful. I know how you feel. Midnight was, sort of, your wedding present."

"I didn't get you one," she replied.

"Oh, yes you did. You gave me the greatest presents of all. Firstly, you gave me my life. You helped to cure me. Secondly, you gave me yourself, my dream, my heavenly virgin and my love. Lastly, you showed your love for me."

Linda kissed him, a deep loving and caring kiss rather than a sexual one. "No Mescalero could express feelings in that way," she said. "We have the advantage from our mixed cultures. I suppose our honeymoon is now over?"

"Yup," replied John, surprised at his own use of the word. "I think we've been summoned."

It took them less than two hours to get everything packed, the horses saddled and loaded. They rode back to the main camp. Mangas nodded them in, a cursory thank you and welcome back, without saying anything. Raven and Midnight were already hitched to a large wagon containing many of the band's valuables, in particular, the hides of the animals they had hunted.

Just as John and Linda had tried, the camp was left clean. To a non-scout, someone who didn't track or trap, it would have been difficult to believe, so many people had lived there for months. That was the case.

John wasn't to know it but the route the band was taking was the reverse of the way Paco had brought him to the Mescalero. They were heading for Mesilla and, within two days, would cross the place where John and Paco had encountered the Mexicans, on the route from Santa Fe to San Vicente de la Ciénega. A further three days would see them reach their winter home in the semi-desert around Mesilla and what is now Las Cruces, not too far from the border with Mexico.

There were no nearby small towns along the way. The population was sparse. Despite his impatience, there was nothing much more that John could do but to remain with the band until the winter camp had been settled. Unlike the Gila Forest, the temperature rarely drops to freezing. There is only the occasional flurry of snow and crops could be grown as long as enough water was available. The horses had sufficient grass and could be ranged. Above all, the mescal plant was in plentiful supply.

It was a tiring journey and the band needed to put down roots again. A key part of the work was to set up the winter camp and a rather more permanent dwelling for everyone, a Wickiup. This is a wooden construction covered in a mix of buffalo and other hides, and brush. That explained the beauty of the wagon and, for the Mescalero, the two Percherons to haul it. As the days developed and the village appeared, John planned his next move. The Mescalero needed to trade and John asked if he and Linda could be part of the group to visit Mesilla. In Council, he suggested, with Linda's further reluctant agreement, they would leave Raven and Midnight to help with the farming and scrub clearance and travel on the ponies Mangas had provided. John also felt that he and Linda might learn more if they travelled alone but not dressed as Mescalero. This caused some consternation, unusual for the band, but John went on to explain.

"We are 'Ndee' but regarded as 'Apache'. We are feared by the Hispanics and the whites alike. Fear of the differences between peoples is what leads to conflict and hatred. The history of the Mescalero is such that they inspire awe. You live in hostile and alien lands, yet you survive and prosper. You find food and water where others find nothing but barren land. You have a proud culture that people outside do not understand. This reinforces the fear."

He took a sip of water and glanced around. In deference, they were listening. Not everyone was in agreement and John knew he would have to argue his case.

"This land is changing. I believe it will change rapidly. The land we are in is called New Mexico. I have already told Mangas and Paco that the Americans, the whites, bought it from Mexico." He glanced at the two of them and held up his hand as he felt anger welling from some of the younger braves in the group.

"There is a 'white man's' government of New Mexico. Whites and Hispanics are allowed to buy land. Even, since the abolition of slavery, black people can buy the land. 'Ndee' cannot."

One of the braves jumped to his feet and shouted. "That is not right. The land is for everyone. If we have to fight for it, we will fight and die bravely. We will live in the legend of the Mescalero, forever." He raised his fist and several of the audience, both men and women, cheered. He looked at Mangas. The stern face told him he should sit again.

As it quietened, John spoke again, almost in a hushed whisper, but projecting his voice as an actor can do in an auditorium.

"I have no doubt about your bravery. You believe that if you die for a good cause you will be remembered forever. You will be part of Mescalero history, a legend of the Ndee. I love you, my brothers and my sisters. I love Linda, Mangas, Paco and even Maria Elena." He accentuated the name of his mother-in-law. That last comment relieved the tension and created a snigger of mirth.

He paused and looked around the group.

"I want them to live. I want you to live. Above all, I want your children to live, prosper and carry on the values of the Ndee. Who will be there to remember you? Will anyone be left alive to celebrate this glorious period? Some of you, who are older, were on the Mescalero march. How many died on the drive into New Mexico. Where have the Ndee been before? Your lands were further east, on the plains, and you were driven west."

John looked around and sensed the air of resentment that was building. He looked at Mangas, who remained quiet, without betraying any emotion. John also knew that no one doubted his bravery and so he continued.

"I am with you and will go along with the decision of the Ndee." He looked at Linda, who lowered her eyes. "We will go along with you. But if you decide to fight, we will lose. We are not talking about tens of people, whites, coming here. We are not talking about hundreds or even thousands. We are talking about tens of thousands. We cannot beat that. But, I think, there is a way we can win. You may not like my solution. However, I ask you to consider it in this council?"

The young braves were about to jump to their feet. Mangas raised his hand and they settled back. He turned to John.

"Continue."

John did just that.

"When the whites, the Americans, came here, it was two hundred and more years back. They moved everything in front of them. The Ndee and others can testify to that. Three years ago, the Americans bought the whole of this New Mexico Territory from the Mexicans. It is not part of the United States of America yet. It's ironic that they found time to do this even in the midst of a civil war, white against white. Now, New Mexico has its own government. The laws are similar to the United States. One of those is land ownership. Since the war ended, earlier this year, many men, many families and many people have been made homeless. They are encouraged to buy land, especially those who were in the army. They can buy in New Mexico as well. They will if they have, or can raise, the money. I repeat, Ndee, Mescalero cannot. Other peoples have been forced onto reservations, not the lands they want, not the freedom they had when they roamed the plains. You have heard of the Indian Territories. You have seen what has happened to the Cherokee and the Cheyenne among others. You cannot trust the white men."

He hesitated for a moment, drew a big breath and looked around at the faces in the group. He pulled himself up and spoke once more.

"I am asking you to trust a white man, your 'Ligai Ndolkah' as my brother, Paco, named me. I can buy the land the Ndee want. We cannot have both the summer and winter lands, but I suggest we buy the summer grounds. In America, and New Mexico, there are 'white man's laws' that protect ownership. It will have to be me, on behalf of the Ndee. I suggest we'd be best there rather than here in the Southern desert. You know how to farm, you know how to hunt and fish. You are great with horses and we can ranch and break the wild ponies in the canyons. Above all, we must own the watershed so that no one can stop our supplies or pollute them with mine workings in the mountains. We will need to learn how to live through the harder winters and maybe build more permanent structures than the Wickiups. But then, no one will drive you from your land. I am in your hands. You, my people, decide."

John nodded his thanks to Mangas for letting him speak. He moved over and sat down next to Linda. She squeezed his hand and gave him a long adoring look and a great smile.

Several people spoke but, though voices were raised and heated, no one, even those against John, said they couldn't trust him. At last, Mangas raised his hand again and everyone waited. He sat quietly for a few moments to let the tension subside.

"My son," he looked at John, "speaks very wisely for one so young in years. I am proud to have him as husband to my daughter, Linda, and brother to Paco."

It was unusual for an Ndee to speak in this fashion and the group was slightly taken aback at the show of praise.

Mangas added more.

"Yes, our history honours those who fight and die for their beliefs. It is becoming harder to live. Even a troop of cavalry is bigger than our band. John is right about the wave that is the white man whether American now, the French, Spanish and Mexicans of before. He may be wrong in that they can change the rules if it suits them. Whites can buy, now includes Hispanics and the black 'whites', since slavery has been abolished. We have seen how our hunting lands have been reduced and many have starved because of the excesses of the white men. Some of you were involved or know those who were on the 'Great March'.

If we can keep the good land in the western forest, we can do as John says. We will not abuse the animals. We will only take for our needs. We can bring the seeds from here to grow there. We can trade our horses, skins and other things for what we need in return. And, if we have to fight to the last, what better battlefield could there be but the forest. We can survive in the wilderness and the mountain-sides. We can fight like guerrillas. The Ndee, the Apache, are the best at that. We will become the Shis-Inday; the people of the mountain forests."

The younger braves perked up with Mangas' words.

"We should make this our last winter in this desert and make our permanent home in the forest. We can either all agree, or we can split into two smaller bands; those with me and those against. Remember the sticks. One is easy to break; two together is harder. If you disagree, leave now."

His wisdom had swung the mood. Even the most flamboyant of braves would be hard-pressed to counter his appeal. Mangas' courage had never been in question. There was no further discussion. The consensus had been reached and the unspoken pledge would be honoured.

The people dispersed to their Wickiups. Mangas asked John and Linda to join him, Paco and Maria-Elena before they retired for the night. It was the nearest to a show of affection that the Ndee were able to show.

The five of them were together in their own family privacy when Mangas spoke again.

"I do not see an end to troubles. I am pleased the band stuck together tonight and common sense prevailed. It won't always be the case. John is right about the treachery of the whites, the Americans."

He looked at John, sitting quietly, Linda holding his hand. John did not react immediately and didn't contradict Mangas' description. He had seen many examples of dishonour already. These people, the Ndee, had the most honourable code he had ever known. He wished Mangas wasn't right. In his heart, he knew he was. John looked up, matched eyes with his father-in-law and nodded.

Mangas continued.

"We will need a plan. We need to see the future and we will have to make sure we take the Ndee along with us at every stage. We must be prepared for the things that go wrong. We cannot let silly mistakes or hot-headed reactions jeopardise the futures of us all. It could have happened tonight. You heard the cheering and the support for bravery and the honour of those Mescalero who die in battle. For a people, who are supposed to show little emotion, it didn't seem that way with some of the sentiments we heard earlier."

The others muttered their acknowledgement.

"John and Linda, I do not wish you to travel with us into Mesilla." He raised his hand as they appeared to want to object. "I want you to go separately. John, you will wear your American clothes; Maria Elena will help Linda to dress as a Spanish or Hispanic lady married to this American. We need to find how the land lies. The team that trades our skins and horses, for the things the band requires, can go in separately. Both can find out different things. We will learn what other peoples, whites, blacks, Hispanics, Mexicans, think of the Mescalero. We will also find out if there are two faces shown to the Ndee. John and Linda may have a totally different perspective when they return. I hold no illusions."

John motioned he'd like to respond and Mangas gave way to him.

"Linda and I will do as you suggest. I doubt we can get everything done quickly, as much as we would like. Mesilla is not that big and I do not know how good its facilities are. My first priority is to let my family know I am alive and," he chuckled, turning to smile at Linda and taking her hand, "that I am married. We don't know how good the telegraph system is this far south. I don't know if the link across the sea has been established yet. We don't know if there is anyone in Mesilla who knows the process for purchasing lands in New Mexico. However, I sense we need to act quickly. Mangas is right. We have to take every precaution. It is not like the Ndee to be devious; in this instance, I think it is forgivable, even for the highly honourable Mescalero."

"Then it is agreed," said Mangas. "It is strange, our liaison and our trust and belief in one another. I married a beautiful Spanish lady, yet we fought the Spaniards and the Mexicans. Our children cross that divide. A white man joins us, marries my daughter and swears his allegiance. Yet, we could not trust the whites from the past and I think we still cannot. In all peoples, there are good and bad. Many of the good are seduced by the bad because of fear. As you, John, said earlier, others call us the Apache; the enemy."

Paco entered the conversation. "Father, I believe you should stay here tomorrow. Let one of the other seniors lead the trading team and not take too many of the younger men. It will be less threatening, especially if there are some women involved in the trade. As you saw tonight, there are potential hotheads in our group. I don't mean they are deliberately looking for trouble with the whites or Hispanics, but they might invite some comments that trigger the wrong reaction."

John concurred. "There is not the same law for the whites and Hispanics in killing an Indian." He tempered the use of the term in his next statement. "We have to be careful." He noted, they recognised he had included himself in that description.

Maria Elena spoke for the first time and directed her remarks primarily to Mangas and Paco. "My husband and son have both spoken well and I am pleased with them. Paco's plan is good in two ways. One it is safer. Secondly, Mangas, it will show your faith and trust in other members of the band."

Mangas pretended to be slightly taken aback, but his eyes flashed across looking at John. "It shows you, even when you think you are head of the family, you still have to do as you are told." They all laughed as Mangas glanced at his wife who was blushing slightly. His honour and respect for her was obvious.

John and Linda shared looks. It was clear how important that same belief resided in their relationship. They were growing up fast. The family broke up. Paco, and Linda and John, retired to their respective Wickiups.

"Just think," said Linda. "Tonight, you have your Ndee wife. Maybe tomorrow, you will have your Spanish lady as your mistress." She gave John a big kiss and laughed, wickedly, her eyes full of fire.

John pulled her close. She admired his increasing strength and health. He was getting bigger, filling out, holding her firmly and gently at the same time. He turned her around so that she was leaning into him. He stroked her sleek, long, black hair as he kissed the nape of her neck, something he knew she loved. She raised her arms so that she could reach back and run her fingers through the long gingery-blond hair. He lowered his hands over her pert breasts and hardening nipples. She wiggled her backside tighter into him, feeling his penis hardening.

She spun around and they kissed passionately as they gently lay alongside on the bed. They were playing and undressing at the same time. They had never discussed how their love life should be. Everything was a new adventure and an exploration. Nothing was forbidden. Implicitly, neither would do anything that hurt the other one. They had learned that the first time they made love.

Linda reached out of the bed and put her fingers in a pot of her specially formulated, herbal cream. She put some of it into her cervix, around her clitoris and deeper into her vagina. She applied some more to John's penis, already hard and erect. But, she was making sure it was done slowly, sensuously and in a controlled fashion. She was taking charge and John loved it. She ran her thumb over the very sensitive tip, feeling him react and moan. Then she turned, sitting on his face and bending so that she could suck him while he licked her. John loved the herbal taste of her and the increasing wetness as he worked his tongue around her clitoris. She loved his increased stamina, the better control, the size and thickness of his penis, a gorgeous fit inside her small body. Well, she wasn't that small inside. She smiled to herself.

Linda turned again and lowered herself carefully on to John. He kissed her, pulled her nipples and smoothed her hair. Linda's movements in riding John were almost too much for him to contain. She was clever. Her rippling took him high but not quite to the climax. Linda did this time and time again. How John kept himself in check, only he knew. Linda was enjoying it; teasing and going through mini-climaxes in turn. Then, for the first time in their relationship, she grew to an orgasm, holding John inside her, crushing him to give his all. The spasms rocked Linda; her firm tight hold and thrusting gave John the serene pleasure and pain at the same time. He was being sucked dry until there was no more to come. They fell back, encompassed by their joint wetness and stickiness. The kissing was lovingly sweet and gentle.

"Oh my poor baby," giggled Linda. She was playing with John's spent penis as it softened and reacted no more. "Do you call that a man?" She was teasing, her eyes on fire and laughing at John's weakness in her hands.

"You witch!" he responded. "You are a beautiful, wonderful witch!" He kissed her gently, again and again, on all parts of her body. She was still tingling and it was her turn to respond.

"Are you my warlock or my slave?"

"Definitely slave; I belong to you and must do your bidding."

"You can't," she said, holding his limp member. "I shall have to get myself a real man."

"Don't you dare?" John pretended to be all manly.

"I thought you were my slave, to do my bidding?"

"I am, my love. Forgive me for rebelling." Linda hit him playfully.

"You are forgiven, but don't forget your place again."

"No mistress, I shall not."

They laughed and kissed again. They straightened the fur covers and snuggled up to one another. They soon fell to sleep.

John was awakened in the early hours by Linda playing with him. This time, their love making was less frenetic. It was soft and gentle, climactic rather than orgasmic. It was still pleasurable but in a very different way. They dozed off again until it was light.

Chapter Nine

The preparations for the separate journeys to Mesilla were immaculate. The Mescalero band took the wagon and needed Raven and Midnight to haul it with all the merchandise they were trading. Most of this was animal skin of various sorts. The rest of the team were bringing the spare ponies. Paco was with them but did not lead the group. It was a mix of men and women. The chosen women were capable fighters in their own right and not to be underestimated. There was no outward belligerence.

In line with their disguise, John and Linda rode two of the horses which had belonged to the Mexicans who had tortured Paco. It would have been odd for two Americans, Spaniards or white people, to have ridden unshod ponies. They took the third horse as a pack animal to carry what they needed for the trip. Linda was not riding side-saddle. She had a dark female suit and trousers befitting an aristocratic rider who was a good horsewoman. Her hat was a flat Spanish rider's Stetson. Once more, she took John's breath away. She was beautiful. He was so proud of her, so pleased to be her husband and so willing to belong to her and do her bidding.

John's western garb caused some amusement among the Mescalero braves and they had some ribaldry, pretending to shoot him and John pretending to be hit. It was a symptom of the belief and trust that was being engendered in the band and the closeness of the bond.

Mesilla was a very small town, a village, a pueblo. It was on the trail into Mexico and not too far from the border. Its strategic position was the river crossing. It had built up from the trading post and livery stables. There was no hotel, only a 'cantina'. It had its own church, a testimony to the broadly Hispanic mix of people who made up the majority of the population. It was cosmopolitan in a strange kind of way. There was an uneasy alliance of all ethnic groups, a sort of 'live and let live' attitude, but not camaraderie. There was an unhealthy tension that simmered below the surface with a deeply ingrained suspicion of other people's motives. Somehow, the balance was maintained. Livelihoods depended on everyone making a living. The different groups were reliant on trading with one another.

Linda and John felt that there were a thousand eyes on them when they rode into the town. They tied up the horses at the tethering rail outside the trading post. Hopefully, no one would recognise the mounts, or care, that they had once belonged to the Mexican desperadoes. That might involve some awkward questions at best or real danger at the worst. It was a calculated risk.

"Buena's Dias, good morning, Senor y Senorita," came the greeting as they entered the store. "How can I help you?" A storekeeper in Mesilla had to be at least bi-lingual. The man wasn't sure which to use. Linda looked Hispanic. John, once he had removed his sombrero, showing a lighter skin and the ginger-blond hair, didn't.

John answered in English. "Good morning!" His voice was soft, quiet and firm. "My wife and I would like to know if there is a working telegraph here and also if there is anyone who acts as an officer for the Territory of New Mexico?"

The trader, a short, stocky man, swarthy with a large moustache, stepped from behind his counter and came forward to meet them in the middle of the store. He was surprised that two, so young, were already married. He was wearing a long, dirty-white apron to protect his clothes. His smile showed the contrast between his white teeth and the black facial hair. He ran his hand across his mouth and his chin and he gave a thoughtful, considered answer.

"My apologies, Senora, the telegraph office is in the Jaffe's office. I suppose he is the nearest to an official, the sort of cross between a mayor, a town marshal, or a sheriff, maybe. The links are a bit intermittent. It depends on how many times those 'bastard' Indians cut the lines and they have to be repaired." Neither John nor Linda reacted to the man's statement.

"As you saw, when you came in, the cantina is next door and the Jaffe has the premises next to that."

"Gracias, thank you!" Linda responded. They were walking to the door when the man spoke again.

"Don't you need any provisions?"

John turned as he held the door for Linda and replaced his sombrero.

"First things come first. We have a few things to sort out before we decide our next move. Thank you anyway! Hasta Proxima!"

They walked the few yards to the official's office. They entered to see the Jaffe behind his desk. He was a very smartly dressed and dapper little man with the engaging smile of a politician. As John took off his sombrero again, the man greeted them in English.

"Good morning! How may I be of service?"

"Good morning," John replied. "There are two things with which my wife and I hope you can help. One is to send some telegraph messages and the other is to advise us on purchasing land in the territory."

The Jaffe raised his eyebrows as he cast them up and down. He wondered how two people, so young and inexperienced, were already married and could think of setting down roots in this wilderness. He didn't know the half of it and John and Linda didn't let on.

"First of all, I have to tell you the lines are down at the moment and they are more often down than up. Secondly, all claims and purchases of territory land are handled in the capital, Santa Fe. It's the New Mexico Territory Land Claims Commission. Where are you thinking of settling? What are you going to do? Are you aware of the dangers?"

John and Linda exchanged glances and wry smiles. It was Linda who answered. "Yes, we are aware of the difficulties and we know what we are doing." She touched John's hand. "Are you telling us we will have to go to Santa Fe to sort everything out?"

"As things stand, I am afraid that might be the way it is."

"How many days ride is that?" asked Linda.

It was John who answered, having already done most of that distance before.

"It's a good twelve days, minimum. There are some tough, dry patches and *Indian* dangers along the way." Linda entered the subterfuge with him.

"It's just as well I can ride and shoot as well as you then, isn't it?"

John smiled and in an aside to the Jaffe said, "I'd take care before you ever cross this little lady."

The Jaffe laughed and Linda pretended to glower at her husband as if to say "I'll get you for that, later." However, in two contacts already, they had picked up the anti-Indian feeling; Apache not Ndee. They would have to plan very carefully.

They thanked the Jaffe and left the office.

There was a commotion, a stirring out on the street. The rest of the band had arrived with Raven and Midnight drawing the wagon, the remaining Ndee on their ponies. The cart was laden with furs, skins, timbers and carved artefacts for sale, barter or trade. A string of ponies followed as well. There was not the glimmer of recognition between the riders and the married couple. John and Linda joined the townspeople ogling the arrival. They took the opportunity to gauge the reaction of those around them. There wasn't an air of animosity. It was a heady mixture of intrigue, apprehension and curiosity.

The band stopped outside the trading post and the negotiators went inside to trade. The little crowd was starting to disperse, a handful approaching the wagon to see the wares and a couple of men examining the horses.

John took Linda by the arm and they walked to the cantina.

There was a wider choice of offerings than in a standard American saloon. They ordered a couple of tortillas with chilli and beans and black coffee. Both of them suddenly realised how hungry they were. Even this far south, American Union' dollars were far more acceptable than pesos or Confederate dollars. It was the first money that John had spent since before he had seen and met Paco.

They finished every scrap of food and drank every drop of coffee. They spoke little to maintain confidentiality and discretion. They listened, as carefully as they could to other conversations. Not a lot was said about the Ndee, the Apache, so it was difficult to ascertain very much about local feelings.

They left to go back to the store. The trader was still in deep negotiations with the band and some heated debate. John and Linda waited until the dealings had been completed and both parties were satisfied. The band had sold their goods and ponies. They were taking back tools, different foods, especially flour, salt and sugar. There was less willingness to trade weapons.

John and Linda took note. When the band had departed, they went into the store. The owner was quite exhausted but also exhilarated by the extensive trading and haggling. John and Linda used money to buy food, some extra clothing and weapons. The four guns and three rifles were ostensibly for them. They didn't need them but the band did. They were not brilliant but they got the best on offer. The ammunition was crucial. They paid for their purchases, loaded the pony and one of the horses, fed and watered all of them, and departed. They checked to ensure they were not being followed and made their way back to the camp.

They arrived to a hive of activity. The animals were being fed and watered while the wagon was being unloaded, the goods shared out and stored to meet everyone's needs.

That evening, the band got together to discuss the events of the day and the reactions of those involved. The trading had been good and the team had obtained everything they wanted in exchange for their goods. They had sensed wariness about their visit but no obvious hostility. No one had commented on the Percherons, nor Ndee having large horses with shod feet. Similarly, no one had commented about Linda and John's mounts. John and Linda reported the more subtle comments about Indians, but that was it. There was guarded relief all round but, as always, everyone knew that continued vigilance was a priority.

John and Linda reported on their frustrating day. There were the extra weapons for the band. John apologised for their quality not being the best, but the best of a poor bunch. Single-shot rifles, a legacy of the South, ironically, and also the British, were not as good as his repeater. However, there were more guns for the band and his extra purchases had not aroused suspicions.

Then John dropped the bombshell.

"We cannot sort out the land from here. It looks as if Linda and I may need to go to Santa Fe. It is a trial but at least I have connections at the bank and that should help enormously. It does mean that we shall have to be away for at least a month."

There was a silence, a period of reflection.

Mangas broke it.

"Do you think it would be safer to travel with an escort?"

John replied.

"Thank you, Father, but no. Linda and I have discussed it. We will carry my Comanche lance. Overnight, we will take it in turns to stand guard while the other one sleeps. She will dress accordingly to where we are; Ndee on the trail, American/Hispanic when we enter settlements or the soldiers' forts. As a couple, we are less threatening. If other people think we are vulnerable, they are sadly mistaken. My wife is a good shot, and," he said, rubbing his chin, "throws a good punch for a little one." Linda hit him playfully and even the usually taciturn Ndee smiled.

Mangas looked at his wife. Maria Elena remained impassive. Whatever they did, there was an element of danger. She had not said much but she knew John was right about the plan and the need to secure the future for them all.

"Mangas," she said, "I agree with the children. We should respect their decision. I think it is for the best. However, for the first part of the journey to the plains, they could be accompanied by a hunting party. We will need buffalo meat and skins for the winter."

Everyone concurred with this suggestion. They spent the rest of the evening planning the details. Raven and Midnight were to stay with the band to work the land for the winter crops. John and Linda would have the three shod horses and another pony, one to ride and one to carry their requirements.

John spoke again. "Before we go on this long journey, Linda and I will have to be well prepared. We'll have to get more supplies from Mesilla tomorrow and I think we'll get the horses re-shod and the pony shod for the first time. It's a hell of a distance so we can't take any unnecessary chances."

He looked around at the band, speaking very quietly, almost in a whisper.

"I'd like to thank you for your trust. What Linda and I are trying to do is difficult. We may not be able to succeed. We are grateful for your belief in us and you, the Ndee, backing us in what we are trying to do. I am sometimes ashamed to be white. I know I am not American but I have seen the same kind of treachery in the past. We know what has happened to other tribes, Cheyenne, Arapahoe, Kiowa and Comanche, driven from their lands, not given ownership of where they live and given reservations not even fit for Goshe."

The dog wagged his tail at the sound of his name and came over to John to be stroked.

John added, "But, if this works, it will set a major precedent for the future. The Ndee will become the Shis-Inday. It will be land that we can work; we can grow our crops, we can ranch our horses, we can hunt and we can live all year round. It is getting harder to hunt buffalo every year. In the next few days and weeks, some of you may find this to be true. We hope, next year, the valley, in the Gila Forest, will be ours and none of you will be forced onto a reservation."

He raised his voice, louder and firmer, looking directly at the younger braves.

"If the white man does not honour his own law, and we have to fight, we will have a much better chance to defend ourselves there. The enemy will suffer great losses if we are clever. We can use the terrain, the mountains and the woods. We can move much quicker than they can. If it comes to that, please do not fight and die with honour. Fight, run and live. Hit the enemy before he hits you. We cannot afford to lose people; not one for one, not one for ten or even one for one hundred. We must make it so hard for them that they will give up. You know the land. You know your way around it. The whites do not. Make it count! Your lives are so precious. You sow the seed of the future. Without you, there is no future, no history, no one left to tell it. That is not glory. That is pure stupidity."

John stood up, took Linda's hand, helping her to arise. Without a further word, they made their way back to their Wickiup. Linda pressed up against him, proud of her man and what he represented.

The next day, John and Linda rode back into Mesilla with the horses taking them to the farrier to be shoed. They took advantage to go to the cantina while the horses were at the stables.

"I am glad I've seen you." It was the voice of the Jaffe from one of the tables. "Please come and join me as I have some news for you and I can save you a wasted journey." He motioned them to sit next to him.

The waitress came over and they ordered tortillas and coffee.

"I hope you don't mind if I finish my meal," said the Jaffe. The couple nodded. "We got the lines back up again early this morning and I was intrigued by what you asked me yesterday. First of all, may I ask how old you are?"

"I am seventeen," John said. "Linda is sixteen." The Jaffe was not entirely surprised.

"OK," he said. "I managed to get through to Santa Fe and to the Land Commission. They replied and sent me the basic rules. To lay claim to the land, you have to have settled it and proved you have worked it for five years."

He saw their faces fall but continued. "Secondly, you have to be twenty-one years old as a minimum. So if you can do it over the next five years, it will work out just right for you. I got the impression that no one else has any claim. Lastly, they are setting jurisdiction by counties. You will need to find out where that is for the land you are claiming. The Land Commission sends out a surveyor to verify it, measure it and set the correct fee."

"So what do you suggest we do?" John was still a little shocked.

The Jaffe smiled. "Settle where you want to be, work for five years and pay the New Mexico Land Commission when you make the claim. I understand, it is fifteen dollars per square mile. It gives you time to make and save the money. In the United States, preference is given to war veterans, especially those who have been displaced. That doesn't apply to the territories."

The waitress arrived with their food and coffee. John and Linda looked at one another but said nothing. It was a lot to take in. However, John was delighted that the lines were up and he and Linda would not have to make the arduous journey, especially as winter was approaching.

The Jaffe had finished his meal. "Do you mind if I smoke with my coffee?" He got out a cigarillo and lit it, leaning back in his chair and expressing a sigh of satisfaction with the first puff.

John had a couple of bites to eat before he spoke.

"Thank you for all of your help. What you said is both disappointing and heartening at the same time. We were dreading the long journey. We'd have preferred to have settled everything quickly, but if what you say is right, we have no choice anyway. At least we can contact people as long as the lines are up."

"You are very welcome. Whom do you need to contact?"

The Jaffe raised his eyebrows in surprise at John's answer.

"My family in England, our agents in New York and the bank at Santa Fe are the main ones. I don't know if the direct line under the ocean has been completed yet."

"Well, we can but try. When you've finished eating, we can go over to my office and see what we are able to do. Quien sabe!"

John and Linda both laughed at the fatalism shown, John nearly choking over a mouthful of food.

"Thank you," said Linda. "I am so relieved that we do not have to undertake the long trek. I haven't seen telegraph messages before so that's new to me."

They finished up, paid for their food and drinks, thanked the waitress and left the cantina to walk to the Jaffe's office. The telegraph was still up and working.

"I suggest," said the Jaffe, "You let your first contact know that the lines are intermittent. That way, there'll be no surprises if you don't receive or send quick responses."

"That sounds like common sense," commented John. "I'll do exactly as you have outlined."

His first message was to Julio Gonzales at the Bank of Santa Fe. He apologised and explained briefly why he hadn't been in contact for so long, set out his plans and asked that the bank forwarded his message to the New York agents and his family. There was an almost immediate acknowledgment.

"Glad you are OK. We had been worried. We'll forward your message and check out further answers for you."

That lifted their spirits enormously. John was elated that, at long last, he was able to get information back to his family, to let them know he was still alive and that he had recovered from his consumption. He knew it would take some time for the messages to be relayed. The best thing was to take it step by step and come into Mesilla as often as they could. Linda was just pleased to see the weight lifted off her husband's shoulders.

They shook hands with the Jaffe. He seemed delighted to have been of help and he appeared to have taken to the young couple. They collected the horses which had been well-shod and groomed and returned to the camp.

The nights were now drawing in and the early signs of the winter chill were becoming apparent. The band met around the fire for a communal meal, after which, John updated the position.

"First of all, my brothers, sisters and friends," he said, "Linda and I have to change our plans and we have to ask you to change yours."

There was an uneasy buzz and murmur. John held up his hand.

"It's not bad but it is not easy. At this stage, there is no need for us to go to Santa Fe. Next Spring, when we go back to the valley, forests and mountains, I recommend we stake it out the area for the claim and we call it the Lawson Ranch. We brand our animals with my family's sign, as on our ships' flags. I'll draw that for you. We call the valley and the river tributary the Shis-Inday and we make sure we have the whole of that from its source until it meets the main Gila River."

There was noticeable heat in the exchanges that followed. The Ndee were resentful about what they considered their freedom to roam the territory and their right to settle wherever they chose. As before, Mangas listened, quietly, impassively and eventually held up his hand. The arguments subsided and the Ndee listened respectfully.

"The white man is coming amongst us like a plague. If I am right, and we have seen it on the plains and in Mexico, he will take over. Other people, like us, have been forced away from their traditional grounds. Some, and some of you, have known the long march. Many perished; others atrophy in reservations. Although it is against our basic beliefs to own the land, that will be the future. But, I have one major question to ask my son, what guarantee is there that the white men will recognise the claim if the Ndee are living there?"

"The Americans put great trust in the law. They believe in companies. You will, in effect, be working for the company and it is 'white-owned'. But we will make sure it is your land. My family will pay for it. In return, you are not interested in money. You take what you need for yourselves. Any extra, trading horses, selling food, that makes money, goes back to the company. It will pay for the original purchase and it will be there if we need to buy more things or even more land. The reason we need the whole valley is to stop claim jumpers, miners, trappers and anyone else, destroying or polluting our upstream. We will preserve it as it should be for the animals and the Shis-Inday."

"And what happens if you are wrong?" One of the braves was laying down the challenge. "The white man does not follow his own law or he changes it. He doesn't want the Ndee there so he alters the rules. He sends in the army to clear us out and tells you that you cannot have Ndee working there."

"Then," said John, "We will have to fight. We have said this before and we will employ tactics you know so well. I will tell you something about history. There was an empire called Rome and they were attacked by the Carthaginians. The Romans were brave, like the Ndee. They believed in honour and glory in death. But there was one general, one leader, who angered the people because he thought differently. He wanted to win but not by the death of many of his men."

John took a sip of water. The Ndee loved stories and they related to them.

"What did he do?" The questioned was posed by a young boy.

John smiled. "I'll tell you. The Romans pretended to prepare for a battle. The Carthaginians had to stop and prepare also. By that time, the Romans had disappeared. They kept doing this until the invaders were so demoralised and exhausted that they beat them in the battle and sent them packing. If we have to, we can do the same. We hide in our forests and mountains. We live off the land in the ways most whites cannot. We harass them and destroy their supplies so they have to go back. We do it with quiet and stealth. There is no direct confrontation. We melt into the trees and up the slopes. We must preserve your lives. I re-emphasise that. You are the future. We will grow and we will live by trade. We have wild horses that we tame and can sell to the cavalry. If we are lucky or clever, we can make them friends not 'Apache', enemies. We also have one other thing on our side. I have told you about my family's history and the fight against slavery. Many of the cavalry are buffalo soldiers, former slaves. They understand the tribes, and you the Ndee, better than you think. They will not want to fight us, not because they are afraid, but because they feel a kindred spirit. We will play on that to our advantage. We will live in peace in our own land, but we will defend it fiercely if anyone wants to take it from us."

These were stirring words from one so lacking in years. John sensed he had inspired them all, the young and the old, the bold and the careful, the belligerent and the calm.

They dispersed for the evening.

As John and Linda reached their Wickiup, Linda took John's hand and spoke. "Husband," she said, "I am glad we don't have to go to Santa Fe. I have some news for you."

John gave her a startled look. Linda smiled and took his hand, placing it on her tummy. "We are going to have a baby."

She looked at his face, studying his reaction. The look of surprise gave way to silence. His eyes were now moist and then his face grew into a beaming smile. He took Linda in his arms, suddenly realising that he might crush her. He held her close as they kissed passionately.

"What are you thinking?" Linda posed the question.

"It was a whirlwind in my mind. I have come so far and we have come so far in a very short space of time. About eight months ago, my future was uncertain. In fact, I didn't know I had one. I came here in hope and a belief that I may be cured. Then I met Paco and through him met you. You saved my life and made me better. I am stronger, fitter and tougher than I could ever have hoped. I found the love of my life, something I could never have expected. You did me the honour of becoming my wife. And now, you are topping it up by telling me we are starting a family. It's a flood of emotions which have reinforced what we have to do; secure our future and that of all of the Ndee, our wider family."

"I fell in love with you when Paco brought you back. Although you were weak and broken, you were still handsome, blond and white, totally different from any man I'd ever seen. When you woke from your coma and you first saw me, your reaction was wonderful." She giggled. "Did you know you had a hard on?"

"I remember," said John. "I hoped you'd not think badly of me. It's funny how sexy you feel even when you are not well."

"It was natural. You proved very loving and caring. I had to make the first pass at you because you were afraid to do the wrong thing. You treated me like a goddess. That was wonderful. But I also wanted you as a man and I knew you wanted me as a woman. You learned the ways of the Ndee; the language and the custom. You not only brought your horse to me but you gave me your other one. It could be that the baby will have one too."

John furrowed his brow. "Do you mean that Midnight is in foal?"

"My god! You men! You know so much and you know so little. Don't you keep your eyes open?" Linda snuggled up to him again.

They made love very softly and gently. John wasn't sure whether he should but Linda allayed his apprehension. She took charge, giving him some oral sex, spinning so he could lick her clitoris and vagina. She took some of her aromatic, herbal cream she had made, and spread it over and inside herself as well as smoothing it all over John's penis and testicles. How he controlled himself, he didn't know. It was essentially erotic even before she came down on him, letting him suckle her nipples and breasts while she rode and churned him inside her. It was climactic rather than orgasmic but highly enjoyable, nonetheless. Linda made sure she squeezed every last drop from John, crushing him with her movements before she released his failing member. He ran his fingers through her hair as they lay back, gently stroking her breasts and feeling the wet, erect nipples with his other hand. Linda continued to tease his limpness and they kissed frequently. John wondered how he could stay so aroused for Linda and yet not be able to do anything about it.

She was stroking his body, admiring the way his muscles had thickened up, his firm torso and the man he now was. Whatever misgivings they had about the future, Linda believed that they would succeed, no matter what obstacles were put in their way. She was proud of John and what he stood for. He had won the trust of her and her family. Perhaps, more importantly, he had won the trust of the Ndee band.

They were wrapped in one another's arms as they fell to sleep.

Chapter Ten

The months over the winter flew by. The band grew their winter crops in the semi-desert, fertilised with the horse manure and ploughed in by Raven and Midnight. Some of the band went on hunting trips. John went on one of the longer ones in search of bison. The Comanche lance proved to be a gesture of friendship on this travel in their encounters with other tribes. With the advance of the mule skinners and the homesteaders on the plains, peace was something of a premium for hungry Indians.

The herds of bison were not as prolific as they had been. Hunting was becoming increasingly difficult. The party came across evidence of carnage in which skins had been taken, the flesh left to rot and even the calves had been slaughtered. Little was said. It was clear that they all had sick and sinking feelings. To add to this, John felt guilty just for being white.

The guns, John had obtained, proved invaluable when they did find a small herd. They chose the targets carefully so as not to decimate the adults and, especially, not to leave the young animals bereft of cows. It was the unspoken code to only take what was needed and what they could carry.

In between the work, John and Linda went into Mesilla as often as they could. There was now an irregular stage line and John used that for letters and the telegraph to make better contact. It took time but he was able to let his family know what had happened and what he was trying to do.

George dropped the bombshell saying that he and Ann wanted to visit the following Spring or early Summer. George wanted to see if John's plans were viable; Ann wanted to be there for the baby and to celebrate her son's recovery. No explanation of the dangers or difficulties was going to dissuade John's parents. George even toyed with the idea of sailing to San Francisco and visiting from the west.

Underneath, despite his apprehensions for their safety, John was pleased. He would have his father's clear vision for the way ahead. He needed a mentor and someone to whom he could turn for advice. Linda was worried about meeting his parents and what they would think of her. Overall, the prospect was exciting for both of them. Despite not showing any outward emotion, Linda and John felt that her parents were of a like mind. This was going to be a very unusual family encounter.

Mangas and Maria Elena were pleased about the forthcoming baby. Linda's mother had guessed before her daughter had told her, her female instinct coming to the fore. They were pleased for John that he had made solid contact with his family and they looked forward to the visit. The baby was due about June or July, so an early summer arrival was great timing.

Over the winter months, John started making signs for the ranch and the Shis-Inday valley. The Lawson name was also used with the family logo, a stylised letter L, similar to a pound sterling sign. John also got this made up into branding irons for all the animals. It was going to be impractical to fence or wire the range, about two hundred and fifty square miles. Even if they did, people travelling through would cut it.

John also found out that the New Mexico authorities were setting up claims divisions by county, as the territory developed. The new town of Silver City, it was still San Vicente at that time, a day's ride south of the Gila Forest, was to be their centre. It was establishing rapidly because silver had been discovered in the area. Luckily, the deposits were to the south rather than in the more northerly forest.

The band bade their farewell to their winter, desert home for the last time. It was April, 1866. John was concerned in case anyone else had attempted to settle the Shis-Inday valley before they returned. It was unlikely because it would have been too inhospitable over the colder months.

The journey back proved uneventful. Linda, under much protest, rode the wagon drawn by Raven and Midnight. She and John had had their first argument about her riding a pony all the way. However, Maria Elena had come down on John's side and told her daughter, in no uncertain terms, to be sensible. Linda sulked for a short time but common sense prevailed. The journey at six or seven months of pregnancy was still going to be tough. She also realised just how much her family cared for her.

There was a lot of hard work ahead for everyone when they returned. No other people had appeared to have attempted to settle the area. They chose a site for the village on a plateau within the valley but above the flood plain. It was sheltered from the north by a bend in the river and the forested upper stretches of the slopes. Trees had to be felled to build the stronger wickiups needed for the more permanent homes. The ground had to be cleared and fertilised for the crops and the band still needed to hunt and fish for food. The ranch signs had to be taken around the whole valley, all the way up to the watershed. On top of that, John had to update the claim situation and keep in touch with his family by travelling to Silver City. Linda wanted to go with him and loathed letting him travel on his own. The logic was overpowering. It was for the best.

It was late in the month when John rode into Silver City for the first time. It was a raw, shanty collection of buildings, centred around a gambling saloon and an assay office. There was the hustle and bustle of a fast-developing frontier town. It had attracted people of all sorts; miners, gamblers, opportunists, outlaws, adventurers, drifters, drunks, whores, saloon girls, various nationalities and yet, the law, represented by a town marshal. Consequently, John did not warrant any particular attention when he arrived. With his sombrero and shod pony, he was not out of the ordinary.

John tied up at the assay office as the first port of call.

"Howdy! What can I do for you, young man?" The man behind the scales and the counter had horn-rimmed spectacles. He was about five feet seven inches, balding, fair, wispy hair around the patch. He had a bent nose, fleshy cheeks and a rotund body.

"Howdy! I'm new in town and need to find out a few things. I thought you were sort of official and I'd ask you first."

John had an air of politeness that made people feel more important than perhaps they warranted. It was a trait that brought the best out of them. This man was no exception. He puffed out his cheeks.

"Fire away. I'll do what I can to help you."

"OK! Thank you. Firstly, is it you or your office which deals with land claims?"

The man raised his eyebrows in surprise.

"Forgive me for asking, but aren't you awfully young to be enquiring about land? You have to be twenty-one in New Mexico and prove you have worked it for five years."

"I appreciate that," said John. However, without giving away his age, he added the following. "I want to know the procedure, the law and am I talking to the right person in the right place. I understand that the ruling has been changed to county rather than centrally in the capital, Santa Fe."

"That sure is the case. This office handles everything for this county on all aspects for the New Mexico Territory. Where did you want to mine or prospect?"

"I don't. I want to set up a ranch."

The eyebrows were raised even further.

"You'll need to get an approved land surveyor from the Territory. He'll map out and measure the claim so that it can be registered. How big is it?"

The official's eyes nearly jumped out of their sockets at John's reply.

"I think it is about two hundred and fifty square miles or three thousand seven hundred and fifty dollars. That's a rough approximation."

"Jesus Christ!" The man expostulated and then he crossed himself at his temporary aberration and blaspheming. "How are you going to manage that?"

"It's a ranch," said John. "You know hands, stock, crops."

"But it's not cattle country."

"Who said cattle?" John laughed as the man frowned. "This is great horse country and people are going to need more horses. We'll breed and stock them. We have the skills to break them from wild."

The man seemed impressed. "I'll organise the surveyor for you. When are you next in Silver City? I can give you the date then and you can give me directions to your ranch."

"How long will you need?"

"Give me two weeks and you'll have an answer for sure."

"OK," said John, "I'll see you then. Thanks for your help."

While he was in Silver City, John took advantage of the opportunity to get some new clothes, in particular some boots, jeans and working shirts. He found the General Store had a lady's riding outfit and some underwear which he bought for Linda. He bought some sugar candy for the children of the village. Added to that, there was a layette of baby clothes. That strange find had arisen because a family of prospectors had lost a baby and needed money badly. The storekeeper had bought it from them, more in sympathy than in the hope of reselling it. John's chance arrival was a bonus for a good deed done.

Despite the location, the choice of guns was not particularly good. John couldn't find anything suitable for the band. He decided to leave it.

John departed from the township as quietly and discreetly as he had arrived. There were one or two smiles or guffaws at the layette but they were tinged with best wishes for the new baby.

There is a misapprehension about the American West. People think about the carefree, undisciplined cowboys and drifters, plenty of villains and gunfights, wars and skirmishes with all sorts of Indians, Native Americans and general lawlessness. Like all stories in history, the dramatic and unusual are taken out of all proportion. This was a time when the population of the territories, New Mexico, and Arizona as the separation was about to become, both grew rapidly, about tenfold in fifteen years. The land would never have been settled without great co-operation amongst those living there. There was no insurance. Homesteaders and prospectors grub staked one another. Those people who failed were bailed out by their neighbours for another year. It was the realisation of 'there but for the grace of God go I'. That was how the west was won. It was co-operation rather than competition. They had enough trouble in battling the elements, the terrain and the extremes of weather, without having to fight one another. Of course, there were exceptions.

So, having said that, John took all precautions he could on the trail. He covered his tracks in the way the Mescalero had taught him. He had no wish to be followed or to be easily traced. On top of that, until the band was well established in the Shis-Inday valley, he wanted no interference in their affairs. A time of reckoning would come and they had to be prepared for that eventuality.

When he camped out overnight, he made two beds, the false one being nearer the fire as it died. He slept in a more hidden position. It was just a precaution but it was now instinctive and had been learned and ingrained. However, on his journey back, he encountered no one and there were no incidents of note.

When John returned to the village, everything was in order. He held up the bars of sugar candy and the children came running. John made sure that every boy and girl received one. There was much excitement. He dismounted wearily as Linda came to meet him and give him a welcoming kiss. She grimaced a little. He smelt awful from the trail. John realised this and laughed. Paco came forward and took his horse.

"I'll look after him," he said. "You look beat!"

"Thanks," replied John. "Can I just show and take the things I bought for Linda and also for the baby?"

Linda's eyes widened. She unwrapped the packaging around the layette and looked at all its contents of baby things. "Oh! It's beautiful. Look, Paco." She showed everything to her brother. Several of the women and girls gathered around, some of them mouths open in awe.

"It's lovely," said Paco. "This is some lucky baby."

He turned to his mother in the group and showed her. Maria-Elena was pleased for her daughter. She smiled but said nothing.

"You haven't opened my present to you." John was almost protesting to Linda.

She removed the wrapping to reveal the beautiful riding suit.

"It's lovely," she said. Then, in an aside to her mother, "But he's not letting me ride yet."

"No! But that's not forever. After the baby's born, you'll soon be back in the saddle." John was forthright, not recognising that Linda was pulling his leg. It was one big tease.

The company laughed and John suddenly realised he had been taken. He started to chuckle with them as Linda kissed him on the cheek and whispered "Thank you! Now go and clean yourself up so I can hold you and kiss you properly."

John went back to their Wickiup and pulled the wooden bath off the wall. He filled it from the water barrel and stripped off his dust laden clothes. It was a relief to wash off the dirt of the trail, to clean his hair and to have a shave, even if it were with cool water. Linda walked in while he was in the middle of it. She smiled, wickedly, moved his dirty belongings and fetched him a clean change of attire. She also brought back an herbal deodorant, the soap and shampoo she had made. Despite her pregnancy, she knelt down and scrubbed John's back.

"Are you OK with that?" asked John.

"Yes, of course. I'm having a baby, not dying."

"I just didn't want you to overdo it."

"Why? Aren't you enjoying it?"

John responded by pulling her into his wet arms and giving her a big kiss.

Linda rose and got her own back by dunking him into the bath so his head was under.

John came up spluttering and laughing at the same time.

As he dried and dressed, they talked some more.

"How was your trip? What happened? Did you get any further?"

"Yes. We need to have the land surveyed by the Territory Representative, get it registered and work it for five years. I have to go back to Silver City in two weeks to see the agent and set the time for the survey."

"Does that mean no one can take the land from us?"

"Not legally, they can't, but we'll still need to be careful. We'll do everything we need to do properly."

"But, you are still concerned, aren't you?"

"The authorities still want to move all Indians on to reservations. They can always change their own laws if it suits them. I don't have much trust or faith in them. But company law may be harder to overturn. We are not buying the land as individuals."

"I don't understand the difference."

John looked serious for a moment, pondering whether to say what was really in his mind. He looked at Linda carefully and realised she deserved the answer.

"Let's say you, the family, the Ndee all trust me. Mescalero people cannot buy the land. I buy it and everything depends on me. If anything happens to me, you and the baby are my next of kin. They would find ways to disinherit you and force everyone onto a desert reservation. The company is inanimate. It doesn't depend on one person. Whoever takes over would honour the way it works because that's the way we'd set it up. Everyone who is here, everyone of working age, becomes an employee and works for the company. If the employees were driven off, the company would fail. To prevent it we'd have company law, injunctions and legal redress to prohibit the authorities. It would take time for them to change the law and they won't have anticipated what we are doing."

Then, looking at Linda intently, John spoke calmly.

"It also means that it's not worth anyone's while trying to kill me and claiming the land from our family."

Linda had gone pale at his words.

"Do you really think that? Do you really think there is going to be trouble?"

"As sure as eggs are eggs, I am." Seeing her frown, John smiled. "Certainly, I do."

He took her hand in his.

"Listen to me, my love! It will be relentless. More and more people will come west. They will want someplace to stay and to make a living. Most will be genuine, homesteaders, prospectors, miners, shopkeepers and other trades. Amongst them, there will some who are thieves and murderers. They do not

108

understand the way of life as it has existed before they arrived. The ranchers and the trail herders on the plains didn't understand the farmers, their own kind. What chance do you think they have of understanding the native Indians, Ndee or Apache as the case may be?"

"But, if we keep mostly to ourselves, on our land, stay peaceful and just trade, surely we'll be accepted?"

"We might be lucky, but I wouldn't chance it. Do you really want me to tell you how I see it developing?"

"You've troubled me and intrigued me. I suppose you'd better tell me what you perceive of the future."

"We register a claim for the whole of this valley in the company name. We also make sure it is a legally set up company in the United States of America, probably registered with the agents we have in New York. That's where I need my father's help and agreement. As more people come, there will be those who try to claim our land; trickery, robbery or violence. They may say they were attacked by marauding, savage, Apache warriors. They will demand the army comes in to drive them out on onto the reservations. But, we will pre-empt as much of that as we can."

Linda looked at him wide-eyed.

"What can you, we, do to prevent that?"

"We ranch, farm and hunt the land, much in the traditional way. We preserve it as it is; its beauty, its animals and its vegetation. We kill and we use only what we need. You've seen what is happening with the buffalo. We can capture and breed the wild horses and trap them in the large box canyon. We arrange to trade the surplus ones with the army. They'll need horses in this terrain. They will be ours because they will have the Lawson brand. We grow all sorts of crops near the river. The horses will supply loads of fertiliser. We have many fish in the river and animals on the land. We can eat well. We can build better homes with the wood all over our forests, plenty of which will supply our fires. We'll build separate hidden places in the mountains and forests in case we are ever attacked. That way, the Ndee can escape and regroup."

"If it did get bad, how would our small band, men, women and children, be able to defeat a larger number coming to drive us out?"

"You heard me tell the braves about Scipio. I also said it was important to preserve the lives of our people. We become guerrillas. We hide in the forest. We live in the forest and out of the forest. We harass the aggressor from cover. We are snipers. The Apache is great at being hidden. Our enemies do not know how to fight that way. They will have great difficulty bringing heavy weapons up this valley. Hopefully, it will never come to that. I hope talking and an open, honest argument will prevail. I am not banking on it. I want the best but I'll prepare for the worst. The young braves are beginning to understand. They can see how other tribes have fared. A glorious death is no answer; our small band will just decrease to nothing. Too many people still believe in the honour of war. It is harder to stay alive and care for your family. Our tactics will demoralise anyone who is against us. Now that I think you have cured me, I want to see our child, our children, grow and in turn to see their children develop. I don't want to die for any cause, no matter how noble. You and our children are what matter now."

"You are a strange warrior, my lord. I like what you say and the way you present it. I hope it will work out for the best and the rest of the Ndee will see it that way. By the way, you said, 'our children'?"

John laughed.

"We're not sticking at the one, are we? I wouldn't have done this without a lot of thought. The band took some convincing of my suggested plans. Your father and mother believe in that way forward. Your mother has never said much to me in true Ndee tradition. I suspect she listened a great deal and persuaded Mangas it was the right way to go. I shan't forget the way he supported me with the braves and that made them think hard. They looked surprised at his stance and listened to his wisdom. Maria-Elena appeared to take all in her stride, almost as if she'd accepted it. Hopefully, we'll have no hotheads, amongst the braves, who will do something stupid to destroy everything that is good. We can't afford slip-ups."

They kissed and cuddled for a while.

"Now, I've been home all this time and you've not told about yourself and 'bump'." John gently laid his hand across Linda's tummy. It was a fortuitous moment because he felt the baby kick. For a moment he was startled and surprised. Linda laughed.

"We have a couple of months yet, but the little one seems well and active with a great appetite. I am eating like a horse or should I say a bear."

"I hope my parents will make it here on time and we can conclude the land survey before it arrives."

They were silent in their own thoughts for a moment before John spoke again.

"I know it's not normal practice for Ndee or for white people, but Linda, do you mind if I am with you for the birth?"

She kissed him on the cheek.

"That would be lovely. I don't know if the other women and, my mother in particular, would object. But, it's our decision. Your being there will be of great help to me and we should share the experience together."

Linda giggled with a wicked thought.

"If the birth's that difficult, I might not ever let you touch me again. So then, we'll only have the one."

John grabbed hold of her, held her tightly but gently, and kissed her.

"Fat chance of that," he said.

Just then, there was a noise outside the Wickiup. Mangas had arrived but had made his presence known discreetly. The young couple invited him in.

"Welcome back John," he said. Turning to his daughter, he continued. "Your mother wants us all to eat together tonight and won't take no for an answer."

"How can we refuse?" asked Linda. She glanced at John who had a bemused look on his face. He nodded in agreement.

"See you at sundown," said her father. He retreated without another word.

John and Linda took advantage of the time to rest and be with one another. They lay down and dozed in one another's arms.

They rose as the sun was setting, cleaned themselves and made their way over to join Mangas and Maria Elena. Paco joined them. Maria Elena had laid out a kind of Smorgasbord of Mescalero and Mexican foods; breads, tacos, wild guinea fowl, buffalo and deer meat, beans and salads. Everyone suddenly realised how hungry they were and tucked into the feast with relish.

When they had finished, they sat round the fire and John told them of his trip to Silver City. He didn't go into the details of the prognosis he had discussed with Linda. He stuck to the facts.

Mangas waited until he had finished. He took a thoughtful drag on his pipe.

"What is the next step you are suggesting?"

John had it very clear in his own mind.

"We work hard over this coming summer, build up this ranch and secure it for all of us. That means building some second homes which I recommend are at the edges of the forests above and around the box canyon. There are two reasons for that. Firstly, if we are caught out in the winter by any sudden snows, those working with the horses will have a close sanctuary. We'd need to make sure

111

there is a supply of food, water and fuel as well as shelter. Secondly, if we are ever driven from this part of the valley, we have an escape for all our families. I'd also set up a cross fence which we can build at the neck of where the canyon becomes steep. If we are followed or attacked, we can cut the lines and drop it from the top, trapping our pursuers. As I said before, we will be guerrillas, snipers and cannot afford to lose any of our people. If our enemies, our 'Apache', don't accept us as we are and leave us be, we'll have no choice but to vanquish them. Like you, I hope it won't come to that."

Paco knew his brother-in-law well. He looked at him and spoke.

"I think you believe we won't be left free and untroubled." It was almost a question.

John considered his answer carefully.

"I think that, by being prudent, we might make other people wary. If they recognise our defensive strength, they might think twice about attacking us. We know there are lots more people moving out here. Our horses will be our lifeline and our trade. If we are trading with the army, we can build a reputation and we'll have many of the soldiers on our side. However, we'll have to be disciplined and not let any of our braves go wild. One incident, one killing of a *'white man'* could be the end of our dream."

John let his words sink in before continuing.

"If you agree, I'd like Paco to take charge of the canyon for now. In two weeks, I shall have to go back to Silver City to pick up the Territory Surveyor and find out when my parents are coming. I don't want to be far from Linda, as I want to be there for the birth of our child and to see it come into this world." He turned and smiled at his wife.

"That is not our tradition." Maria Elena was quite adamant turning her glance to Mangas for his confirmation. The older man continued to suck thoughtfully on his pipe and said nothing.

"It is not the tradition from my background, either," said John. "But, Linda and I have discussed it and she'd like my support."

Linda responded. "I would like him there, Mother," she said.

Maria Elena glowered at her daughter to no avail. Linda was remaining firm.

The men smiled but thought it best to keep their own counsel.

"Talking about the baby, have you thought of any names yet?" Maria Elena was relieving the tension.

Linda looked at John and, turning to her mother said.

"There are two or three alternatives or combinations that are obvious to us. For a girl, Maria, Elena and Ann, after you and John's mother; for a boy, William, George and Mangas, after our respective fathers' and grandfather's names."

Everyone seemed pleased. John caused a laugh.

"We couldn't have another Paco," he said. "That would be much too wild."

With that happy note, the evening broke up and retired to bed.

The next two weeks went quickly with normal work; growing and weeding crops, making herbs, hunting and gathering and Paco leading the team working with the horses and developing the structures around the canyon.

The time came for John to go back to Silver City.

Chapter Eleven

John rode back into Silver City and went straight to the New Mexico Territory office where he was greeted warmly.

"Welcome back, young man, muchacho. How are things? Has your newly little '*gringo*' arrived yet?"

There was laughter and a smile in his eyes.

"Not yet," replied John. "He or she is due in about six weeks. I hope I don't miss it by being with the surveyor. How did you know?"

"I heard what you bought when you were here."

The man chuckled.

"Well, I have two good bits of news for you. Firstly, the surveyor is in town and is happy to go back with you now. Secondly, we have had a wire that your parents are due on the stage to arrive in two days. That means that you and the surveyor can get all your work done in the days after that, return to Silver City and sign all the necessary documents."

Things were moving fast.

"That is brilliant," said John. "It's killing several birds with one stone."

The official frowned. He hadn't heard that English expression before but it seemed to make sense.

"OK. Let's go. I said we'd meet him in the saloon. His name is Hank Warren and he hails from somewhere back east. By the way, mine is Luis Delgado."

"Thank you, Luis. I can't wait."

The saloon was bustling and noisy. As they came through the swinging doors, their nostrils were assailed by the rich smells of stale tobacco smoke and rough whisky. It was not a particularly pleasing combination.

Luis introduced the two men. Hank was smartly dressed in a brown riding suit with a white shirt and black tie. He was slightly smaller than John, around five feet nine inches, still tall compared with most men in New Mexico. His hair was long with a mousey brown colour. He was clean-shaven and in his middle to late twenties. He had very penetrating blue eyes which seemed to laser straight through you but not in a threatening way.

Having just come off the trail, John had not had time to clean up. He felt a little embarrassed. The two young men eyed each other up and down. There was an instant rapport and mutual respect.

"I apologise for my appearance," said John, as they shook hands.

"Hell man," came the reply. "You ride through the dust and dirt astride a fleabag." Hank smiled as Luis roared with laughter. "Let's see how I am after spending the next couple of weeks or so with you?"

Hank and John sat down at a table while Luis went to the bar to order drinks. Hank continued.

"Luis has given me a rough idea of your plans. I have just started as a land surveyor for this territory, so this is a very exciting project. I qualified back east, Philadelphia to be exact. Then the war erupted."

He looked sober for a moment. The smiling face had gone.

"Let's just say I was lucky to get through. My education made me an officer. I tried to look after my men. I'd rather not say anything more about the last four years. Coming out here is my therapy."

"It seems we've both had our trials to get here," said John. "We've got more to come. Let's hope they will be happier ones all round?"

Luis returned with the drinks; tequila for him, beer for Hank and lemonade for John. John saw Hank's quizzical look.

"I had consumption and came here from England in the hope of being cured. The sea journey, the trip across the United States, the drier climate of the territory, meeting my wife, her medicinal treatment and the baby which is imminent, all seem to have done the trick in improving my health. I can't take the alcohol."

Both Hank and Luis looked impressed.

"Christ, man, you've packed in an awful lot of life into a short time." Hank was genuinely in awe.

John got down to business.

"So as you can see Hank, time is pressing. Can you tell me what you need to do and how I can help you?"

"Well, first of all, you'll have to show me the extent of your land. I'll need to bring my equipment to mark it out, take the measurements and map it as accurately as I can. We file the paperwork and claim here with Luis. Once it's been ranched uninterrupted, throughout for five years, and I gather you've evidence going back at least a year, you pay the land fees and the land is yours."

"Can we wait till my parents arrive and all go together? The ranch is named after the family company and it will be that rather than mine."

"That's not a problem. If you're staying in town, you can share with Luis and me for now and we can eat at the cantina. It will give us time to plan our trip properly and take the necessary provisions. Do your parents ride?"

"Luckily, yes. Though I don't know how they'll get on with western saddles. They've both hunted in England, so they should be OK. I didn't expect them to arrive so quickly and I didn't bring any spare horses."

Luis intervened. "We'll get you a couple of hire horses. When you return to sign all the papers, you can bring them back then."

"It seems we've settled it," said John. He raised his glass. "Let's drink to all-round success?"

They clinked glasses and drank.

"Right," said Hank, "we'll have time to do some preparatory work when we get back to the office. I have some broad, original maps of the area from early surveys. I must tell you they are pretty rudimentary. So I am also killing two birds with one stone as I can improve the mapping and the detail for future reference." He grinned.

"How much do you know about the place?" asked John.

"In what way do you mean?" Hank responded with a question.

"Well, I am talking about the people, the terrain and the landscape."

"It's mostly what I know from the maps. I've not been there. The country looks very varied and the river valley you are talking about is a tributary that feeds into the Gila system."

John looked a little pensive and there was a pregnant pause.

"I am going to have to put a lot of faith and trust in the two of you and ask you not to betray any confidences." John glanced at both Hank and Luis who nodded their agreement. "As I told you, I was very ill and I came here, as a last resort, in the hope that the drier climate might cure me. On the way, I had several adventures including running into some Comanche braves on the Santa Fe Trail. They gave me the Comanche lance which is attached to my saddle as a gesture of safe passage. It was their response to my feeding carrots to their ponies. Later, I saved the life of Paco. He is now my brother-in-law. I won't go into detail other than to say he is half Mescalero and half Spanish. In turn, he saved my life when

116

I collapsed and got me back to his village. It was his sister who cured me with her herbs, medicine and nursing. We fell in love and married. The Mescalero Apaches are generally nomadic, going south for the winter and north for the summer."

John took a drink before continuing. Both Luis and Hank were agog and concentrating on every word with a deep fascination.

"However, we have to recognise that the days of the open ranges are numbered. Your work is part of that. The American government is encouraging settlement of the west and homesteading. The Indian tribes are being corralled into reservations and this cuts across most of their cultures. I persuaded our band that we should settle in one area, basically the Summer lands, preparing ourselves to live through any harsh Winter weather. The Mescalero are great horsemen. They are also agricultural. In their own language, they call themselves the Ndee, which means 'the people'. The word, 'Apache' actually means enemy. Because of the area, and the fact that the river is as yet unnamed, we are proposing it is known as the Shis-Inday. That means the people of the mountains. Under American and New Mexico laws, the tribes are not allowed to own land. They have agreed to be part of our company and it will be the Lawson Ranch. That is where the importance of my family, in particular my father, matters. We are legally registered as both English and American."

He took another drink as the message sank in to his two companions. Hank looked at Luis who seemed stunned. He turned to John. "Bloody hell, John that is some story you are telling us. But, why are you doing this?"

"All over the west, the Indians are being forced on to reservations. They are rebelling and fighting their cause. They will eventually lose because they will be overwhelmed by the mass of settlers. There is already considerable fighting especially around the plains. It will spread. Our band is giving up a nomadic existence for greater peace and security. I can tell you, they took a hell of persuading, especially with the younger and more belligerent braves voicing their traditions and the courage expected. But, they listened to me, because of what I had done for Paco, what he did for me and because he showed his faith in me. Most of all, wiser heads, older heads prevailed and I can't thank my father-in-law enough for that. I have to repay them the best way I know how."

"Senor, that is very honourable. I salute you." Luis raised his glass and took a drink.

"What are you going to do if they pass laws in New Mexico to force all Apaches on to the reservations?" Hank was genuinely concerned.

"Truthfully, I don't know. First of all, we will try to pre-empt that. Making it company land is one way. In effect, although it is their land, technically the Shis-Inday people are company employees. As there are mixed races and ethnic types in other businesses that will make the situation difficult for the authorities. Indian scouts work for the army; Chinese are on the railroads. This land is still predominantly Hispanic and there are Indian and Mexican cowboys.

"Secondly, to survive, we will need to trade, especially for tools. One way is to breed horses and sell them to the army. But settlers, moving here, will also need horses. The Shis-Inday riders are great at breaking them and this is an outlet for the aggression of the younger men. To be honest, that is my only fear, that some members of the band will become fed up and act as mavericks because they feel there is no honour. We'll just have to see what transpires."

"You've got balls," said Hank. "I've got to give it to you." Turning to Luis he said, "I don't know about you, but I am prepared to back John on this. I tell you what, meeting your family and your band is going to be some adventure. I am really looking forward to it. As far as I am concerned, we go ahead on the basis of what you have said and I'll maintain as much discretion as I am allowed about, what you call them, the Shis-Inday."

Luis murmured his agreement. "I hope I get the chance to visit your home."

"Of course," said John. "You'll be welcomed any time. The more friends we have, the easier it is going to be."

They drank up and went back to the office. Luis had his living quarters in the back and showed John where to put his gear and bunk down. John took his pony to the livery stable to be stabled, fed and watered. He returned to the office to get cleaned up and change clothing.

"You look human, don't you think?" Hank winked at Luis who responded with a wry smile. "OK, John, let's get down to some preliminaries?"

He had laid out the maps he had of the unnamed valley. John was quite impressed with the work that had already been undertaken years ago. The outlines were already more accurate than he had expected.

"The reason we want the whole valley is so we protect ourselves from any upstream water interference. That means owning everything up to the watershed. An example of problems could be blast mining."

"You've really thought about this, haven't you? I can see your logic."

The rest of that day and the following, John and Hank set about planning the details for the trip, what they needed to take with them, who was doing which work and what were the timings. They arranged hire of the horses they needed to carry the equipment, for Hank and for John's parents to ride. It was all set.

John found it difficult to sleep on the second night. There was so much going through his mind and there was the excitement of seeing his mother and father again, a future he hadn't dare to anticipate when he had left home. He wondered how his mother would react and how she had coped with the arduous journey to get there. How were they going to take his plans now they were meeting face to face? What would they make of Linda and her family? Eventually, he drifted off into a fitful doze, but his mind was still whirring.

The stage was due in at eleven. It was more like twenty to twelve when it did pull up and the extra wait did nothing to calm John's nerves.

His father was the first to step down from the coach. He recognised that huge frame and beard instantly though it was more greyish than the ginger he remembered. He turned to help Ann down.

"Hallo, Mum, Dad," said John. There were tears in his eyes.

Ann looked at him in astonishment, this fit, young man, who had grown and thickened out as a tall, blond, fit and healthy Adonis.

She threw her arms around him and kissed him all old English propriety and etiquette thrown out of the window. His father nearly crushed him in a massive bear hug.

"God be praised, son." Ann spoke. "You look fantastic! Are you totally cured?"

"You can see that for yourself," said George, before John could answer.

"Was your journey OK?"

"We're both tired and a little 'back-side' weary from sitting on trains and stages," said George. "We can't wait to see where you are living and this family ranch you are planning."

"I can't wait for the baby to arrive," Ann intervened. "That's more important than anything."

They collected the luggage from the stage, thanked the driver and the shotgun rider, and John took them to meet Luis and Hank. Once introductions had been made, John outlined the plan.

"I am sorry to add to your bum weariness," he laughed at his mother's shocked look, "but I am afraid we'll have to ask you to endure some saddle

119

soreness. It's a day and a half's ride to the ranch and you can only do that by horse. We've hired them for you, to carry the bags and equipment and for Hank to undertake the survey. When Hank comes back in two weeks, we'll bring them back and you can use our ranch ponies. If you want to wash up and change into riding gear, we'll have a meal in the cantina and set out this afternoon. If you need anything, we can get it from the general store."

His mother replied. "The sooner we get going, the better. We are," she said looking at George, "longing to see the place and Linda. We're not too late for the baby, are we?"

"We better not be." John laughed. "But we might see another birth has taken place." They looked at him quizzically.

"Our horses mated and Midnight should have foaled by now. Paco, Linda's brother, is a fantastic horse person and he'll have made sure she's OK."

They got ready and went for the meal. George and Ann's riding attire was typically English, even gentry, but it was OK for the trip at this time of year. Both had headgear. However, John went and bought some extra slickers in case of inclement weather. Ann proved not too fond of the chilli, beans and tacos but she appreciated they needed food of substance for the journey. George wolfed his down with relish as though he hadn't eaten for a week.

On the journey, while Ann and Hank exchanged conversation and histories, George rode alongside John.

"Nathan told me what really happened with the Shamrock. Nobody else but me seemed ready to question the story and I was willing to let it lie. But I could see he was troubled so I got it out of him."

"They are good men, Dad. They are very loyal to you, to me, to the family, the company and one another. How are Nathan, Joseph and Jimmy?"

"All of them were well when I last saw them. For this trip, your mother and I came over on the Crosby. Nathan's taken the reins of the company in my absence so Jimmy is now the skipper and Joseph first mate. They were all pleased to hear you were getting better and making it out here."

"Well, I miss them. We got pretty close during that trip and the crew also got nearer to one another. Loyalty means a lot."

"Several of the Shamrock crew joined us when they got back home. They needed better training but our lads licked them into shape. I tell you son, we've got some bloody, good crews."

"It's down to you Dad. You treated them properly and they responded positively. It's in the bible; you reap what you sow and that's what I am hoping we are doing here."

"Tell me about this ranch and the Mescalero. I realise you couldn't say much over the telegraph."

"It's like everything. People fear the unknown. There are different skins, different colours and different cultures. Add religion and prejudice into the mix and you have a lethal cocktail. In simple terms, they cannot own the land. We can. Better than that, as an American company, the law is even stronger on our side, at least for now. New Mexico is more diverse than any other part of the USA and it hasn't joined the union yet. Not only can we make a living from it and make it pay, but we may also have hidden assets like the silver found around here. The economy will grow fast. Horses are the only way, for now, to get around much of the territory. We breed them, break them and sell them."

"Can you trust them?"

"You can more than most Americans. Their word is their bond. It applies to other tribes as well. Look at what the Comanche gave me for safekeeping."

He handed his dad the lance. "That was a gesture of trust and friendship. I didn't threaten them and they never threatened me. It was much more valuable than the carrots I gave their ponies."

They camped that night near a creek. John managed to shoot a wild turkey just before dusk. They were able to pluck it and cook it on the fire to supplement the usual boring beans. John's mother and father were not used to sleeping outdoors and on the ground. They hadn't realised how tired they were; they soon went off. John and Hank shared guard duties, Hank's instincts from his army days still haunting him.

The next day, they awoke to the sounds of all kinds of bird and mammal noises. It was quite a cacophony. It was beautiful and raucous at the same time, very different to the dawn chorus of West Derby.

Everyone was excited about the last leg of the journey. Ann wanted to see the girl who had won the heart of her son and see how well she and the baby were doing. For George, it was the intrigue of meeting different people and starting a new leg of the family business empire. In Hank's case it was the challenge of the role, successfully completing the survey and improving the quality of the map of the valley and the surroundings.

121

Their arrival was known well before they reached the village. The signal had been spread by outriders well in advance. As they came to the village, the reception committee was there to welcome them. Despite everything, Paco was taking pride and place leading forward a small, stocky, black filly.

"Look, John!" he shouted. "Isn't she beautiful?" He was so excited, he was almost ignoring everything else about the importance of the occasion.

"Yes," said John, "she is. But, she's Linda's by right, as Midnight is her horse."

Linda came forward to greet them. She was more restrained and demurer. Inside, she was bursting to greet John as throw her arms about him, but she was uncertain how to conduct herself in front of his parents.

John sensed her dilemma and took charge of the situation. He dismounted, took hold of Linda with his free arm, firmly but gently, pulled her towards him and kissed her, long and passionately. By that time, George, Ann and Hank had also dismounted, Ann being helped down, rather gingerly, by her husband.

"Mum, Dad, this is Linda, your daughter-in-law."

Ann came forward and took Linda into an embrace.

"Thank you for everything you have done for John." There were tears in her eyes. "I am so pleased we are in time. You do look well."

"I am so happy to meet you," Linda responded. She turned to John. "You didn't tell me your mother was so beautiful and your father so handsome."

John was quick off the mark. "I didn't want to make you jealous." He laughed.

Ann spoke to Linda. "John never stopped telling us how beautiful you are, how much he loves you and how much he was looking forward to the birth of the baby, in all his telegraph messages. He didn't lie."

All the introductions were made; Hank, Mangas, Maria-Elena and Paco.

"Have you decided what you are going to call the new horse?" John asked Linda.

"I thought it would be too big, too quickly for our baby, so I'd like to give her to Paco and let him name her." Linda had not discussed this with her brother.

Paco was delighted and looked at John for approval.

"I told you it was her horse," said John. "You deserve it as far as I'm concerned, especially for the way you have built the stock on this ranch."

"Thank you," said Paco, as he kissed his sister on the cheek. "I shall call her 'Lindanegra' in honour of my sister. I think, in English that means 'Black Beauty'."

Mangas spoke. "I know there is so much to say and so much to talk about. But, you must all be tired and weary after your ride. John, why don't you and your guests get cleaned up and we will get some food and drink ready for everyone?"

Chapter Twelve

They sat around the meal and gravitated into two natural groups. Although Linda sat alongside John, her mother-in-law was next to her, followed by her own mother. Hank sat on John's other side, followed by Paco, George and Mangas. It gave them all a chance to develop a better bonding; the women discussing and anticipating the imminent birth, the men planning the survey and George and Mangas, in particular, creating a better understanding of one another. There were occasional moments of misinterpretation, but with George and Ann knowing some Spanish, a mix of the languages got them through.

With the baby due in about three weeks, John was anxious to get on with the survey and then concentrate on the birth. Paco was willing to go with Hank and replace John, but it was decided that he was best placed to continue his role as a foreman and head wrangler with his Mescalero team. Both George and Mangas were keen to go with John and Hank over the whole area.

Agreement was reached. The ladies would stay together, preparing for the baby. The four men would conduct the mapping under Hank's guidance and Paco would continue to manage.

While John had been gone, a separate Wickiup had been built to accommodate George and Ann. However, while the men were to be away, the three women would stay together. Overnight, while he was in the village, Hank was to stay with Paco.

At last, John and Linda were alone together. Linda sank down gratefully on the bed, glad to get the weight off her feet and to be able to kick off her moccasins. John sat beside her and kissed her gently.

"Are you OK?"

"I am better now you are home. I hope the baby doesn't come too early before you all get back, but I don't want to feel this heaviness too much longer. The other women tell me that the first baby is always late. But, you make sure you're back in time."

"You're looking great. It's what we call 'blooming'. You also look contented in yourself. I can't wait either. That's why I am trying to get things done quickly."

"I know. I am being selfish. I just want everything to be perfect."

"You're not selfish. I want things to be perfect as well; for you, the baby, our band and the ranch. That was lovely what you did for Paco. Did you see his face? He'll love that horse to bits."

They were quiet for a few moments.

"Tell me, how did you get on with my mother? How did she get on with yours?"

"All three of us were apprehensive when we met. To be honest, we didn't know how an English lady would take to the Ndee. But she was so pleased to see me, she got on with my mother straight away, she didn't push herself on us and her understanding of Spanish made it easier to speak to Maria-Elena. I think your father kept in the background a bit to let us get to know one another better. But, I am sure my father and he got on well and they'll get to know one another better while you map the ranch."

"I wondered how Hank would fit in. However, he seems to have settled quickly and he and Paco seem to like one another. I think he is going to be very useful to us."

"What makes you think that?"

"He's an ex-army man but not really a soldier. He doesn't want to talk about the war. It's the only time he stops smiling. I think he saw some terrible things and doesn't ever want to see the like again. All I know is that he was an officer, probably as a result of his education, and he had a command. But his links with the army and the New Mexico authorities will be useful to us in selling horses. I also think he is trustworthy."

"That's good. We need friends in all quarters. That goes for all of us, as well as you, me and the baby."

"What do you mean, baby?" queried John, feigning horror?

"Don't push it mister? The way I am feeling now, I might not let you touch me again." She laughed and pulled him down on the bed, snuggling as close as she could, kissing him. They settled down in one another's arms and went to sleep.

The next day, the men set out for the northern part of the valley and the ranch. Two extra pack horses were needed for Hank's equipment. Paco rode with them towards the box canyon where they corralled, broke and trained the wild horses.

Hank had explained how he'd set the measuring rods and the rest of the team could help him. At the box canyon, Paco left them and Mangas, George, Hank and John rode on to the top of the Shis-Inday valley and the watershed. From there, they worked their way back and diverted into the box canyon for the first night, making camp with Paco and the rest of the wranglers.

John was pleasantly surprised to see how much work had been done. The team had built Wickiups, on the slopes and just behind the edge of the forest. They were not visible from the base of the canyon but they were being used by the men while they were working the ranch. There was fresh water tumbling down a stream and a waterfall into the canyon.

The dual functionality had already been achieved; a haven for winter if suddenly trapped by the weather and a sanctuary for the Ndee should they need to escape the main village. It was a perfect spot.

John also noted that they had created two, drop-down, trestle fences where the canyon narrowed. They could trap any marauders, or indeed wild horses being driven up the valley, leaving them at the mercy of the band. The higher defensive positions were impenetrable from below and provided perfect cover for snipers hidden from their enemies.

It was not far from dusk when the four men arrived to join Paco's band of workers. John introduced his companions and thanked the team for their hard work and what they had accomplished. Everyone was in good spirits. The braves were enjoying their work, and play, with the horses. It was hard, but it was channelling their energy and their macho aggression in a very positive way. What was most important was that the whole band was committed and saw the sense and purpose of what they were doing. They were not as free as they had been historically but paradoxically, they were trading this wild, nomadic existence for greater security and longer-term freedom. Their destiny was in their own hands. It was going to be shaped by them, not by their enemies.

They mapped the box canyon on the second day out, again staying overnight with the wranglers. On days three and four they completed the middle section of the Shis-Inday enabling them to return to the village for nightfall.

"George, what do you think of the ranch and John's plans?" asked Ann, as they met up for the evening to eat as a group?

George answered with a sideways look at his son. "It's a wonderful place. The scenery is unbelievable and I can see why he's fallen in love with it and," he looked at Linda with a smile, "with our beautiful daughter-in-law. It is a risk to invest here but the potential is vast. Remember how Britain failed to understand the opportunity that was America. We mustn't, in our own small way, make the same mistake. Hank, Mangas and Paco have also convinced me that this is right."

"I'm glad you feel like that. The women have shown me what they do while you were away. I didn't realise just how much they got out of the mescal plants and the crops they can grow here. Have you seen the animals and the fish?"

"I've been told. I also know how important the Ndee think this is, preserving it as it is. They know what is happening to the buffalo. So Ann, John, Mangas, Paco and the team have my backing as obviously as they have yours."

"Well, that goes without saying. George, will you be able to sort out the finances in Silver City when Hank has finished?"

George grimaced. "I am not sure. It depends on how much I can get done upfront with Luis. The banking system is a bit fraught around here in the early days of the town, so we might need to settle things with Santa Fe. I'll wire them, if necessary, in the next few days."

The next three days were to be spent mapping the south and south-western ends of the valley to the confluence with the main Gila River. Hank said his farewells to the ladies and to Mangas. It was felt to be unwise him going into the town. The team didn't want to draw any unnecessary attention. It was too delicate and fraught a time and there were potential dangers in a new frontier town. However, Paco was to meet them in Silver City as he was bringing in a string of horses to sell in four days' time.

The weather remained hot and dry. The work was completed with George, Hank and John feeling tired, dirty and dishevelled but also elated at the achievement. They got back to Silver City just before dusk and were warmly greeted by Luis. Once they had tended to the horses, they cleaned themselves. The cantina, food and drink were most welcome. To Luis' amusement, the travellers showed how ravenous they were.

"Hey fellows, slow down! No one's going to take your food away."

John laughed.

"Sorry about our manners, Luis. I don't think any of us realised how hungry and thirsty we were. We've spent the last three days intent on getting the job done."

"I can see from your faces that it was successful and I am pleased for you. It's an exciting time."

"Will we be able to sort out everything tomorrow?" George managed to ask this without betraying any signs of anxiety.

"If Hank's work and measurements are complete, there shouldn't be any problem." Anticipating George's next query, Luis added, "And we can sort out all financial transactions by telegraph. Both you and the territory have accounts with the Bank of Santa Fe. It's safer than carting any money around. You'll have the certificate of ownership, as many copies as you need, one filed in this office, one with the New Mexico authorities and one with the Bank of Santa Fe."

John raised his glass and a toast to Hank for his hard work and Luis for his support. George endorsed it. Hank replied with his thanks.

"This was a great challenge to me and Luis. If you succeed, it will be good for us as well. Our reputation will grow in handling land sales and surveying the territory. The maps will be a boon as the territory grows and the place becomes more civilised."

"I am anxious to conclude everything," said John. "The baby is due in two weeks and I hope it hasn't decided to come too early."

"Here's to the Lawson bambino, whatever it is." Luis was in an ebullient mood.

They slept like logs that night.

The following day, they were able to conclude the business. The financial transactions were completed over the wire with the help of the Bank of Santa Fe. John sent his best wishes to Julio and Enrique and got their greetings in turn. Hank was busy compiling his maps and Luis all the official details of ownership. One set of copies was to be taken by John.

George and John prepared themselves for the trek back with Paco when he had brought in the horses. They also returned the hired horses from George and Ann's arrival. It was then a case of relaxing and waiting.

Paco arrived with the horses late in the morning. George and John met up with him at the livery stable. The sales were agreed and Paco's horse left to be fed, watered, cleaned and rested. They went back to the office, introducing Paco to Luis and enabling Paco to clean himself up. While Luis and Hank were finishing off their work, the other three went to the cantina.

He was drunk as he staggered out of door, crashing into Paco.

"Gerrout of my way! Hey you're an 'Injun' or a 'Mex'. 'Fellas'," he shouted to the other miners or drifters that were with him, "What am I 'gonna' do to teach this animal manners?"

Over nothing, the tension was rising. John sensed Paco's hackles erupting and his instincts would be to take this man on.

John touched Paco's arm lightly and stepped in front of him. The drunk was confused.

"You'll have to take me first, before you can get to my friend." John knew Paco would be annoyed but he was thinking fast. The consequences of getting this wrong could be dire. John moved forward to be nearly on top of the man before his companions joined him. He was smaller and more thickset than John, dark, swarthy, unshaven and smelling of alcohol. The other men seemed to be becoming aware of what was happening but their drinking had also dulled their senses.

The drunk's bluster had turned to fear. His eyes met John's fixed gaze and the sense of fright showed. He went for his gun only to find John grabbing his wrist. As it came out of the holster, John used his other hand to direct the man's arm and weapon hard and straight into his temple. He was out cold.

"Get him some coffee and cold water and look after him." John was addressing the man's companions. "That's not a request, that's a bloody order!" John was furious and shouting. His steely look, the penetrating, cold, blue eyes showed that he meant business. If there had been any thought of aggression to George, Paco and John, it was gone. The men carried out the prone drunk. A semblance of calm was restored.

They sat down and John ordered coffee. Paco was still angry. George seemed to be nonplussed.

"Why did you interfere?" Paco tore into John. "I could have handled the situation. You are not my keeper. You don't have to keep 'saving my life'. So what is it with you?"

George looked at John, quizzically. Paco was still, quietly seething.

John took his time to reply making Paco even more furious.

"Paco, I have no doubts in your bravery and courage. You are not thinking straight and you are not going to like what I am going to say to you. You haven't thought through the consequences. So be angry, but listen to the brother who loves you before you explode."

The coffee arrived.

John took a sip and continued.

"Paco, you could have handled the situation and you could have knocked the guy out without any difficulty. The other men would not have stood for that.

129

Right or wrong, they don't consider you as white and not as equal. They would have had to do something about it and the whole thing would have escalated. When I stepped in, it took them back. Once they are all sober, they'll probably forget about it. If it had turned into a gunfight, who knows what would have happened. If we had come through and you had killed anyone, no matter what the extenuating circumstances, it would be a lynching. If I had killed him, it could have been seen as self-defence. That is what I have been trying to impress on you and the band these past several months. Don't tell me about fairness. Don't tell me it's wrong. I know that very well. But it could spell the end of our band, our family. That's why I argued with the young men. One mistake and the Shis-Inday are tarred with the same brush; in your words, Apache not Ndee. We have a lot to lose but a lot to gain if we can keep our heads."

George entered the conversation before Paco could reply.

"He's right Paco. If you think straight, you'll know he is. Our family has seen this all over the world with our ships in many lands. That's why we run the ships as families. We want our men to protect one another. I know your pride may be hurt. This country is changing. It's changing fast and that creates fear among those who cannot adapt. It has always been like that and I suppose it always will be. John doesn't doubt you; I don't either. What's more, I've seen the pride your own family has in you. Now, there is more tension and trouble building. The authorities, I know white, are trying to put all the Apache on to reservations. If we can keep out of that, with the ranch, how much better is that going to be for the Ndee?" He sipped some coffee and carried on. "With the marauding bands causing trouble, right or wrong, we cannot afford to be labelled with them. John is right; one incident and everything we've worked for could be lost. If we get into conflict with any of these bands, the reverse situation may occur. We might need you or Mangas to step in and face them and John would have to swallow his pride. We mustn't fight amongst ourselves."

Paco was calming down. Neither John's nor George's words were lost on him. There was still the simmering fire in his eyes, now more of a golden, brown ember.

"I am not used to thinking in that way. I have been brought up to be strong and proud, standing up for my beliefs. If I find it hard, how much more difficult is it going to be for the young men of the Shis-Inday? The older men like my father may understand better."

"It will be tough," John conceded. "We might fail to prevent any trouble, but we are going to try. Have you thought what we'd do if a wandering band of Ndee wanted to join us because they were being chased by the troopers?"

"We couldn't turn them away, could we?" Paco hadn't thought about it before.

"I guess not," John replied, "but it might depend on what they had done. That's why I asked you to build those traps in the box canyon. Whatever our decision, we are likely to have trouble thrust upon us."

At that moment, Hank and Luis burst in. For the first time, since John had seen them in the town, they were wearing sidearms. News had travelled fast.

"I hear you had a little ruckus," said Hank, slightly breathlessly, "but you dealt with it."

Luis added, "I think that it's OK. They are four miners from a claim about twenty miles south of here. They had struck it a little lucky and had celebrated too much. They've taken the one you knocked out back to camp. I think you really scared them. They are not gunmen and they sobered up pretty quickly with the shock. I don't think there will be any repercussions. No one else is interested."

"Thanks," said John, "I knew from looking at their hands and the way they carried their pistols that they weren't gunmen. I certainly don't want to be targeted as a killer so that some young whippersnapper can get a notch on his belt for shooting me or Paco. Come on, have some coffee with us and let us know how you are doing."

Hank and Luis sat down and ordered some coffee. The Hispanic waitress, who brought them across, continued to look a little shaken by what had happened and the language used hadn't been lost on her. However, she managed a smile at Paco and he responded. She blushed a little sheepishly. The other four men grinned as Paco's gaze followed her small, slim, long dark-haired figure away from the table.

"You've made an impression there, Paco." Hank was laughing at him. George, Luis and John joined in.

"She's the owner's daughter," said Luis, "and he guards her with a rod of iron."

The smiles increased, at Paco's expense. John put his arm round Paco's shoulder but had it roughly removed. However, now the girl had returned behind the bar, he couldn't stop looking at her and she, in turn, couldn't take her eyes off him.

Hank brought them back to business.

"I've done the first sets of documents, so you can take your copies now, the deeds and maps in particular. Luis has put the New Mexico Territory seal on them. Because this is company land and paid for, you don't have to wait five years. It belongs to you. The Lawson Ranch is now official. Congratulations! There is one other thing. Part of my job is to map out these lands and supply those maps to the army. Earlier this year, they set up Fort Bayard, just south of here. Their job is to support the settlement of New Mexico and protect the people from the marauding Apaches, at the moment mainly around here rather than in the Gila Forest area. Now, I'll have a word with the sergeant who is the Quartermaster. The fort is expanding to over three hundred soldiers and they will need plenty of horses. They also use Indian scouts, mainly Kiowa and Apache. This might be a dual opportunity for you and some of your lads. Prove that you are peaceful, settled and cooperative, sell them as many horses as you can and the pressure to move the Shis-Inday will ease."

"Thanks to both of you," said John. George murmured his approval. Paco was more reticent.

"Hank, I hope you are not suggesting we betray our brothers. We'll never turn them away if they seek sanctuary with us."

"Paco, I am trying to help. It may come to it that you'll have to take sides. But, if the nomads calm down and show themselves to be peaceful, things will settle. If you fight the army, there will be no going back. If you harbour fugitives, it will make life difficult."

"We'll have to fight if they try to drive us from our land. We're not going to any reservation, to starve on infertile land, eke out a poor existence and lose all our pride." Paco looked at John in particular.

"We'll cross that bridge if, and when, we have to. That is why it is company land. There will be no betrayal. I, for one, could not face it if I did not support you, your family and the rest of the Shis-Inday. However, there is more than one way to skin a cat, a 'Ligai Ndolkah'." John grinned at Paco following his analogy.

"I suggest we have something to eat, and Paco, if you and your horse are OK after your long ride, we should get going so we'll be home by tomorrow night. I am anxious to get back, as you can all understand." He then added, rather cheekily, "Unless Paco, you have some other business to attend to?"

The others laughed as Paco glowered at him but there was no malice in his eyes.

They ordered tortillas, beans and rice. It was noticeable that the waitress had shown her favours as Paco's plate was noticeably fuller. They smiled but did not comment. However, John got Paco to settle the bill up at the bar and this gave him time to talk to her.

"Gracias por servicio." He spoke in Spanish. "Thank you for your service. I am Paco Faraones."

"Thank you!" She replied in English. "You are welcome. My name is Juanita Zapatero."

"Well, I hope I get the chance to meet you again and get to know you."

"That would be nice, Paco. The Pharoah and the Shoemaker." They laughed.

"We've got to get back to the ranch so I am not sure when we'll be back. John, the tall young blond man, is married to my sister and the baby is due now."

"Good luck! I hope everything goes well for them. Hasta Proxima!"

"See you soon!"

They returned to the office, picked up the deeds and maps, their bags and saddles, made their farewells and went to the stables to retrieve their horses. As they left town, a certain little figure waved to them from the door of the cantina. George and John looked at one another but kept silent.

Chapter Thirteen

They were all anxious to get back as fast as they could and make as much headway as possible before nightfall. There was a natural, quiet urgency. All three of them were lost in their own thoughts. Even so, neither Paco nor John forgot to cover their tracks and maintain the usual precautions.

When they made camp that night, Paco and John took turns to take guard. George was intrigued.

"Why are you going to such efforts, John? Are we in real danger?"

"It could be, Dad. We don't know for sure. There are more and more moves to get all the Indians on to reservations as the new, white settlers advance west."

"I notice you said 'white'. Aren't there others: black, Hispanic, Chinese?"

"It's mainly the whites who are the problem. They change the laws, legal and natural. The Indians, in the main, lose their lands, ancient hunting, culture and domain. We may have enemies all around; nomadic Indians including various tribes of Apache, political, moneyed and business land-grabbers, thieves, villains and murderers of all sorts. You never know. You just keep your wits about you."

"It doesn't change, son. We've seen it before, all around the world. You are a chip off the old block. Your grandfather fought slavery and I have had to fight sharp business and political practices. You've found a new cause, but you've also got a business in the making. Let's do everything to keep it together."

"Thanks for your support, Dad. I couldn't have done it without your help and Mum's backing as well. I think the Ndee were surprised how well you fitted in with them and accepted their traditions. You've seen how hard they work and how clever they are in carving out a living. You've also seen how good the braves are with the horses."

They banked up the fire and settled down to sleep. A few hours later, Paco woke John to take over his stint of guard duty.

"I have been thinking a lot since our conversation in town and the events of the day."

"Yes," John replied.

"I remain troubled as to what is the right thing to do. The Ndee cannot live if they are not men. We have to be proud and strong."

"You will be, Paco. You and the other Ndee braves are doing it in a different way. That takes great courage, much more than to fight and die for lost causes and needless honour. You are building a legacy for the Ndee, the Shis-Inday. This ranch will be yours. It will contain your history and your culture. People will learn much from that and from your descendants, the family of Mangas, Maria Elena and other Ndee, who will carry it on and develop it. Get some sleep. Have some sweet dreams about seeing your little Hispanic girl again."

There was a wicked glint in John's eyes and a chuckle as he said it. Paco hit him, in a friendly way. John sensed he had blushed, although that couldn't be seen in the dark. He smiled in turn.

John repaired the fire again and moved around the perimeter of the camp to take guard. He took a sip of water from his canteen, checked his Spencer and settled down to await the dawn. He was really longing to be up and away, to get home, to see Linda and, hopefully, not to be too late for the birth of the baby. It was an exciting time.

The horses were suddenly restless. John tensed himself but kept still and wary hidden in the brush. A figure appeared moving lithely, silent and with purpose. Whoever it was, he was stealthy, smaller than John. It was too early to challenge him; there may be others. John remained silent. His caution was rewarded as other figures appeared. They moved nearer the fire. John counted seven of them and knew he'd have to act before they were too close to Paco and his father.

Instinctively, he called out "Ndee; friend!" In the split second that followed, also out of the shadows, Paco shouted "and here too," to be followed likewise by George. Paco's alertness had awakened him. In turn he had roused George and they had taken strategic cover.

"Move towards the fire." John spoke in the Mescalero tongue. He was guessing and hoping.

"We outnumber you," came the reply. "By the way, your accent is horrible." Despite the situation, the intruder hadn't lost his humour and he and the others had relaxed, slightly, at the native language.

John laughed. "Yes, but we have you covered from three angles," was his rejoinder. "Who are you?"

They did as they were told and waited by the fire as John, Paco and George emerged from the shadows.

"We are Chiricahua braves. We have been chased by the cavalry who are setting up the new fort at what they call Bayard. They are trying to confine us to the desert lands south of there. The hunting is poor, we are all hungry."

The dawn was approaching fast and the light improving by the minute.

The seven braves looked bemused when they saw two white men with a Mescalero.

Paco and George still had them covered as John approached and lowered his rifle. "You are welcome to join us for breakfast."

He looked them over. They were gaunt and dishevelled. Their clothing had seen better days. The defiance and pride was still in their eyes. Their weapons were poor except for the bows. The guns were ramshackle and rusting. They hadn't had time to look after them while evading their pursuers. They were brave but young, possibly not even as old as John himself and unwilling to admit they were scared. They were intrigued and curious about who their hosts were.

"How far are the cavalry behind you?"

"Maybe they are two hours behind. They have a Kiowa scout with them and he is good. He'll be on the move already."

"OK! We'd better move too." John grabbed some sticks of jerky. "Better eat these for now. Get your horses and come with us. Ten horses and three shod will cause some confusion for a time. We want to get back quickly for other reasons. We can talk later. In the meantime, you are our guests and welcome in true Mescalero custom."

The seven Chiricahua nodded, took the food and raced off to get their ponies.

George, Paco and John broke camp in record time.

They moved as rapidly as the terrain allowed. John and Paco agreed, in view of what had been said about the scout, there was little point in spending time to cover their tracks. However, they decided it might be worth the diversion at the confluence of the Shis Inday and Gila rivers. Despite taking great care to ride up and down the mainstream and the tributary, they thought any tracker, worth his salt, would be able to follow them. However, there was no sign of their pursuers at that stage.

They got back to the village to be met by virtually everyone. The lookouts had seen them coming and had warned of the unexpectedly large numbers. Linda was there. John was relieved to see she still hadn't had the baby.

He jumped off the horse, handing the reins to Paco, raced towards her, then remembering her condition, slowed, held her and kissed her gently.

"It's alright. I am not that fragile." She laughed. "But, who are your companions?" Mangas and the other Mezcaleros were eyeing the newcomers warily; the Chiricahua were uneasy.

Paco broke the ice. He dismounted holding on to the reins of both his and John's horses.

"These Chiricahua are being chased by the cavalry from the new fort. They are supposed to go to a reservation in the southern desert. They cannot live there and survive. We met them early this morning. We believe that the soldiers will be close on our heels so we have to move fast."

"What are you suggesting?" Mangas was now eyeing his son warily.

"We change horses so that we all have fresh mounts and I'll take them up to the canyon. John and George will have to stay for the baby. So, it's up to me. When the soldiers arrive, tell them they are employees of this ranch and were caught up with the Chiricahua when delivering horses south of here. They have been racing for home because they feared no one would believe their story." The braves nodded their agreement.

"We are putting our trust in you on this," Paco continued. "You will need to work with us as wranglers and not get involved in any fighting. Somehow, we'll find a way to re-unite you with your people."

The Chiricahua looked at one another and signalled their response in unison, placing one arm, horizontally, across their chests.

Almost on cue, a flashing signal was being sent from the surrounding hills. All the delaying tactics had failed to slow down the pursuers. They had less than two hours grace.

The team moved fast. Paco seemed to have gained an extra wind. The young newcomers were driven by a mixture of fear, adrenalin and gratitude to the Ndee for supporting them. Their ponies were corralled and now they had Lawson brand ponies. Mangas made sure that the new horses were fed, watered and branded. Paco and the seven strangers had headed for the canyon. Everyone else started to calm once they had gone, preparing themselves for the imminent challenge.

John and George took the opportunity to clean their selves, getting something to eat and drink and then, once they were more settled and relaxed, reacquainting themselves with Linda and Ann respectively. The conversation turned to the baby.

"I am so glad you made it back on time," she said as she hugged John as closely as she could. Ann also looked relieved to see her husband's and son's return.

"Actually," John said, "that's another excuse to add to the story as to why we were moving so fast to get back." He didn't sound convincing but it lifted everyone's spirits.

"I think we should get some food ready." Maria Elena proposed and everyone murmured assent. "That will help to keep things on an even keel and we won't appear to be threatening."

They busied themselves with their various tasks, all the while, receiving signals from the look-outs as the cavalry troop approached.

By the time they appeared, the Ndee were ready. The soldiers rode up from the river, across the flood plain and up to the village rise. There were about fifty mounts. At the front, they were led by the Kiowa scout and a sergeant. There were no officers. The most noticeable thing was that they were all buffalo soldiers. They had ridden hard and they looked tired, dirty and dishevelled. They were very surprised to see two white men and a white woman with the Mescalero.

John and Mangas stepped forward to greet the troop. They deliberately wore no weapons but the soldiers were still very wary.

"Howdy," John shouted. "Welcome to the Lawson ranch. I am John Lawson. This is my father-in-law, Mangas Faraones. I'll introduce you to everyone else when you've dismounted."

The sergeant responded in kind. He was a little more relaxed. The Kiowa scout remained very stiff, not giving anything away. "Howdy, I am Luther Jackson, leading this troop out of Fort Bayard."

"Come and join us," John said. "You look exhausted and we can let you have some food and water, for you and the horses."

"We've got to keep moving. We have been chasing some renegades who've escaped from the reservation and we've tracked them here." Sergeant Jackson appeared adamant.

John responded quietly. "You are not going to make much progress unless you rest your horses and your men. You are wrong about the pursuit and we need to explain." He was talking to Luther but looking at the Kiowa. The scout remained impassive, remaining perfectly stony-faced.

Luther realised he needed to compromise. The horses had been drinking at the river but they did need feeding and resting. His men certainly needed food, water and rest. He understood that any threats of violence were not going to achieve a purpose. Ploughing on would be unproductive.

He turned to the cavalry. "Dismount. We've been offered feed for the horses and food for ourselves." The soldiers remained uncertain but they allowed several of the Ndee to show them where to take their animals, clean them and feed them, then clean and feed themselves. One of the corporals took the sergeant's and Kiowa's mounts to look after them.

Luther and the scout joined John and Mangas and the introductions were made. The Kiowa was known as Little Hawk.

As they ate and drank, John explained what had happened.

"There has been something of a misunderstanding. We have just been to Silver City to register the ranch in the name of the family company. On the way back, we met up with some of our wranglers who had been delivering horses and somehow got caught up with you following people who had escaped from the reservation. We needed to get back quickly because, as you can see," John was pointing to Linda, "our baby is due very soon."

Luther motioned his congratulations to Linda.

"So where are these men now?"

"They've returned with the foreman to our horse canyon to look after and break new beasts."

Luther turned to Little Hawk. "It looks like, for once, you got the wrong trail."

Little Hawk did not even blink. He did not betray a single twitch. "I read the signs."

"We'll have to check this out." Luther was clear.

Mangas intervened. "I'd best go with you." He wanted no trouble and he knew John wanted to be there for the baby.

George was thinking along the same lines and suspected his presence would help to maintain a level of calm. "I'll come too."

Maria Elena and Ann realised that their husbands had done this to allow John to stay with Linda. John was quietly grateful to both of them.

"Before you go," John said, "we want you to know we have a large horse ranch here. Fort Bayard is growing and you'll need all the horses you can get. Pass that back when you return and we'll deal with your quartermaster on a regular trade. This is a family business and the people, you see here, work the ranch. I think that would prove far more productive for you than chasing a fool's errand."

"I'll bear that in mind and I'll take that back." Sergeant Jackson was adamant. "We have a job to do." Then, he added as an afterthought, "We'll take care not to do anything stupid."

"That's all Mangas, George and I want. Let wise heads prevail all around. Make sure you take the advice of the older people."

As they mounted their horses and prepared to move out, Luther noted that both George and Mangas had better weaponry than his own troop.

Chapter Fourteen

At last, John and Linda were together and on their own. Events were moving so fast that they had hardly had time to catch up. Everything was ready for the baby. It was now time to wait and be patient.

They cuddled up and kissed.

"I am so relieved you got back in time. I am sorry that our fathers and Paco have had to sort out more problems and may not be here. It was good of them to share the onus." Linda was voicing her thoughts aloud.

"I hope it works out for everyone. I know we are both worried. The soldiers didn't believe us but, if everyone sticks to their story, there's not much they can do about it. I should be with you. I should be helping our fathers and Paco. I feel torn. Just tell me I did the right thing."

Linda stroked his face and kissed his cheek. "You could not have done much more. If the three of them can't control what's going to happen, your being there would have made little difference. The baby is the future. It represents what we want for the Shis-Inday. We are building a new world, a new civilisation. We are showing that mixed cultures and religions can work together. I think that made an impression on the buffalo soldiers. They got more respect from us than they get from their officers. That wasn't lost on them."

"I hope you are right, my love. It won't stop me from worrying. As you say, there's nothing more for me to do for now except to concentrate on the baby."

They fell asleep as dusk fell.

Linda awoke feeling warm and wet. Her waters had broken and it was still dark. She roused John. He was up in an instant. Despite herself, Linda had to laugh.

"Settle back. It's not going to be that soon. The other ladies tell me the first baby always takes the longest. We have a few hours yet. There's no need to wake anyone else."

She winced as another contraction came. "Stay with me, hold me, talk to me and help me take my mind off the pangs."

John got a towel and wiped and kissed her forehead, settling back alongside her. "Just tell me what you want and when you need it," he said. "I think I am more nervous than you."

"Don't worry. I am sure everything's OK. We've got everything ready. I'll let you know when to get our mothers and the rest of the helpers." Linda grimaced again.

The dawn soon arrived. It was going to be another, hot, bright day. Linda's contractions were becoming more frequent and now down to about two minutes apart.

"I think it's time to get everyone in," Linda said. "Can you also make sure we have some hot water and you keep a fire going?"

John was up and dressed in a moment. He found Maria Elena and Ann already awake and ready. They seemed calm on the surface, were not rushing and had already eaten. They followed him back to Linda.

Maria Elena still wasn't happy about John being at the birth. However, she respected her daughter's wishes. She gave John his orders.

"Make sure you keep the fire going and we have plenty of warm water. Test it with your elbow before you give it to us. And, make sure you keep yourself clean."

"I know," said John. "I've been given my instructions already."

Maria Elena glowered at him; Ann had a slight smile of amusement but kept the sisterhood.

"You had better get on with it, son."

The ladies looked after Linda while John was in and out with his chores. At one point, Linda had screamed at John. "I'm never letting you near me again, once this baby is born."

The two mothers looked at one another with their own secret acknowledgment and agreement. John flushed, but they deliberately ignored his embarrassment. In between times, John was holding Linda's hand and she clung on very tightly at critical moments.

"Keep pushing," was the regular advice.

"What the hell do you think I'm doing?" was the pained response.

Suddenly, John shouted. "I can see the head. Keep going darling, you are nearly there."

Linda was pale and feeling exhausted. She was too tired to argue now. John mopped her brow and, a few pushes later, the baby appeared.

There was that dreadful silence that accompanies a birth. Everyone was holding a breath. So it seems was the baby. Then suddenly, there was a piercing cry as it took its first gulp of air. A flood of relief went through the two grandmothers, John and Linda.

"You've got a little girl," Maria Elena announced. She and Ann cleaned her up while John tended to Linda.

"We've got a daughter," Linda almost whispered to John. "We've got a beautiful, little girl." She took her from her mother and clung to her, now wrapped up in a blanket from the layette. She started to smile as she showed their little child to her husband.

John recovered from being dumbstruck. "Yes," he said. "You did really well, my love." He turned to the grandmothers. "Thank you for all your help. I don't think we would have done half as well without you."

"We wouldn't have missed it for the world," said Ann. "I am so glad we made it here, and I'm so sorry, Mangas, Paco and George are not here to share this moment with us."

Linda was recovering and so proud of her baby. "I have something else to tell you," she said. "John and I discussed it beforehand. We are going to call her Marianna, after the pair of you."

Neither grandmother betrayed any immediate response but it was clear that they were delighted with the announcement.

"Marianna Faraones Lawson," mused Ann. "That's lovely. Thank you!" She looked and smiled at Maria Elena.

"She's a greedy little beggar," said Linda, as the baby startled suckling. "She's not giving me any time to recover."

"I'll just have to make sure you're well-fed," said John.

John helped the ladies to clean up everything while Linda nursed the baby. Maria Elena took charge of the placenta which was soaked up in the waste, fabric materials and mescal fibre. While her daughter and granddaughter slept, she hurried away to bury the remains in the consecrated ground. It was a tradition not to jeopardise the child by allowing the placenta to be eaten by any animals. Different indigenous tribes had their own approaches. This particular group of Mescalero people had decided on sacred burial.

Despite their tiredness, John and Linda were torn between conflicting responsibilities. Though they concentrated on little Marianna, their thoughts were with their fathers as well.

Later that day, John, Linda, Maria-Elena and Ann were together when Linda, feeding the baby said, "John, I know you want to stay and help but I think you'd better find out what's happened to our fathers and Paco." The two mothers murmured their approval.

"Are you sure?" John replied. Linda touched his elbow and smiled.

"You can see Marianna's OK. Between the three of us, we'll look after her. At least you were here for her birth and that was the most important. But, we are all worried about what's happening up at the canyon. The sooner you get there, the more you might be able to help."

John kissed her and the baby. He raced around to saddle a horse and take basic food and water provisions. He made sure his gun, rifle, ammunition and bedroll were in order, went back to give his final goodbyes to Linda, Marianna and her grandmothers, then departed. As it was now late afternoon, he knew he'd have to camp out overnight before getting to the canyon.

Because they had left the previous afternoon, the cavalry, Mangas and George had also had to stop overnight. Paco took advantage of the extra hours of grace to brief all the wranglers and set up the traps in the canyon in case they were needed. He was dramatic about discipline and this applied to the Chiricahua as well as his own men. The newcomers were given buddies and told to work with them, looking after the horses further up the canyon. Some of his Ndee team backtracked down the valley to set up a series of lookout points and signals on the pursuers. The rest were to lay in wait, undercover and, if necessary, spring the traps. By dawn they were ready. There was nothing more to do but wait.

By mid-morning, the first of the signals was being relayed up the valley. Paco was relieved to hear that his father and George were leading the cavalry. He informed the men lying in wait and that reduced the tension, enormously. However, they remained on guard and maintained their disciplinary stance.

Leaving the rest in position, Paco rode down with a small party of three Ndee to meet the arrivals, at the point where the canyon and a stream adjoined the main river valley.

It was obvious that the greeting party was not a threat. Mangas led up front while the soldiers were ordered to dismount and care for their mounts.

Mangas, George, Luther and Little Hawk approached Paco and the three Ndee wranglers.

"This is my son, Paco, and some of our team. They round up and manage our horses in this part of the ranch." Mangas turned and introduced those with him. "This is Sergeant Luther Jackson and Little Hawk."

Luther was surprised as Paco stepped forward and proffered his hand in the 'American' way. He removed his glove and the two shook hands. Paco and Little Hawk exchanged nodding acknowledgements and no more.

Mangas took control to make sure the wrong things were not said.

"Sergeant Jackson is here to bring back some renegades to the reservation from which they escaped. Little Hawk has tracked them here. George and I told both of them that there has been a misunderstanding and that the men, they were trailing, were our men returning from a mission delivering horses in the south."

Luther was a little nonplussed to have some of his thunder taken away from him and his authority usurped.

"Now look here," he said, "I will still need to see these men and ascertain that they are who you say. It's an offence to protect renegades and you could all be in trouble if that is the case."

Paco responded. "They are working employees of this ranch and we have a responsibility for their protection."

George intervened. "I have a solution to your problem, Luther. Why don't you allow us to write out an affidavit that these are our men? You can take that back as proof you accomplished the mission and satisfy your officers."

"What the hell's this 'davit' thing?" Luther was getting increasingly fraught.

George spoke softly. "An affidavit is a signed, legal document that can be given as proof in a court of law. Luckily, I have some paper with me and I can draw it up for you."

It suddenly came to George what was spooking Luther. He had come out of the Civil War and been promoted in a time of conflict. He didn't go through the normal channels and, being an ex-slave, couldn't read nor write. Presumably, none of his troop was capable, either. They wouldn't understand how valuable or how useless this testimony was. He wasn't going to embarrass them.

George continued. "There is a way out of this impasse. I'll write up the document while you, Paco or one of the team, bring the men you have been trailing here. All of them, Mangas, Paco and I will sign or mark the declaration. You, Luther, can take that back to Fort Bayard with you."

Luther was caught in a cleft stick. If he tried to force the issue, there might be a fight. How many of the Ndee possessed superior weapons and how many of them were there? Alternatively, if he did what George suggested, what would his superiors, back at the fort, make of that?

He decided that caution was the better part of valour. His men had been through enough with the Civil War and its aftermath.

"OK."

"Good," said George. "With the agreement of Mangas, Paco go and fetch the men. Paco, please re-assure them that this is in order and they'll be safe."

Paco looked at Mangas, who half nodded and acknowledged a positive agreement with his eyes, almost like a silent bid at an auction.

"Make sure they understand the importance of this, son. We can't look after people if they don't comply with the rules of the ranch." Mangas was staring hard at Paco. "In the meantime, we'll camp here."

"I may not find everyone before the morning," Paco said. "I'll get everyone back for then."

As Paco departed, the soldiers set about their tasks, continuing to settle and feed the horses, putting up tents, collecting wood, building fires and cooking food. There was an uneasy truce and much wariness. The crackling in the fires reflected the tension in the air. As darkness descended, shadows lengthened and apprehension grew, the atmosphere becoming more highly charged.

George had a quiet word with Mangas.

"Should we ask Luther to share the tipi with us? The fact of us being together should relieve tensions all round and he can share a meal with us as well."

Mangas mused for a moment and gave George a hard stare. "Wise words," he said. "Yes, I think everyone would feel more relaxed. It will probably be even better if I ask him."

They strolled over to the soldiers and approached the sergeant. "Luther, would you like to join us for a meal and stay in the tipi with us?" Mangas added, "You might like to see how you like our mescal drink."

Luther was taken aback. His whole background had been one of distrust and disrespect. Even in the army, it was only his stripes that gave him any authority. The reason for the buffalo soldier units was still a racist one. Forget the end of slavery and the Union cause, there was little love shown between blacks and whites. Yet, in his eyes, here was a red man and a white man showing courtesy and respect.

He looked back at the two of them and hesitated. George and Mangas both sensed his quandary and allowed the pregnant pause. Luther's mind was racing. He didn't want to upset his hosts but he wasn't sure how this would look to his men, never mind the authorities back at Fort Bayard. His two corporals were with him. He looked at them.

He spoke clearly with authority. "I shall leave you in charge of the men, sentry duties and morning call." Turning to Mangas and George, he smiled. "Thank you. That will give us the opportunity to discuss things further and decide on the next possible steps. Oh, I may be able to lay my hands on a good bottle of bourbon."

If Mangas and George breathed sighs of relief, they didn't show any outward appearances. George just replied, "Right, we'll see you in a few minutes."

Further down the valley, John was also settling himself for the night. He had pulled up on the edge of the tree line and above both the trail and the river. It was precautionary. He had no specific reason to be that careful. It was an ingrained habit. He wasn't going to sleep easily anyway. He made up a false bed near the fire; just in case. When, eventually, he did settle, his mind flew between situations; Linda and Marianna, his father, Mangas and Paco, the cavalry, how the Chiricahua were going to react, possible trouble, what that meant for the ranch and the future of the Ndee, the future for him and his immediate family. He did drop off for short spurts of sleep, but he was soon awake again.

He would have been relieved if he had known how well Luther, Mangas and George were doing. The stories they swapped were full of intrigue. Luther had been brought up on a slave plantation and the war had given him his freedom. His natural leadership qualities had singled him out to manage buffalo soldiers. Mangas told them about the fights for survival, on the plains, against soldiers, Mexican or Hispanic Americans and the 'Long March' of the Plains' Indians. George's stories were about the business, ships and the sea, something awe-inspiring to the other two, and his whole family history in the fight against slavery. The sharing of drinks helped but nobody overindulged and eventually, they settled down for the night in a more relaxed frame of mind.

John was up and about before the dawn, anxious to be at the canyon as soon as he could. He could hardly have timed it better as he arrived just as Paco was bringing in the Chiricahua braves. His news about the baby cheered and calmed everyone. Paco had briefed the Chiricahua very well and told them not to say much. They didn't speak any English and so he had to act as translator.

It was a little farcical and everyone knew it. George had taken John aside and told him of his suggestion for the affidavit. John was surprised and delighted at the same time.

"Will he buy it?" he asked, referring to Luther.

"I don't think he has much choice in the matter," said George. "The real question is, how they'll react at Fort Bayard. By the way, don't let on, but I don't think Luther can read. He's never been taught and he hadn't heard of an affidavit."

Luther wasn't getting much further with the Chiricahua. Little Hawk knew they weren't Mescalero and said as much to Luther; the soldiers didn't recognise the differences in the Apache tribes. The tension was rising again.

Luther decided. He turned to George. "Can I have your signed statement, as you suggested? We'll then get out of your hair and make our way back to Fort Bayard."

George agreed but was slightly cannier. "OK, but I'll make two copies. They can be witnessed by John and by you; you will take one copy and we'll keep the other." He didn't want his affidavit to be declared invalid because it was signed by a Ndee, but he also didn't want to insult Mangas, Paco and the others. Secretly, he was pleased John had arrived.

Mangas and Paco realised why George had taken that step. They were realistic about it and raised no objection. Luther had probably worked it out as well.

"If it's OK with you, sergeant, may we ride back down the valley with you?" George was putting in the last request to make sure there were no changes of mind. "Mangas and I are anxious to see the baby."

John apologised to Paco for leaving him, but both felt it was best that he made sure the Chiricahua settled in with the rest of the Ndee.

"Just give Marianna a kiss and a hug from her Uncle Paco."

"You'll see her soon. Thanks for looking after things up here. You've done a great job. We hope the new guys won't cause you or us any trouble."

The troop, Mangas, George and John departed and set off back down the valley.

Chapter Fifteen

The summer was rapidly drawing to a close. Everyone in the village was busy; harvesting the crops, storing the food, making the products arising from the gathered materials and readying everything for the winter to come. Marianna was doing well and growing fast. Paco had brought down a string of horses to sell in Silver City and had taken the opportunity to see his niece for the first time.

That day, the scouts had signalled a lone rider was coming up the valley. They didn't recognise him, but he was white and not a soldier. As he approached the village, John and Paco saw him immediately. It was Hank.

"Howdy! It's great to see you. What brings you here?" The greeting from both was warm and sincere.

Hank dismounted. "It's great to see you guys as well. You're both looking fit and strong."

"We can't complain," John grinned. "Did you hear about the baby?"

"No. Congratulations! What have you got?"

"Linda had a little girl and we've called her Marianna after the two grandmothers. When you've cleaned up and had a drink, we'll take you to see her. We assume you are staying overnight."

"Thanks," said Hank. "I'd appreciate that."

Paco added, "I have to take a string of ponies back to Silver City tomorrow. If you are going back there, we can ride together."

Hank hesitated for a moment. "Yes, that will be great, but you can decide that after I tell you the news."

"That sounds ominous." John was concerned.

"Maybe, I am just being ultra-cautious." Hank was not smiling in his usual way. "I'd prefer to talk to you all as a family and as friends, if that's OK with you."

"Now, you've got us intrigued, but I guess it would be better we all know things first hand."

Hank cleaned up, had some water, tended to his horse and took his belongings to Paco's wickiup. He then went with John to see Marianna and Linda.

"She's a beauty; just like her mother."

"You mean rather than looking like me." John laughed.

"You said it," said Hank, smiling for the first time.

They arranged that the family would all eat together. If Maria-Elena was put out at such short notice, she didn't show it. She and Ann set about organising everything. It was a lavish time of the year and they pulled out the stops. It was more like a banquet.

Hank had the floor.

"First of all, can I say that Luis sends you his best wishes? He also thinks I am doing the right thing in talking to you. As you know, when I documented your purchase of this land, I had to let the army know and I said I'd tell them about your ranch and the horses to trade. When I got there, I sensed a lot of resentment amongst the officers. To put it bluntly, many of them regard it as a retrograde step to be sent to this 'god-forsaken' place and they despise the Apache. They do not even consider them a worthy enemy after the Civil War. It's pure 'West Point' like arrogance based on how battles should be fought. They don't appreciate guerrilla tactics. Add to that, we have a changing breed of politicians in New Mexico, pandering to the basest instincts and they want the Apaches out. Frankly, my registration of your ranch was like a damp squib. They'll be looking at all means of getting you out; legal or illegal."

Hank's words were being taken in silently by the assembled group. He continued.

"I thought that mentioning the horse-trading was going to add even more fuel to the fire. That was taken out of my hands when Sergeant Jackson returned to Fort Bayard with his troop. His colonel was furious that he had not brought back the renegades they were chasing. He tore up an affidavit, I understand George and John wrote, and Luther was threatened with demotion to Private if he didn't return and hunt them down. He scoffed at any purchase of horses. I have never seen an NCO carpeted like that, in front of his own men. As an officer myself, I would never have belittled any of my men in that way and I thought it was disgusting. I got the impression that the army would rather have a troop of dead heroes than live peacemakers. Whether they move before winter or leave it now till spring, I don't know. However, I thought you needed to know the truth."

"What about the legalities?" asked George.

"I think that's what's holding them up. Unless the authorities can find a way of revoking your ownership of this valley, the army cannot move. If they were able to prove you were harbouring murderous fugitives, they could move in. I do not believe that they are thinking very clearly at the moment, so you had better be prepared for anything."

John surprised himself and took charge of the situation.

"I think the answer is clear. We de-camp the village from here, take all the families, food and belongings to the canyon. We have enough wickiups built already, even if it may be a little cramped for everyone. However, it is a much better defensive position and Paco and his team have done a magnificent job to make it impregnable. I think Dad, you and Mum should go home now. Before you protest, I am thinking strategically. You will do far more for us representing an American company with American authorities and the hierarchy of the army. New Mexico will eventually become a state and the local politicians and cavalry officers will have to take notice of their masters in Washington."

Everyone was quiet, awaiting George's reply. He thought carefully before he spoke.

"I want you all to know that it goes against my basic philosophy to run from a fight." He looked at Ann to check her approval. "The last thing, we want, is to feel we are running out on you. It would hurt us deeply if the Ndee thought we were letting them down. I do see John's point but we'll only go if everyone else agrees."

Mangas also chose his words carefully.

"We have a whole history of dealing with all sorts of people. There are good and bad people everywhere. We know those who are our friends. We know those whom we can trust. John proved himself in many ways with Paco, Linda and now being very much part of us. Hank and Luis did it with the land registration and the courage to warn us of what is happening now. You kept very wise counsel at the stand-off in the canyon, keeping the peace with the soldiers. I do not understand the workings of the 'whites'; territories, states, land registration, deeds, contracts, businesses and ownership. These seem to be of more importance to you. If that's what benefits the Ndee, then I can explain it to the rest of the band, in their language, and they'll understand and back you."

"I think we have a plan," said John. "Mum, Dad and I will leave with Paco and Hank in the morning. They can ride two of the horses that Paco is taking into Silver City to sell. In the meantime, the rest of the Ndee must decamp and make for the canyon. Once Paco and I have sounded out what is happening, we'll return to join the rest of you, there. Dad will have to make contacts within the American authorities to see what sway they can hold over New Mexico politicians wanting to contravene the law."

There was no single objection. There wasn't any dissent. They were of one mind. No one wanted this but it seemed to be the only solution in the circumstances. An early night was called for in view of the preparations to begin tomorrow.

John and Linda were quiet. Neither of them wanted to be separated again so soon. Marianna was asleep, blissfully unaware of the trauma around her. Her parents smiled and held one another in a loving embrace, shivering slightly in anticipation of what was about to unfold. This was comfort and fear rather than sexual. There was unspoken trepidation and neither wanted to voice their perceived dread. At this young age, they had already been through so much and here was another momentous decision. It didn't seem fair that they could not enjoy an untroubled young, married and family life. Despite everything that had happened, this was the first time it had hit them and it had occurred to both of them at the same moment. They cuddled and fell to sleep in troubled mode, only being awakened by Marianna's cries for a feed. Her needs brought them back to the reality of what was required. As they held one another and settled down once more, the second half of their night's sleep was less troubled. Their focus had returned. Their little girl was the future. She was what everything was about and for what the wider family was fighting.

When they awoke, before dawn, Linda leaned across John and gave him a long lasting and sweet kiss. It said, "I love you." It said, "Keep safe." It said, "Thank you."

There were no protracted farewells. Nobody knew what was going to happen. Nobody wanted to tell of their hopes or aspirations nor their sadness. Conversation was limited as the men and Ann made ready to depart. It was time to go. Suddenly, George, Ann, Paco, Hank and John were away, trailing a string of horses. Mangas, Maria Elena and Linda were there to see them off, Marianna cradled in Linda's arms. Maria Elena surprised and delighted the travellers by giving every one of them a food pack for the journey.

They departed without ceremony. Already, the rest of the Ndee were busily de-camping and preparing for their departure. It never failed to astonish John how rapid and clinical was the way this was performed. Once they had left, there would hardly be a trace that this had been a village. The land and the weather would soon cover all the tracks so that only the best scouts would recognise the remaining signs.

They hit Silver City at lunchtime on the following day. The town was still bustling and growing, manifested by the increased rowdiness. They left the horses at the livery stable to be fed, watered and groomed before the sale. They then went to see Luis and a chance to clean their selves up from the trail dust.

To say Luis was delighted to see them all was an understatement. He was greatly relieved.

"I've some updated news for you, but I'll make the coffee while I tell you. The good bit is that the soldiers are not coming for you again, at least not for now. There have been several break-outs from the forts and reservations all over the south and south-west of New Mexico. It is stretching the army, no end. The cavalry are up to their ears in chasing small bands all over the desert. At the moment, they do not have the time to be troubled by you. Their resources are too thinly spread."

John knew he could trust Luis. He explained what they had done with the village and how they had planned their defences.

Luis showed some concern. "How are you going to grow your crops and feed yourselves in the canyon area? Surely, the growing conditions are not as good as the flood plain?"

"It's not ideal," John agreed. "It means that we shall have to do some more hunting. However, if you are right about the army being stretched, it gives us more time to prepare for our needs."

The conversation turned to other things. The men left it to Ann to talk about Marianna. She was bubbling over and obviously missing her already. Paco had been very quiet and John knew he wanted to get away on his own for a while. There were other practical considerations. Luis and Hank had work to do. George and Ann needed to arrange travel. They agreed to meet up at the cantina later.

John, George and Ann headed for the stage office while Paco went to the cantina. Juanita was serving as usual. As Paco came through the door, her whole face lit up. Paco's heart was thumping as he managed a smile.

"Hello," she said, surprising him by speaking in English. "Is it just a table for one?" Her dark eyes flashed as she looked at him. Paco was stunned into silence for a moment. Then, he recovered. "Just for now," he answered. "The others will be along for a meal later. May I just have a coffee and a 'boccadillo con jamon y queso' for now?" He summoned up the courage to ask. "Would you care to join me?"

The place was quite empty. The other clients were mostly Hispanic, engrossed over their coffee and tequila, not taking much interest in anything else that was going on. Juanita glanced around nervously. Paco was about to speak again when she answered. "Yes, I'd like that. Just let me get you your food and drink and I'll take a short break."

She came back out of the kitchen a few minutes later. On the tray were two cups of coffee and the 'cheese and ham roll'. She set them on the table and sat down opposite Paco. She still seemed somewhat apprehensive.

Paco thanked her and spoke softly. "Are you worried about your father?" he asked.

Juanita nodded. "He doesn't like me conversing with the young men around here. I don't want to speak to most of them, but you seem different and much more likeable. Tell me about yourself."

"I am what you call the Ramrod, at a horse ranch we have, about a day and a half's ride north of here. You have seen me bring horses in for sale every so often. It's my job to help train my men to catch and breed wild horses and break them for people to ride. The tall, blond, young man, who was with me before, is married to my sister, runs the ranch, and the ginger-haired man and the older lady are his father and mother. They are all English."

Juanita looked at him wide-eyed in amazement. "But you are both so young to have all that responsibility."

Paco bristled a little with pride. "It's a long story as to how we got here and I'll be able to tell you much more as we, hopefully, as we get to know one another better."

"Is that something you'd like to happen?" she asked.

"You know it is," Paco replied, gently. He took a sip of his coffee and, in putting down the cup, touched Juanita's hand across the table. She glanced around, startled, towards the kitchen door, but there was no movement. However, she carefully moved her hand away.

"I'd like that," she said, "but we shall have to be cautious."

"I understand," Paco answered. "Do you think, if I asked you and your parents to visit the ranch in spring, they would be better disposed towards me?" He was studying her face while biting into his food and awaiting her answer.

Juanita laughed. "I see you have spent some time with the Englishman. That was a very quaint way of putting it. I'll have a quiet word with my mother first and maybe she'll persuade my father. He's going to be the difficult one. I'd better get back to the kitchen now." She rose and left the table, leaving Paco to finish eating and drinking.

The stage was due to depart for Santa Fe the following day. George and Ann were booked on it. They returned to the office and Luis invited them to stay with him overnight. George was pleased that he'd have the opportunity to find out how the political landscape lay when he got to the city and to visit the bank to check all legalities were still in place.

All five of them headed for the cantina so that they could eat before John and Paco started back, and farewells could be said. Paco was waiting at the table. By his face, John knew immediately that things had gone well.

Paco had finished his snack and his coffee. The team sat down together. Juanita came over to take their orders. John looked at her face and smiled. She blushed a little and John couldn't resist a smile while turning to look at Paco. He didn't get the glower he expected in return and that made him smile even more. Paco was keeping his cool. Hank also noticed the glances between them but said nothing and gave no hint to his understanding of what was going on. Luis, Ann and George remained oblivious.

Juanita took their food order into the kitchen and returned quickly with their drinks. As they sipped the cups and glasses, and settled back into their chairs, George triggered the conversation.

"Ann and I haven't got a fixed plan. We are going to suss out the lie of the land and what is going on business-wise and politically. That's why Santa Fe is our first port of call. We'll see if there is anything we can do with the authorities and take it from there. From that start, we shall have to play it by ear, depending on what we find out there and what we think is the best course of action. It's unlikely we can easily let you know what we are doing and we are loath to do much by telegraph. You never know who might intercept valuable information."

The men looked at one another and nodded in agreement. Ann remained silent.

Hank added his suggestion. "Before you leave, I'll give you some higher army authority contacts."

They finished their meals before John spoke. "I hope you will excuse Paco and me. We need to get some more things together to take back home for the

155

winter and we also have the best part of two days ride ahead of us. If we leave soon, we might just make it for nightfall tomorrow." Paco nodded his agreement.

They let Paco pay the bill so he could quietly say goodbye to Juanita. There was a lingering moment where they touched hands, both wanting to kiss one another and hold each other tightly.

"Hurry on the spring," she whispered. "I do hope I get the chance to see your ranch and that our families can meet."

"I may be down during the winter," Paco replied in a soft tone. "It depends on our needs and the weather. I'll be thinking of you every day."

Juanita hid the little tear that had appeared. "I'll be carrying you in my heart too, my handsome man."

The men shook hands and John hugged his mother. They then left the cantina. While Paco went to the livery to fetch the horses, John headed to the merchandise store to buy some more provisions. Paco returned with six horses; two for them to ride and four to carry the purchases.

John had not forgotten to buy extras such as candy for the children and tobacco for the smokers. The main needs were tools, such as hammers, saws and nails, flour to supplement the agave bean bread and extra ammunition. Despite the growth of the city, the weaponry was still poor and John was reluctant to waste money on it.

They loaded the horses and hit the trail in the early afternoon. Both of them remained cautious. Two men and six horses, four fully laden, would be a prime target for any outlaws or marauding bands of 'Apache'. However, Hank was probably right, in that everyone was preoccupied with what was going on in the south of the territory. As a consequence, the journey back to the new home was uneventful. They took all the usual precautions, covering their tracks, taking turns to guard at night and, just generally, keeping their eyes and ears open, maintaining their wits.

Chapter Sixteen

It never ceased to amaze John. He and Paco had reached the old village on the second afternoon. If it hadn't been for the remains of the tilled fields, you would not have known that there had been a village there three days previously. The Mescalero were very proud of their devotion to their surroundings, of being at one with the earth, the air and the water. Nothing had been left behind. Nothing was wasted. It was probably more natural to Paco, a built-in part of his psyche. Inside, John was swelling with pride with his admiration for the band.

"I don't know how they do it," he said.

Paco frowned. "Do what," he asked?

"Leave the place so clean," John replied. "In a few days' time, you'd need to be a tracker to know a community, a whole village, was here."

"It's what we always do," said Paco, in a very nonchalant way. "What we take from the land, we give back to the land. It's also a matter of religion, our spirit and safety. Anyway, getting down to mundane, practical matters, we'd best camp here tonight, with the good grazing for the horses and the ease of getting water, and we'll be back to the canyon by early afternoon tomorrow."

John agreed. He was both amused and bemused about how Paco was changing, managing him rather than letting him make the decisions. They were becoming more of a management team which, despite their youth, was becoming more mature by the day. The extra time allowed the horses to eat more plentifully and to get their fill of water. Following the chores, the men were able to rest their aching and weary limbs and settle for the night, taking turns to share guard duty.

Despite this, they were both up early and ready to crack on at dawn. Both were eager to get to their new home for lots of different reasons. John was anxious to see that Linda and Marianna were settled and well. Paco was concerned that the move had gone without any hitches and that the wranglers had prepared everything for the tribe in advance. Their excitement was tempered with care for the heavily laden horses. This prevented them from journeying too rapidly. Neither of them let their frustration show.

As it turned out, this slowness of pace was to prove to be an advantage. The scouts in the hills were able to relay their homecoming well in advance of their arrival. When they did reach the top of the canyon, there was quite a greeting party. There had been no slacking in security while they had been away. The children were honoured to be trusted with sentry duties in the hills above the Shis-Inday tributary, relaying messages back upstream through their version of semaphore.

The band had been busy. The homes were more permanent wooden dwellings. There was obvious new building activity that could be seen from the trail. There was a real buzz that emanated from the band. This was their land. Even more, this was their home. The new buildings would ensure no one was cramped by the time winter set in properly.

There was no ceremonial dignity when the riders dismounted. Linda did not perform her usual teasing. She quietly gave Marianna to her mother and walked over to John, putting her arms around his neck and kissing him passionately. She hadn't said a word; no mention of his stinking from the trail or his unshaven visage. John, for his part, smelt her herbal fragrance, his whole body tingling to her touch. He responded to her kiss and held her tightly.

One of the wranglers took the reins of the horses from Paco and led them away to be unloaded, fed and watered. Paco joined his mother and father, embracing Maria-Elena and his niece in one. John took Linda's hand and walked over to take his daughter back from Uncle Paco. The little girl's delight, at seeing them both, melted both their hearts.

John broke the silence. "It's so good to be back. You've all done so much."

"It's everyone," said Mangas. "They worked so hard. They have even built wood stores for winter fuel from the trees felled for the buildings. Anyway, you guys get cleaned up. We can all eat around dusk and get updated then."

"I'd like to speak to our five Chiricahua friends first and update them with what is happening. It's not good news for them but Paco and I are obliged to bring them up to speed." John was showing his concern.

"They are working as a team with the horses in the canyon. You can see them at sundown, when they return."

It wasn't till after the meal that John and Paco had the opportunity to talk to the Chiricahua braves. The five youths listened in silence with their heads slightly bowed.

"Nobody is going to think anything less of you if you decided to leave and tried to find your friends and families. We cannot help you in that search. New Mexico is a vast territory and your journey would be long, dangerous and arduous, carrying no guarantee that you'll succeed in finding anyone. However, equally, you are more than welcome to stay with our Ndee band, the Shish-Inday. Any of your friends and family can join us at any time, whether you leave or stay." John could not have made it fairer or clearer. "We don't expect you to make up your minds instantly. We think it might be better for you to stay and see what is happening in the spring. We may know better, what is happening then."

The young men departed quietly without giving any indication, one way or another. John and Paco did not press them for an answer.

However, in the morning, before he rode out to join the wranglers, Paco was able to tell John that the nomads had decided to stay. They reasoned, despite their skills, that they, and the people they were searching, might wander aimlessly all over a massive area, without ever chancing upon one another. At the same time, with soldiers chasing various bands, they may inadvertently bring their own people into more danger. It was a hard pill for them to swallow. However, logic and common sense prevailed. Being with the Shish-Inday had seemingly calmed their more hot-headed instincts.

It was a strange time as colder and darker days descended. There was an eerie calm as they awaited the next development. Everyone was working hard to finish all the accommodation and gather fuel and food for the winter. Paco did make one more trip to town to trade horses and bring back fresh supplies. It had given him the brief opportunity to meet up with Juanita and the chance to update himself with the news.

On his return, he acquainted John and his father.

"I saw Hank and Luis," he said. "Apparently, the army is being run ragged across the whole of southern New Mexico, chasing various 'Apache' bands. It seems, that they can't spare Luther's soldiers to chase after our five Chiricahua, so we look to be clear until the spring."

Mangas and John murmured their appreciation.

"There's no further news from your father or mother. They did say they'd be reluctant to use the telegraph or letters as this might be too indiscreet."

"Thanks," John replied. "I expect you are right."

"My young men," said Mangas, in a slightly pompous and condescending way. "You have worked very hard this year and we have all been through a lot of turmoil. I think you two should go off for a few days and do some hunting. That will give you a break and you can bring us some fresh meat."

John and Paco looked at one another, neither being sure how to respond. On the one hand, it was an appealing opportunity to get away from the drudgery of work. On the other hand, both had been hoping to wind down; John to spend more time with Linda and Marianna, Paco just to rest.

John broke the silence. "Can we just sleep on it and let you know in the morning? We appreciate you thinking of us. I, for one, must talk it over with Linda."

Paco nodded his agreement and said nothing.

To say Linda was none too pleased when John told her of Mangas' suggestion is an understatement of massive proportions. She flew off the handle.

"Who does he think he is? My father! I bet he didn't discuss this with Mamma in advance. But, what annoys me more is the look on your face. You'd really like to go and, to be honest, I am jealous because I'd like to go with you and I have to stay home with Marianna."

"I think he was contemplating several options. He wants some more food for the whole band. He thought we needed a break from the routine and the problems the band is facing. Paco and I have the best weapons, we are the best shots, especially to get fast-moving deer and, between us, we have the best horses to bring back the supplies."

"By that, I suppose you actually mean, *my horse*," Linda emphasised the ownership, "or don't I have a say in the matter?"

John knew he was beaten and reached over to kiss and cuddle her. She moved smartly away. "Not so fast, Mister! You are not getting around me that easily."

However, the more they talked, the more sensible it seemed.

Next morning, it appeared that Paco had come to the same conclusion. They were able to tell Mangas that they would go.

"Will you organise something for our return?," John asked Mangas. "Can you get the team to dig us an ice house near the stream? That way, we can keep our meat better and longer when we return. As the weather worsens, this will be of great benefit to the village." He outlined a drawing of a typical version, similar to those found on Victorian estates in England. Mangas was intrigued, but agreed to the request.

It took some planning to go on a hunting trip. The first consideration was the horses. The more they took, the more they could potentially bring back. However, that meant they had to carry more provisions for the horses, themselves, largely because of the wintry conditions and the lack of natural food on the trail. In the end, they took the three Percherons and four ponies. The larger horses would carry the loads and the men would ride the ponies, swapping them around periodically. He might prove a nuisance, but it was obvious that Goshe wanted to come as well.

It was already getting quite cold when they set out. There was a bite in the wind from the north. The terrain was changing as they climbed higher into hills and towards the mountains beyond. The trees were becoming more sparse, the grassless lush and there was ever-increasing scrub with the thinner, less fertile soil. The hues and colours were mottled and altering in vivid and dull tones. The scenery was awesome; raw, beautiful and spectacular. Both men appreciated the vista in silence, taking in the views and breathing in the cold, clear air.

It was approaching dusk as they neared the edge of the tree line and the start of the more barren, snow-lined, rocky, climb towards the mountain range. They were looking for a suitable place to camp, to settle for the night with suitable water and shelter.

There was a sudden reaction, stiffness and a bristling of nostrils from the horses. Goshe stopped and crouched emitting a low growl. Both men had their rifles out of the scabbards, laying horizontally across their thighs, in readiness. Then suddenly, out of the scrub, she appeared. It was a beautiful, female cougar, starting to develop her lighter, more camouflaged, winter colouring. She turned and faced them, showing her perfect fangs and snarling.

John had raised his rifle but he didn't fire. Paco whistled, almost silently, under his breath. "I named you right. You do have an affinity with the cat, 'White Cougar'."

The mountain lion turned and moved away from them to be followed by a cub of similar, light colouring. It turned to look at the men, horses and dog, letting out a snarl and baring it's teeth in the same way as its mother. John had lowered his weapon and was watching intently, intrigued.

The spectacle was not over. A second cub appeared, followed by a third. Each one, in turn, reacted to the party in the same way as the first sibling, then turned to follow the mother, soon to be hidden into the rough vegetation. They all looked extremely healthy, going into the winter, a testimony to the success of the cougar as a huntress.

There was no doubting the admiration both men felt. Cougars could be a bane to livestock but, like the men, they hunted for food. It wasn't killing just for the sake of it. The same could not be said of men, although the Ndee prided themselves on not wasting anything.

"They seemed to be well-fed," said Paco. "Nevertheless, I think we should find a better place to camp for the night and to stand guard over the horses." John nodded in agreement.

The darkness was setting in rapidly when they came across a grassy knoll on the side of a stream. There was a cluster of trees offering shelter from the northerly wind, but a wider expanse of a clearing beyond that. It would be hard for a predatory animal to sneak up and surprise the men, the horses or Goshe. For the time of year, the grazing was a welcome substitute for the dry grains and the horses settled down to take advantage. The men gathered kindling and broken branches to build a fire. They set up the tipi and then prepared themselves and Goshe some food, putting out extra grain for all the horses as well. For once, the dog was proving not to be a nuisance, seemingly taking his guard duties and care for the horses as his brief. Overnight, John and Paco took it in turns to sleep and keep watch, making sure the fire was maintained.

They were both up with the light. It was too cold to sleep too much and a warm breakfast and coffee were very welcome.

"I think we should make our way south, doing our hunting on the way back." Paco was being practical. John concurred, just nodding in agreement. While both men had enjoyed their little adventure and exploring further afield, both now wanted to get home.

On the second day back, they came across a small herd of white-tailed deer, in a forest clearing. They carefully approached, downwind, making sure to only take out six of the larger animals, while the rest of the herd scattered. They altered the loadings on the horse so that every one of the Percherons carried two carcasses and they were relieved of as many of the other supplies as the spare ponies could carry.

By the time they had trudged back to the canyon, the men and the animals were cold and exhausted. The team had done them proud and built and flooded the ice house. The ice had already formed and wooden slats fixed just above it.

Mangas took charge of the village team to cut up the carcasses. The offal was to be used immediately for everyone to eat fresh. The hides were removed and stretched out for drying. Some of the meat was removed and cut into strips for jerky. The bones were removed for food for the dogs, other uses as tools and buttons or loop fasteners for clothing. Hooves were made into gels and glues. Brains were used to make a version of brawn. The bulk of the meat was cut into chunks and stored in fiber bags, lowered into the cold of the ice house. Nothing was wasted. Many members of the whole community, men, women and children, were involved in the operation.

The wranglers took care of the seven horses, while John and Paco went to clean up and get some rest. John was lucky in that Marianna was asleep. Linda greeted him with a loving kiss and soon heated water for him to have a bath in the tub. She gave his aching body a loving scrub with her herbal scented soap, easing his pains and relaxing him all over. He got out of the bath and Linda started to dry him off, sensuously rubbing her body against him, teasing him and arousing him.

They clambered into bed and made love longingly and passionately. There was no talking. Everything was natural, playing, changing positions, multiple or not quite climaxing and then a final last orgasm which they shared.

At that, they fell asleep, entwined in one another's arms. Because of their own workloads and the recognition of how exhausted John and Paco looked, they were left alone. Linda and John only awoke to Marianna's cries, when she woke, needing a feed. John's heart melted when the little girl gave him a smile, a recognition that 'Daddy' was home. The smile was still there when she turned to 'Mummy'.

While Linda continued to feed the baby, John stoked up the fire and put a pot of stew on for their own meal. By the time they had finished feeding, cleaning and playing with Marianna, until she had gone back to sleep, their own food was ready. It was now dark, they were still tired, so it wasn't long until Linda and John went back to bed, this time for a deeper sleep.

Chapter Seventeen

The next few months, into the spring of 1867, were busy for everyone in the village. All the building work was completed and the fields prepared for the planting of crops. The wranglers made sure the horses were fed and watered, branding was up to date and new foals were given the necessary care. The lookout system, down the Shis-Inday tributary, was maintained, whether or not the weather was clement. It was testimony to the maturity of the children that they played a big part in the security of the Ndee.

However, there were no visitors, friendly or otherwise. On the other hand, there was no news. So, while this was a peaceful time, there was apprehension as to what would happen next. The Chiricahua braves were also getting more anxious as they had no idea what was happening to their families.

The Ndee still needed to trade. Paco was eager to visit Silver City and catch up with Juanita. John wanted to find out if there were any messages from his father and whether Hank or Luis could update him with what the cavalry were doing.

It was decided to hold a council meeting, as usual, presided over by Mangas. John suggested that he, Paco and two of the Chiricahua braves should take a string of horses to trade in the city. All of them should avert attention by being dressed in American or Hispanic clothing. Paco had stressed the need to the wranglers, they were not to get into any trouble, they were to listen, learn and watch. Any information, however little or informal, could be crucial. Any recklessness could jeopardise them, their families and the Ndee. Discipline was the key.

The weather had improved sufficiently by March, to make the trip. They took their time. It was a good two days ride from their new home. They wanted to arrive in the morning at Silver City to maximise trading time. It also allowed the horses to graze more on the journey. This should enable them to be seen at their prime and, hopefully, command better prices. To enhance that, John and Paco had kept records of the horses bred in captivity, so the birth dates of most yearlings were known.

The usual precautions were taken en route; two sleeping, two guarding. It led to some light relief amongst the four men, remembering the circumstances in which they first met. Levity is a good basis for lasting friendship and trust. There were no incidents and no meetings with anyone on the trail.

Silver City had grown rapidly since the Autumn. John and Paco were both surprised at the speed of the development and the pace of construction. They corralled the horses with the ostler, leaving the details with him, to come back later for a negotiation.

John gave the braves some money so that they could go and get something to eat and drink, maybe to learn more about current events. In the meantime, he and Paco went to see Luis.

"Muchachos, amigos." Luis was obviously delighted to see them. "You are in luck. Hank has just returned from one of his surveys and he'll be in later this morning. In the meantime, I suspect you'll want to clean yourselves up. You know where everything is. While you do that, I'll make some fresh coffee."

John and Paco refreshed themselves quickly and rejoined Luis for the coffee.

"What news have you got for us?," John asked.

Luis responded. "First of all, despite the growth of the city, little has altered. The cavalry are still chasing bands of Apache, excuse the expression, all over south, south-west and west New Mexico." (At that time, before they became separate states, this was the huge area that included Arizona.) "Hank has heard of no moves to challenge you, but he is doing less work for the army and more local surveys as new properties are built. He'll tell you himself when he arrives. Similarly, we have heard nothing from your father, but he did say he'd not trust the telegraph for sending important information."

"We brought two of our wranglers with us and we asked them to keep their eyes and ears open for further news." Paco did not volunteer the information that they were Chiricahua, who would, no doubt, learn the same message.

They chatted as friends for a while until Hank arrived. Luis, in particular, wanted to know about Marianna and Linda. When Hank came, he was equally delighted to see them and embraced both John and Paco with great big bear hugs. They updated him with their conversation of earlier.

Hank said, "I am not so close to the army as I was. My instincts are not to trust the officers who are at Fort Bayard. Other than that, I cannot say. You will need to be prepared for anything."

"We re-established the village at the top of the canyon," said John. "Paco and his team have done a great job of making a surprise defence and trap for any intruders. They have built a more solid range of dwellings close to the stream that feeds the Shis-Inday river. The only disadvantage is that the immediate area is not so fertile for growing crops. We also have an early warning system if people approach. Lots of the children are involved and this has enhanced their esteem and importance. The signalling system gives us ample time to prepare."

Paco intervened. "Shall we go and get something to eat? After two days of grub on the trail, I could do with a decent meal."

The others smiled. Was Paco blushing? They all knew his ulterior motive but they all agreed. However, Luis couldn't resist a wicked tease.

"Do you want to try one of the new places in town, or shall we go to the cantina?"

"The cantina's fine," said John. "The food's terrific and reliable." Then he added cheekily, "The waitress service is excellent." He put his arm around Paco, while he, Hank and Luis, roared with laughter. Even Paco had to laugh at his own expense.

Juanita's face lit up as she saw them arrive. She ran over to Paco and gave him a big kiss. "Don't worry about Papa," she said, "I have told both him and Mama, and of your invitation to come and visit in the spring. They are happy about that."

Paco was relieved and excited. "That's great," he said, his face breaking into a big, beaming smile. "We'll decide that later when we've all got time to talk together."

The four men sat down and ordered their food. John suddenly realised how hungry he had become. When they got it, all four of them attacked it with relish. They settled back to drink their coffee.

"I hope you respect our confidences in what we have told you." John was looking at Hank and Luis. Both of them wore pained expressions.

"John, if I didn't trust you and Paco, I wouldn't have told you about my feelings for the army. There is no way Luis and I would betray you. We really have no news to relate to you." Hank was quite hurt by the suggestion and his face and tone of voice showed it.

"Sorry," said John. "I was just thinking of careless whispers and loose talk. We thought we might hear some around the town today. I didn't mean to impugn your honour."

"You are our friends. There is no way we would let you down." Luis had just made John feel smaller.

Paco broke the awkwardness. "Look, the wranglers may have picked up some information. We still need to pick up some supplies and trade the horses. I need to see if I can make arrangements for Juanita and her parents to come and see us. In view of what we are talking about, that may need to be more flexible than firm, but I'll explain that discreetly. If I do that now, John can you find our riders, start the negotiations for the horses and organise the supplies? I'll join you at the General Store or the Livery Stable, as soon as I am able. Depending on the time, we can decide if we leave tonight or go tomorrow morning."

John was taken aback by his brother-in-law's forthrightness and his taking charge. His work as foreman and ramrod had matured him into a decisive young man. There was no arguing.

They paid up and went about their various tasks. Hank and Luis went back to the office. It was into the afternoon so the cantina was quiet. Juanita and her parents were able to sit at the table with Paco. He took some time to explain what was happening and why the invitation to visit had provisos. While Juanita and her parents were disappointed, they appreciated Paco's honesty and his trust in them.

Meanwhile, John had found the Chiricahua braves, in the corral by the livery stables, looking after the horses they had brought in. He thanked them for their hard work and checked if they had any different news. They had got some food and something to drink, overhearing snippets of conversations. Some of the soldiers had been talking about chasing various groups of Apache all over the territory. There were several bands still at large. The braves were both alarmed and reassured at the same time. The news had reinforced the futility of leaving the Ndee to try to locate their kin, the same decision they had made in the autumn. While they continued their work, John went to see about selling the herd.

Because the horses were in fine condition and were well-shod and groomed, John got good prices. The records for those that had been bred were seen as a bonus and set new standards for further transactions in the future. He went to the General Store to purchase the needs for the village. The plan had been to return with twelve ponies, four for the riders and eight to carry supplies.

Paco caught up with him there.

"How did it go?" asked John, with a wicked gleam in his eye.

"Very well," Paco replied. "Everyone understood our difficulties and the need to keep quiet. They'll all be disappointed, not just Juanita, if they can't visit us soon, but they accept the reasons and they are pleased we are being very honest with them. In turn, knowing how much we had to do, Juanita's father suggested we stayed with them tonight, and our two companions can make up beds in their back store. The family has two spare rooms. They also reasoned that we'd do better starting back, tomorrow, after a full breakfast."

"That was really good of them," said John. "It also means we'll be fresher, won't need to camp out so near to Silver City, on the first night, we can load the horses in the morning and give them the extra rest, tonight, as well. While I finish up here, getting our list of supplies ready for first thing tomorrow, you tell your wranglers, I'll pop back to tell Luis and Hank, and we'll meet back at the cantina. By that time, you can have given our thanks and gratitude to Juanita's family."

The braves were a little uneasy about sleeping in the store, but the winter up the Shis-Inday, had shown them the benefits of sheltered accommodation. They'd still have the next two nights in the open on the journey back.

The evening went very well. It was such an unusual grouping of people, but a bond was developing and the chemistry was there. Juanita's parents set the tone with their welcome. Having trusted friends in Luis and Hank proved to be a massive bonus. The two braves were accepted into the party and quickly lost all inhibitions. Juanita and Paco had the opportunity to get to know one another better. John and Paco related how they had met, to the horror and amazement of the company. Juanita's family was reassured that Paco was the right man for their daughter.

The next morning, everyone was up early, to a very substantial, Mexican-style, breakfast. There was a mixture of pleasure and sorrow, hope and anxiety. It was wonderful that Paco had been accepted by Juanita's family. Their immediate parting, again, was a great sadness. The friendships that had been struck, by people of different cultures and backgrounds, gave much hope for the future. The impending actions of the army were a source of trepidation.

The goodbyes were brief. John, Paco and the wranglers had a lot to do; feeding and watering the horses, loading them, settling the bills and contracts and getting on their way. As the horses were fully laden, they couldn't move rapidly. The team recognised the desirability of maximising the distance they could make away from the city by dusk. In particular, they felt they'd be safer, once they were past the confluence of the Shis Inday and Gila rivers.

They took all the necessary precautions. There were no incidents on their way home and they saw no other travellers on their journey. They arrived back at the village, in the morning, two days later. The sentries had given plenty of notice of their arrival. They were greeted back with enthusiasm, especially by the children, all of whom knew that John would not have neglected to bring them some special treats.

Linda and Marianna were just pleased to have John home. They got together with Mangas, Maria and Paco, that evening, to update everyone what had happened and the little information they had. Paco's parents were delighted with the news of his relationship with Juanita and his acceptance by her parents.

Chapter Eighteen

There was an air of tension as the spring progressed. Everyone was busy, planting the crops, looking after the horses, continued building and maintenance, and increased vigilance. Nothing appeared to be happening. This was not a case of 'no news equals good news'. More, it was a case of heightened anxiety. There was no let-up in security.

And then, all the preparations and precautions paid off. It was early May. The messages were being relayed back thick and fast. They were confusing, actually more puzzling, to start. There were two groups of men coming up the Shis-Inday. The leading twenty or so were followed by a further thirty, trailing a little way behind them. It was not a chase.

Paco was incredulous. "What in heaven's name are they doing?," he asked his father and John. Neither one gave him an answer.

The continuing observations gave them the information. The leading group was white; the following group were all buffalo soldiers.

John grinned. "They are playing into our hands."

"In what way?" Paco was still uncertain. John glanced at Mangas. He was as impassive as ever, but John knew he understood.

"Shall I explain, or do you want to brief Paco?" John saw Mangas consent to him continuing. "Paco, it's their arrogance that's going to be their undoing. Whoever is in the front group has no respect for the soldiers and is making them eat dirt. We will use that to our advantage, separating them at the narrow front of the canyon. So, let's get everyone organised."

They got the wranglers together and John gave the briefing, emphasizing exactly what needed to happen. "There is to be no shooting and you are to stay undercover. I don't want anything happening to any of you. We split into four teams, either side of the neck of the canyon. The front two will drop the trellis fence once the leading riders have entered, trapping them from going back. To stop them from getting up the canyon, the rear teams will drop the second fence.

They'll be in a cage, like when you trap the wild horses. The soldiers won't be able to help. I emphasise, once again. Don't be seen, stay undercover and do not use any weapons! I guess we have two hours, so let's be ready."

The Ndee maintained their discipline and their silence. They watched from the top of the canyon as the riders approached. They were still in the two groups as the scouts had signalled. The leading ones all appeared to be white men with a gap back to the cavalry, the buffalo soldiers.

The leading group had entered the narrow neck of the canyon when the Ndee dropped the fence. All hell broke loose as the men fired at their non-existent opponents. Some tried to ride up the valley, to escape, only to be confronted by the second fence at the end of the canyon neck. All the firing was coming from them, without any reply. The soldiers had pulled back into cover, further down the canyon and remained non-combatants.

As quickly as the firing had begun, it subsided, when the trapped men realised there was no incoming fire. There ensued an eerie silence. It was broken by John's voice shouting from the top of the hill.

"Who are you and what do you want?"

"I am Herbert Corrigan and these are my men. I own this land and I have the papers to prove it. We have come to escort you back to Silver City as you are trespassing on my property. The soldiers are under orders to support us."

John was not to be moved. "Okay, Mr Corrigan. We want no trouble so listen carefully. Tell all your men to place all their weapons, guns, knives and ammunition belts, in a pile, on the valley floor, so that we can see them. That includes you. You alone, will walk up to the second fence, where we can meet and you can show me your deeds to this land. Remember, you are trapped and we can shoot all of you down if you don't comply. If you don't believe me, watch the rock just above your head!" John fired, splitting the chosen rock into two.

Corrigan protested. "We can't do that. You won't get away with it."

"All you have to do is prove this is genuine and we'll obey," John shouted down the valley. He looked at the worried Paco beside him, whispering, "Don't worry, he's bluffing." Louder, he shouted, "Luther, is that you leading the cavalry? Can you vouch for my honesty? Tell Corrigan, will you?"

Luther shouted back. "Mr Corrigan, he's genuine. Besides which, we can't defend you. Do as he says, so we can get this resolved and go back home."

Corrigan was annoyed and frustrated, but he kept his temper in check.

"Men, do as he says and then take your horses back to the fence."

Corrigan's men did as they were told and the arsenal piled up on the valley floor. The observers, on the hilltop, remained unobserved, but watched every move very carefully.

"Get your horses," John shouted. "Now take them back down the valley. We'll lift the fence to let you through." The men were too shocked by the events to do otherwise. "Raise the fence and let them through." The wranglers, still hidden, pulled the fence up. Once Corrigan's men were through, John ordered them to drop it back. "Right, Mr Corrigan, disarm yourself and put your weapons on the pile. Then walk with your horse up the valley and we'll meet you there. Then you can show us your proof."

Momentous events sometimes occur as a result of the strangest decisions. John and Paco were going to meet Corrigan. Linda insisted she came too. She had already left Marianna with Maria Elena. Despite her husband's and her brother's protests, she remained unmoved. She wouldn't listen to her father nor mother. In the end, they all resolved to let her have her way.

They rode along the canyon rim and came down to the floor near the top fence. The rest of the Ndee remained hidden. The three of them dismounted and walked down the valley towards the barrier. Corrigan was already there, waiting.

"Raise the fence," John called. The barrier was lifted.

John motioned Paco and Linda to wait. He handed his rifle over to Linda and the reins of his horse to Paco. He moved forward to meet Corrigan.

"So, what is this proof of ownership?"

Corrigan reached in his pocket and produced what looked like a document. He had obviously not realised with whom or with what he was dealing. He handed it to John.

It was written in a poor way, claiming ownership of the whole Gila valley and its tributaries. There was no seal for the New Mexico Territory and no land agency signatures.

John reached into his inner pocket and produced his own copy. He showed it to Corrigan. The colour drained from Corrigan's face.

"The Indians cannot own this land. It's illegal."

"They don't," said John. "It's company land, fully registered with the territory and a copy lodged at the Bank of Santa Fe." He took the deeds back. "Now take yourself and your men off our company land. Get back to where you came from. Don't trouble us again."

He turned to walk back to Linda and Paco.

What was going through Corrigan's brain, no one could ever judge. Maybe he thought John was the only white person around. Maybe he thought he could escape up the valley and through the mountains. Or was it just a moment of madness? A shot rang out. Linda was trembling and screaming at the same time. Corrigan was dead, shot through the heart, a derringer clasped in his lifeless hand. "He was going to kill you." Linda ran up to John, shaking all over. She was sobbing as she held him, shivering and clasping him close.

"I've never killed anyone before." She was shaking uncontrollably. John held her firmly, his mind racing. He took the rifle back from his wife.

Even Paco looked shocked. "What are we going to do now, John?"

John was quiet for a moment, continuing to support Linda. "They will have heard the shot down the valley. They'll be wondering what's happened. We three are the only ones who know, apart from any of the Ndee watching from the top of the fence. Paco, get back down the rim of the canyon. Shout to Sergeant Jackson to come up the valley with two of his men, but no one else. They can keep their arms with them. But make sure the fence is down once they are through and no one else gains access. Linda and I will stay here until Luther arrives. You can then explain to Mangas and Maria Elena."

Paco didn't query or hesitate. He was on his horse in an instant, racing to the said roof of the canyon.

John was now shivering himself. He got Linda to sit down with him and they clung to one another.

"Thank you for saving my life, once again."

Linda kissed him, passionately, shaking with relief.

"What are we going to do now?" She was still very frightened.

"We show Luther and his men the evidence and tell them the truth. They can take Corrigan's body, the derringer and his horse back with them. We'll keep the false deeds."

"And then, what's going to happen? Won't they send the soldiers back in force to attack us?" Linda was struggling to keep control.

"I'm thinking," John said, now calmer. "You are going to have to trust me on this, to save you, me and the Ndee. We'll find a way out of this. In the meantime, settle down until Luther and his men get here."

Paco had got back to the top of the canyon and quickly briefed his father. There was no time for a detailed explanation. There was uproar amongst Corrigan's men, but they were powerless without their arms.

Paco shouted down to the troops. "Sergeant Jackson! We need you and two of your men up the valley. No one else. I repeat, no one else. We shall shoot anyone who disobeys. You are to give the order to the rest of your troop to hold back and to keep Corrigan's men in check. Do you agree?"

Luther bellowed back. "What is this all about? What was the gunshot? Where is John?"

"Please do as we ask." Paco was firmly insistent. "John will meet you and your men at the head of the valley. Everything will be explained then. Please keep your weapons buttoned-down as you come through."

Luther issued his command. "Corporal Riley, take command of the troop. Privates Freeman and Woodstock, mount up, keep your sidearms buttoned down in the holster and your rifles in the scabbard and come with me. The rest of you," he said, distinctly looking at Corrigan's disarmed followers, "stay put and calm it down until we return."

The fence was raised to allow the three soldiers through and then was lowered again immediately behind them. Paco re-mounted his pony and rode back along the rim to rejoin John and his sister.

He arrived back just as the troopers were being allowed through the second fence.

John walked forward to meet them. They couldn't fail to see Corrigan's body, ironically, with his horse grazing quietly, nearby.

"What in heaven's name happened here? For God's sake, John, what have you done?" Luther was more perplexed than angry. He and his men dismounted to talk to John. None of them, as battle-hardened cavalrymen, was fazed by the sight of a dead body.

"We needed you to see it exactly as it was, so you can report back, truthfully, in every detail." John's voice was sad but firm. "As you know, Luther, Sergeant Jackson, we disarmed everyone in the trap, making them ditch their weapons. Corrigan's men, in disrespecting you, making you take up the rear and eating their dirt, gave us the advantage. When we separated you from his men, we ensured your safety. We kept our heads down, as ordered, and did not return their panic fire. You saw all that and how we asked them all, including Corrigan, to lay down their weapons. Once they had done that, we released them and asked Corrigan to prove his ownership of this land. We met him up here and he showed us this."

174

John handed Luther the deed and continued. "I don't want to embarrass you guys, but you will see that it is shoddily, drawn up, it is badly misspelt in places and it has not got the seal of the New Mexico Territory. This is our copy of the company's ownership, and it is registered with a copy in the Bank of Santa Fe, for safekeeping." He showed them the real document and pointed to the seal. He took both sets of paper back.

"So what happened next?"

"I had walked forward to meet him, unarmed, as I am now. I had given Linda my rifle. I don't know what madness overtook him. Maybe he thought, with me out of the way, and only the Mescalero here, he could get away with it. Linda saw him pull out the hidden gun, screamed and fired before he did."

Luther looked at the still distraught Linda. Instinctively, he knew he had just heard the truth. "We are under orders to remove you all from this land and take you to one of the reservations in the south. As you know, Indians, Mescalero, are not allowed to own land. Corrigan and his men would then have taken possession. You also know that it's the officer corps that want you out. My men and I are stuck in the middle. We were carpeted when we didn't bring in the ones who escaped last year. We had a lousy winter chasing Apache bands all over the south of the territory. I know what you are telling me is true, but if I disobey orders, what is going to happen?"

"There is only one way of resolving this," said John. "We cannot destroy this ranch, our company and the livelihood of the people who are part of this. Neither can we return the arms to Corrigan's men nor reduce our security. Paco, Linda and I will bring the truth and the evidence to the authorities in Silver City and at Fort Bayard. You'll have to take Corrigan's body and his horse back with you. You will also have to make sure that his men go with you. Just remind them that, with him dead, they are not getting paid, and any attempt, to try and oust us, is risking their lives for nothing but revenge. For us, it is our home, our whole way of life and our livelihood. In other words, everything. You can tell your officers we are coming in, but under our own terms and maintaining our own safety."

"I don't like it, but I don't see another alternative." Luther was philosophical. "Just make sure you get there quickly. We, I include my men, will report what we have seen and heard, but I cannot say what the outcome will be. Don't let me down, John."

"We'll do our best, Luther. I can't promise any more. Now, let's get Corrigan's body strapped to his horse, so you can take him back with you. We'll keep the derringer for evidence, but you'll have put that in your report, along with the forged deeds. You have seen both."

They loaded the body. The two fences were raised to allow the troopers back down the valley and replaced immediately they had passed through. There was nothing that Corrigan's, disgruntled men could do. Without their weapons, they were powerless. They could only voice their anger, but there was no other action they could take.

John, Linda and Paco returned to the rim, watched the intruders departing down the valley and returned to the village. Several of the wranglers went into the canyon to collect the pile of weapons. They were not all the best quality, but there were some, which demonstrated Corrigan had hired some professional gunmen. They were a useful addition to the Ndee's armoury.

Chapter Nineteen

The family was together in the Ndee Council. One of the other mothers was looking after Marianna so that all five adults could attend. Mangas chaired the meeting. He started by thanking everyone for maintaining their discipline and for being so brave. He then called on John to address the membership with what had happened.

John outlined the sequence of events. He stuck to the facts. He did not speculate, nor did he venture any opinion, as to why things had turned out as they did. Depending on where the Ndee had been positioned along the canyon, not everyone was aware of everything that had transpired. Only those at the top of the canyon had seen what had happened to Corrigan. Linda had still not recovered her composure and found it difficult to keep it when John described the shooting. Maria Elena put her arms around her daughter. There was nothing other than admiring glances from the rest of the assembly.

However, there was some consternation about future action. Why should Linda, Paco and John put themselves at risk? Mangas, as usual, kept his calm and listened to arguments. Eventually, he held up his hand and there was a respectful silence.

"We have made this our Ndee home, the Shis-Inday valley. We've built somewhere to live and we have a livelihood we can sustain. We have constructed good defences and an early warning system of danger. We have also learned from our past that we cannot resist the relentless surge of American settlers encroaching on our lands. We could defend an attack on our home for a short while. There would be much bloodshed and, eventually, from the weight of numbers, our enemies would win."

There were murmurings in the audience. Mangas continued.

"My view is that we have tried to do everything within the new laws of this country. We will need to trust in the good judgment of those who manage those rules and that true justice will prevail. I emphasise, the alternative is the certain end of the Ndee; not necessarily today or tomorrow, but certainly, in the none too distant future. So, I propose, with a heavy heart, that Linda, Paco and John, report to the authorities in Silver City and Fort Bayard and we take it from there."

Despite the misgivings, no one disputed what Mangas had decided. His authority and esteem went unchallenged.

The rest of the evening was spent in preparation. Maria Elena was going to care for Marianna. To add to the trauma and all the misgivings, this was to be the first time that Linda would be without her little girl. John and Paco had to remain strong and look after her. They would take six ponies; three to ride and the others to carry essentials.

They left early in the morning but planned to get to Silver City on the second evening, entering the town under the cover of dusk. They had no idea of what might await them. The soldiers and Corrigan's men would have arrived earlier in the day. However, they did have one advantage. Only Luther and his two troopers could clearly identify them; Corrigan's men had seen nothing.

Despite all this, they took precautions. It seemed clear that Corrigan's men had not hidden a secret cache of weapons and were not doubling back. They settled for the night, downstream from the old village but before the confluence of the Shis-Inday and Gila systems. They camped in scrub on the edge of the valley, off the main trail and hidden from view. The two men took overnight guard duties, insisting Linda got some sleep. There were no encounters on the way or overnight. Because of their planned timings, there was no rush to rise in the morning. Paco had taken a second watch and deliberately not woken the couple. Truth to be told, no one really slept well. Their minds were all racing. But they took time in the morning to care for all the horses, busying themselves in the necessary chores and preparation of food and coffee. Little was said, but they all exchanged glances with one another, everyone checking that the others were as well as could be expected. It was an eerie, unspoken communication. Their occasional touches were unlike the usual behaviour of Ndee. But, then again, Linda and Paco were half Hispanic and John was English.

They met no one on the way into Silver City and the dusk had already settled. They tethered their horses behind the land agency offices. To their delight, Luis was at home. He ushered them in rapidly, even though he was delighted to see them. Hank was there as well. He greeted Linda with a huge embrace.

"What in the of God has been going on?" Hank asked as Luis made them all coffee.

"What have you been told?" John answered his question with a question.

"The story is chaotic, mixed and confused. It is all conjecture and doesn't hold together properly. In essence, Corrigan's men say they were separated from the soldiers, ambushed and only just escaped with their lives after Corrigan was murdered. They had to surrender their weapons to escape. They say the soldiers ran off as they are all cowardly 'niggers'. Sergeant Jackson delivered Corrigan's body to the Town Marshal, but said nothing other than he'd report back to Fort Bayard." Hank paused for a moment. "What didn't make sense to me was why there was only one casualty and no one was wounded, not even a scratch."

John didn't know whether to laugh or cry at Hank's account. He related the exact train of events as they had occurred. Luis was agape, the edges of his moustache nearly sucked into his mouth.

Hank was smiling in awe. "Heck man, what a fantastic wife and sister you've got." Linda was feeling much better as Hank and Luis gave her huge smiles of admiration. "You guys should rewrite the military manuals. These guerrilla tactics are superb."

The conversation took a more serious turn. "What are you going to do now? Why are you here? Aren't you putting yourselves in real danger?" Luis was really concerned.

"We wanted your advice." John looked at both their friends. Paco and Linda nodded their agreement. Hank and Luis exchanged glances. It was clear they felt honoured to be entrusted so much.

"In which way can we help?" Hank was slightly perplexed.

John continued. "We are unclear on the law in New Mexico. As a territory, it is not a state of the USA. If we do nothing, we will bring down the forces of the authorities to crush the Ndee. If we prove our innocence at a trial, our legitimacy is reinforced and the legality of our claim will be proven. The question is, do we submit ourselves to the Town Marshal under civil jurisdiction, or would we be better surrendering to the military at Fort Bayard?"

Hank looked at Luis and turned to speak to John. "I can't speak for Luis, so he can tell you if he thinks differently to me. I have not trusted the officers at Fort Bayard for some time. They would probably like to make a scapegoat of you and clear the Shis-Inday off the land, company law notwithstanding. The cavalry were only incidental to the land grab. You made sure they came to no harm. The only casualty is a civilian, Corrigan. Martial law only applies to the south and west of here, not your land. However, I do not know how far the Town

179

Marshal's jurisdiction goes. My suggestion is that you hand yourselves into the Town Marshal tonight. The army may declare a widening of martial law, but that would be retrospective. It could be argued that your case pre-empts that. I wouldn't hold too high hopes that that would deter the officers at Fort Bayard. However, if a civil trial were set up quickly, you'd have a better chance to choose your jurors, some of whom, probably, have fallen foul of Corrigan before now. In the meantime, Luis and I, if he agrees, can get all the evidence together to support you. I shall get in touch with your company, family, agents, Bank of Santa Fe and my Washington army contacts, to see what else can be done."

Luis nodded his agreement. "I go along with Hank, totally," he said. "I shall also let Juanita and her family know what has happened."

A flood of relief appeared to come over Linda, John and Paco. Hank had made the case perfectly and decisively.

Linda stepped forward, putting her arms around Hank, hugging him and kissing him on the cheek. She did the same with Luis.

All three of Linda, John and Paco, murmured their thanks in unison. There was a relief that they had come to an agreed decision. The backing of their friends had been instrumental. It endorsed the feeling that they were not on their own and many people would support them.

Luis suggested that he'd look after the horses while Hank took Linda, Paco and John over to the Town Marshal's office. They left their arms at the house.

They arrived just as Marshal Tom Holland and two of his deputies were about to do a walking inspection of the town. He was an extremely phlegmatic lawman, showing little emotion when John introduced himself, Linda and Paco. He was unworried about despatching the deputies to carry out their duties, despite their obvious apprehension of leaving him alone with three 'murderers'. The Marshal had no such misgivings, realising, from all his experience, lawbreakers do not give themselves up, especially unarmed, nor do they come in with a well-known local citizen. All he said to the deputies was not to tell anyone what was happening.

He was that relaxed, he invited them in, asked them to sit and offered them coffee. Hank declined and said he was returning to help Luis.

"Well, this is a turn up for the books," said Tom, as he handed round the drinks. "Sergeant Jackson said to me, on the quiet, that you were going to come in, but he didn't know whether you'd come here or go straight to Fort Bayard. I got the impression he thinks very highly of you."

"We didn't know which was the right thing to do," said John. "We didn't know the extent of your jurisdiction or martial law."

"To be honest, it's difficult to judge. Martial law doesn't apply to your ranch, but my legal responsibilities extend to the city limits. However, Corrigan was a citizen here, so I am taking responsibility for now." It wasn't lost on the three visitors that Tom had called it 'their ranch'.

They were eyeing one another, ascertaining what they were like. The Town Marshall was a thick-set man, in his middle forties, about Paco's height, a little smaller than John. He was dressed in typically Western garb, the badge of office pinned to his vest. He carried a Colt 38, but it was not slung low as a gunslinger would carry it. His craggy features were not handsome but there was a twinkle in his blue eyes with laughter lines at the corners. Above all, his demeanour was reassuring to his visitors.

In turn, Tom was surprised how young they were. He sensed their fear and trepidation, admired their courage for what they had done and was astounded by their maturity.

"I think you'd better tell me what happened." He opened the drawer of his desk and got out a pencil, a penknife with which to sharpen it and some writing paper.

John related the events that had led to Corrigan's demise. He spoke slowly, giving Tom time to write down his statement. It was clear, from his writing and spelling, that the Marshal had had a decent education. He showed Tom the written documents; their deeds and Corrigan's forgery. As he finished, the deputies returned, obviously relieved that nothing untoward had occurred. In turn, they had nothing major to report from their tour of the city.

"Okay, 'fellas'," said Tom, "grab yourselves some coffee off the stove, sit down and listen up."

He repeated what he had written in response to John's story. The deputies were agog. "Is that an accurate account of what you told me?"

John nodded as did Linda and Paco.

"And is it right," Tom said, looking intensely at Linda, "that you were the one who actually shot Corrigan?"

Linda shuddered, as the memories of that fateful afternoon came flooding back. She steeled herself long enough to say "Yes, that is true." John took her hand in his, squeezing it gently.

Marshall Holland took control. "I need all three of you to sign this is an accurate account of what happened." He turned to his deputies, once Linda, Paco and John had put their signatures down, "Now, can you guys countersign this as witnesses?"

He turned to the trio. "I am going to have to detain you. I am sure you expected that. At least one of the three of us will have to be on duty. We'll try to be as accommodating as we can and you can share the cell. I'm sorry that the personal hygiene standards may not be entirely to your liking. We'll try to help to meet your requirements."

"What happens next?" John asked.

"I shall lock this statement and your documents in the safe. In the morning, I'll seek out the judge and we'll take it from there." Tom turned to his deputies. "Not a word to anyone! I don't want to deal with any drunken, misinformed mobs. Neither do you." His words were most forceful and the look on his face matched that.

Paco intervened. "Our friends, Hank and Luis know we are here. Could you also tell Juanita and her parents at the cantina?"

Despite the seriousness of the situation, Tom smiled. He realised that this request was more than asking for food and drink. Everyone else relaxed as well. "I shall sort that out first thing in the morning. I am not knocking up anyone this time of the night." Tom was firm.

Chapter Twenty

They awoke next morning as it became light One of the two deputies was on duty. Not long afterwards, there was a knock on the door. The guard unlocked it to let in a rather shaken Juanita. She had brought breakfast for all four of them, the deputy included. The moment she had put down the food, and the guard had opened the cell, she rushed in to throw her arms around Paco. After they had embraced, she was introduced to Linda.

"I am so sorry," Juanita apologised. "We heard such awful stories yesterday, and I was really frightened for you all."

"That's why we want you to keep as quiet as possible," the deputy interposed. "If the Marshal can persuade the judge to conduct a speedy trial, we might be able to keep a lid on an explosive situation in the city."

While they ate, Paco explained to Juanita what had happened. John was pleased to hear that his testimony bore out exactly what he had said and the Marshal had written. The fact that the deputy was listening, and would have found no deviation in the story, was a minor, added bonus.

After they finished eating, Juanita gave Paco a loving kiss and took the remnants back to the cantina. The deputy, reluctantly, locked them back in the cell.

Tom Holland returned, accompanied by a rotund, little man, in his fifties, wearing a fancy vest, from which, hung a watch chain.

"This is Judge Augustus Forster," the Marshal announced. "He's agreed to hold the trial as quickly as we can arrange it."

John asked a question of concern. "Will you be sure to get all the relevant witnesses? I am thinking of Sergeant Jackson and his deputies in particular."

"Young man," said the Judge, "You are in no position to demand anything." He thrust out his chest in a rather pompous manner. He was about to say, "And if you think, the testimony of three n*****s is going to help…" but thought better of it once he saw the complexions of Paco and Linda.

Tom sat the Judge down at the desk, opened the safe and showed him the signed, written statement, the true and false deeds to the ranch and Corrigan's derringer. The Judge's demeanour altered as he read the documents in front of him. There are times the truth is patently obvious. However, he said nothing, only taking in how young the accused trio were.

"What do you think?" asked the Marshal.

Augustus Forster was in his element. "You did the right thing coming to get me so quickly. There is the obvious 'prima facie' evidence for a trial. We'll set it up at the courthouse tomorrow. This must be a civil not a military matter."

John tried again. "What about getting legal representation?"

This time, the Judge did not reprimand him. "The prosecution can get whoever they can find and, frankly, good luck to them. You have a close friend with education, integrity and no little legal knowledge in Hank Warren. As an officer, he has taken part in military trials. I doubt you'll find anyone better. His participation will also give the army less of an excuse to impose martial law, neither retrospectively, nor over a wider area."

John glanced at Linda and Paco. Both of them appeared to be more reassured now they had seen the reaction of the Judge. Added to the way they had been treated by the Marshal and the way the deputies had relaxed, they were feeling more confident about a positive outcome. Linda smiled back at her husband. Paco's eyes matched John's without a flicker.

"Thank you," said John. "We'll take your advice."

"I'll set the trial proceedings to start tomorrow." Judge Forster was adamant. He looked at their slightly shocked faces. "Look, the more we delay, the more things can go wrong. I am an experienced Judge and Tom is an experienced lawman. We know the truth when it hits us. If I give the prosecution too long, Corrigan's men might concoct all sorts of stories. A short period will make it difficult for them to corroborate one another, without being tripped up under cross-examination. It also gives less time for the army to interfere if the officers are of a mind to intervene. It will also pre-empt any trouble being built up in the city. Tom and his team can do without that. You should prepare your defence evidence, marking the submitted documents you have already shown me. They will need to be shown to the Prosecution Counsel as well. The initial part of the trial will be to select a jury. You will be able to question and challenge individuals in advance as will the prosecution. I shouldn't be surprised if they will try to make it an all-white jury. So, think very carefully about the questions you ask of prospective jurors. Right, let's get moving." There was a spring in Judge Augustus' step as he departed. He was looking forward to this trial and proving to be an arbiter of justice in New Mexico.

Tom organised Hank to undertake the defence. He was pleased to be asked to handle the defence. He had already telegraphed the bare details back east; the Lawson company and its agents, the Santa Fe Bank regarding the deeds of ownership and his army contacts in Washington.

The news of the trial spread around Silver City like a wildfire. The interest was phenomenal and the speed of events took people by surprise. Judge Forster had not only organised the notices. He had already sent subpoena requests for the key witnesses, pre-empting them being chosen for jury service. This included all of the Ndee's friends and business associates, Corrigan's men and his business associates, Sergeant Jackson and his two troopers. A despatch rider was sent to Fort Bayard in case the telegraph lines failed.

Chapter Twenty-One

The opening session of the trial was set for 10:00 am next morning. The selection of the jury was the first issue. Irwin Stanton was the attorney for the prosecution, a dark-haired, angular-faced man with an aquiline nose on which he would perch reading glasses for close notes. The cut and thrust of the questions to the prospective candidates meant several were rejected by either Irwin or Hank. Eventually, the jury was settled at six white and six Hispanic citizens of New Mexico.

The courthouse was packed out, with people standing at the back and even some trying to hear from outside the open doors. Judge Forster brought down his gavel on the desk in front of him to set the scene.

"This is the trial on the charge of murder, that the three defendants, John Lawson, Linda Lawson and Paco Faraones, did individually or collectively, conspire to murder Herbert Corrigan, earlier in this month of May, 1867, in a box canyon off one of the tributaries of the Gila system."

"Hang the bastards," came a shout from the room. There was a murmur of approval.

The judge banged the desk again. "I will have no interference with the workings of the law. Anyone raising remarks like that again, will be arrested for contempt of court and fined $50 on the spot or a month in jail if they haven't got the money." The groans of dissent subsided immediately. "Now, I am telling you, the jury, you are to decide the outcome of this trial on the evidence laid before the court, not your own prejudices and not any hearsay from outside of these proceedings. You will also dismiss, when ordered, any unauthorised remarks, such as you just heard. When you are dismissed, to determine your judgement; you will elect a spokesman from amongst you, and he will speak on your behalf. Is that clear?" The jury nodded.

Augustus turned to the defendants, addressing each in turn. "I want a simple answer to the following question, either guilty or not guilty. Do you, (followed by the name), plead guilty or not guilty to the murder of Herbert Corrigan?"

All three entered the plea of 'not guilty'.

Augustus turned to Irvin. "May we hear the opening remarks for the prosecution? Remember to stick to the facts."

Irwin stood. "On 11th May, 1867, Herbert Corrigan and his men, accompanied by a troop of US cavalry, rode up the north-eastern tributary of the Gila River, to reclaim his land from squatting Apaches."

"Objection, on three counts." Hank was on his feet. "We have not established ownership rights, whether squatting was taking place and, finally, the use of the term 'Apache' is derogatory, as it means 'enemy'. For the purposes of the court, may we use the term 'Ndee', which is how this group of settlers, describe themselves."

"Objection sustained. Mr Stanton, I did ask you to stick to the facts. Jury, disregard the prosecution remarks."

Irwin was a little shaken to have been reprimanded so early. He quickly recovered his composure. "Mr Corrigan, and his party were going up this valley to reclaim ownership of property, for which he had deeds, purporting the land to belong to him." He paused, but there was no further intervention. "At the entrance to the box canyon, they were separated from the cavalry by a trellis fence, trapped at the head of the valley by another fence and, after a short gunfight, forced to surrender."

"Objection! There was no fight. Mr Corrigan's men panicked and started firing at shadows." Hank was forthright.

"Objection overruled, at this stage, until we have established the facts, one way or another." Judge Forster was being impartial.

Irwin Stanton felt he was on more confident ground.

"Corrigan's men were forced to leave their armaments, to depart from the valley without them, once the bottom fence was raised, leaving Corrigan behind in the trap. They could hear him being told to go to the head of the box canyon, round the bend and out of sight. The next thing they heard was the shot of him being murdered."

"Objection!" Hank was furious.

"Sustained. Mr Stanton, I shall not warn you again. It is up to this court to decide the outcome of the murder, not you. Jury, please note, it will be up to you

187

to decide the issue of murder, after you have heard all the facts. Prosecutor, please rephrase your address and avoid inflammatory language." Augustus was in his element.

"After the shot, Sergeant Jackson was requested by one of the defendants to come up the valley with two of his troopers, wearing only their side arms, buttoned down. Later, they returned with Mr Corrigan's body, tied to his horse. The party returned to Silver City, reported to the authorities and the coroner, and the cavalry returned to report at Fort Bayard." Irwin concluded his opening statement.

Hank's opening statement was longer, more detailed on the facts. He explained.

"John Lawson had come to New Mexico, in search of a cure for his consumption. He had been found by Paco, alone and ill, in the desert, and with the skills of Linda, now his wife, appeared to have made a full recovery from the disease. To repay the Ndee, who could not own property under New Mexico law, he had purchased the land in the name of his family company and established a ranch, as they named it, in the Shis-Inday valley. This was done legally, all dues had been paid, the land surveyed by me, the deeds drawn up, registered with the New Mexico land office. The documents had the official seal of the territory and the original copy kept in the safekeeping of the Bank of Santa Fe. The Ndee had been nomadic, despite the fact that they were largely agricultural. They spent winter, further south, nearer to, or over, the Mexico border. John had suggested that they settled in the summer location as a fixed residence, constructing better dwellings to overcome the winter. The Ndee were to be employees of the American arm of the Lawson company. This is no different to those employed as scouts to the army, those on the railways, or the ones employed as cowboys. Indeed, Mezcaleros, the Ndee, are renowned for their ability with horses. The terrain and the valley are most suitable for horse ranching. The plan was to develop the ranch and trade with the growing population of New Mexico."

Hank paused to take in a sip of water. He took the opportunity to look round the room and to see these, hard, bitten men, totally enthralled by his story. Even Irwin Stanton found no reason to raise objections and was equally engaged with the story.

"The army has been trying to remove all of the Apache from New Mexico. When Mr Corrigan approached them with his claims to the land, this was an opportunity seen as too good to be lost. As a consequence, the officers at Fort

Bayard sent a troop under Sergeant Jackson to accompany Mr Corrigan on his quest. Following that, the defence is broadly in agreement with the prosecution. The fence trap was set to separate Corrigan and his men, simply because they had insisted that the cavalry followed behind them." Hank was clever enough to not say, 'making them eat dirt', but his inference was not lost on the listening audience. Irwin Stanton could not raise an objection.

"Once the trap had been sprung, it was Corrigan's men who were firing at shadows. My clients insist that there was no return fire. Once the call had been made to lay down their arms, Corrigan's men were told to leave the valley, the gate was raised and Mr Corrigan was left alone. He was asked, by the defendant, John Lawson, to go to the top of the valley, to present his documentation to Mr Lawson himself and, if shown to be genuine, every trespasser would depart his land. The top fence was raised to allow Mr Corrigan through to meet the three defendants. Mr Lawson left his horse and weapon with his wife, walking forward to see Mr Corrigan. There was an exchange in which both parties showed their deeds to one another."

Hank was awaiting an objection, but none came. "The defence maintains that it was clear that Mr Corrigan's deeds were invalid and there was no seal of approval from the New Mexico Territory. I am told, at that point, the defendant Mr Lawson turned to walk back to the other defendants. Apparently, Mr Corrigan had secreted a derringer on his person. He is alleged to have taken it out in an attempt to shoot Mr Lawson in the back."

"Objection! This is an assumption based on hearsay."

"Sustained. The jury is to disregard defence counsel's last remark."

Hank was nonplussed. "Mrs Lawson perceived that Mr Corrigan was drawing his gun behind her husband's back. She screamed and shouted a warning as she fired John Lawson's gun, killing Mr Corrigan in the process."

"Objection! That version of what happened is unproven."

The Judge was more ambivalent. "I'll neither sustain nor overrule your objection, Mr Stanton. However, I must impress on the jury that they must weigh up the testimonial evidence of witnesses, not the statements of either counsel."

Hank concluded. "The follow-up is much as my Learned Counsel for the Prosecution has outlined. Mr Faraones returned to the top of the canyon to ask Sergeant Jackson to come to the top of the valley with two of his troopers. They were debriefed on the events by the three defendants, returning with Mr Corrigan's body and his horse, bringing them back to Silver City."

"Thank you, counsels, for your opening statements. I shall now ask the prosecution to present their case. I appreciate, that with the speed I arranged this hearing, not all of the witnesses have responded to the subpoenas at this stage. We shall proceed with the available witnesses and allow for some testimonies to be out of sequence. The counsels will be able to re-address any imbalance with their closing statements. I hope that is clear to all parties and the jury." Judge Forster reinforced who was in charge.

The Prosecution case started with the assertion that Mr Corrigan was reclaiming his ownership of the land. This was immediately challenged by Hank as invalid as the document submitted, was not recognised nor approved by New Mexico Territory. The witnesses to the events of what had happened at the canyon were proving to be unreliable. They could give no reasonable explanation as to why, in their words, having been 'fired upon', not one of them had been injured, even in the slightest, and how they were deprived of their weapons. On cross-examination by Hank, not one of Corrigan's men was able to say that they had witnessed his killing.

Sergeant Jackson and Privates Freeman and Woodstock had not responded to the subpoenas at this stage. With such short notice, there was the question of them travelling back to Silver City for the trial. Judge Forster was concerned that the army would try to block his request although, to be fair, there weren't any negative vibes to date. He decided to call an end to the day's proceedings and to reconvene at 10:00 am the next day.

To the immense delight of the three defendants, Sergeant Jackson and his two troopers arrived in Silver City soon after dawn. Their testimonies were exactly in line with the true events. Any disparaging remarks, towards the Buffalo Soldiers, were silenced by Judge Forster, with the reminder of his power to fine or imprison offenders for contempt of court. Between them, Irwin Stanton and Hank Warren, with their questioning and cross-examination, elicited the facts. In particular, none of the three cavalrymen had witnessed the actual killing. They were released from their court summons and allowed to return to their duties at Fort Bayard.

Unbeknown to the court, behind the scenes, Hank's dispositions back to the East and George's submissions to the authorities in Washington, had jointly proved to be decisive. A replacement officer corps had been despatched to take over at Fort Bayard. The existing team were to go back east in disgrace, rather than as the reward, for which this reassignment would normally be seen. The army was working in conjunction with the civil authorities rather than against them. The experiment, with the Lawson Ranch, was being viewed as a positive response to quell lawlessness in the territory. The only sign, of this change, was that the three troopers appeared to be easier in their minds, less tense and knowledgeable in that they had the support and respect of their new officers.

That ended the case for the prosecution.

The defence opened with Hank calling John to testify. Everyone in the court was agog as he reiterated the reasons for his coming to New Mexico, the perils of his journey, even though he, deliberately, omitted the sea battle and the exact circumstances of his meeting Paco for the first time.

Irwin Stanton asked the Judge whether all this testimony was relevant to the case. Hank asked the Judge to forbear with the line of questions as the relevance was about to be clear. Augustus Forster asked him to continue, on the proviso that the justification was to soon be apparent.

Hank continued. "So John, when Paco found you, ill, in the desert, he brought you back to his band in their Summer camp."

John carried on his story. "That is the case, although I do not recall the details of the journey. I awoke in a tipi, slowly being nursed back to health. That is how I met Linda," He looked at her and smiled, lovingly. "We fell in love and married once I became better, just before the winter migration."

"What happened next and how does this have a bearing on the case?" Hank was becoming aware of the impatience in the court.

"Once in the new location, I conducted enquiries, in the nearest town, about land ownership. I was aware that Mezcaleros, the Ndee, were not allowed to purchase land in New Mexico. I found out, very quickly, as a homesteader, I'd have needed to have worked a claim for five years and to be aged twenty-one. However, company law transgressed all the obstacles. I persuaded the elders that we would be better settled in the summer territory, constructing more permanent residences to overcome the winter conditions. My family company would purchase the land, protecting it right up to the watershed, so it couldn't be ruined by pollution from mining, or other activities, upstream. We registered our intentions at the New Mexico Territory land office, here in Silver City, with Mr Delgado. In turn, he hired you, Mr Warren, to carry out the necessary land survey. The company bought the land, the deeds were formally endorsed with the seal of the New Mexico Territory. We placed the first copy with the Bank of Santa Fe, for safekeeping and kept our own copy to show the court."

191

The deeds were shown to the court and the jury. Even to the inexperienced or illiterate eye, it was clear that the Lawson Ranch copy was a genuine document.

Hank reinforced the point. "I'll call on Luis Delgado, from the Territory Land Office to confirm this in his testimony. Mr Lawson, may we please move to the events immediately before Mr Corrigan's demise? How did you react to his approach?"

John responded. "The ranch extends from the source of the Shis-Inday river, to the confluence with the Gila system, and the watersheds on either side of the river. We had farmed a more fertile area downstream, last Summer. That was our main living community with the horse ranch near the box canyon. It is a perfect location in which to drive, trap and capture wild horses which live in the area. However, it was clear that despite our legal tenure, the army were trying to move us out, on the pretext of confining the nomadic Apache tribes. This was clear from our first meeting with Sergeant Jackson and his troop, last year. Despite the proof we showed him at the time, it was obvious that his officers did not concur. I understand that he was nearly cashiered for not removing us from the land."

"Objection!" Irwin Stanton was on his feet. "This is pure supposition on the part of the defendant."

"I must agree," Judge Forster confirmed. "The defendant is to stick to the facts, not voice opinions. The jury is to disregard his last remark."

John felt a little smug that he had made his point, but he had been brought back down to earth by the Judge's rebuke.

Hank stepped back in. "Please confine your testimony to the events leading up to Mr Corrigan's visit with his men and the army patrol."

"We have always posted scouts on the higher ground surrounding the Shis-Inday valley. We have a system of signals to relay what is happening back to the village. This gives us time to plan our defence. As the village is now above the box canyon, the only easy approach is up the valley. The look-outs reported back that the visitors were approaching in two groups. Mr Corrigan's men were out front, followed by the cavalry, a short distance behind." John did not say that there was so much disregard for the Buffalo Soldiers, that they were being made to eat dirt.

However, the intonation was overt, not lost on the jury, and not opined so that Irwin Stanton could object. Hank Warren was quietly pleased that John had expressed this so well. Judge Forster gave John a steely look, but he did not intervene.

John continued. "That gave us the opportunity to lay the trap as they entered the box canyon. We separated the first group from the soldiers by dropping the bottom fence between them. There was no way the army could intervene. At the same time, we dropped the fence at the top end of the box. Mr Corrigan and his men were caged in. They started firing indiscriminately. Our people were under strict orders not to return fire."

"Objection!" shouted a rather deflated Irwin Stanton.

"On what grounds?" asked the Judge. "It has already been established that not one of Corrigan's men was injured in the slightest. This seems to confirm that they did not receive incoming fire. I overrule your objection. Will the defendant please continue?"

John did. "Once the firing had died down, I shouted down to Corrigan to disarm himself and to get his men to surrender their arms at a visible point of the valley. They were then to return to the fence. I also shouted down to Sergeant Jackson not to try to interfere as we wished no harm to come to him nor to his men. He confirmed that earlier in his testimony under cross-examination. I asked Corrigan to meet us at the head of the canyon and to present his proof to us, in person. We released his men and their horses by raising the fence, allowing them to rejoin the soldiers, but without their weapons. As requested, the troopers did not intervene. The three of us, Linda, Paco and I, rode up the rim and down to the second fence at the top of the canyon. We met Mr Corrigan there and ordered the fence to be raised. I left my rifle with Linda and my horse with Paco and walked forward, unarmed, to meet Mr Corrigan, personally. We shared the respective deeds the court has already seen. It was obvious to me that his paperwork was not valid and I told him as much. With that, I told him to go home, turned and walked back up the valley to Linda and Paco." John turned his gaze to his wife before continuing.

"It was at that point, that Linda screamed, a shot was fired, by her, using my rifle, and Mr Corrigan was killed. Linda shouted that he had drawn a gun and was about to shoot me. We found the derringer by his fallen body."

Hank passed round the gun which had the initials HC, carved neatly into the butt.

John carried on. "I asked Paco to ride back to the top of the canyon, to explain to our people what had happened, and to ask Sergeant Jackson and two of his troopers to come up the valley to meet us. We knew that everyone would have heard the shot and there would be some consternation. In the meantime, I was comforting my wife, who was highly distraught, as well as thanking her for saving my life. Paco returned, just as the soldiers were allowed through the second fence. We explained to them what had happened and asked them to take Mr Corrigan's body and his horse back down to Silver City. We also told Sergeant Jackson that we would come in and submit ourselves to the legal authorities, as soon as we were able. For example, we had to ensure that our baby, Marianna, was able to receive the necessary care. That concludes my testimony."

Judge Forster turned to Prosecutor Stanton. "Do you wish the cross-examine the defendant, on his witness statement?"

Irwin Stanton rose. If he was to make an impression on the jury, he had to discredit John.

"Thank you." He spoke calmly and then turned his attention to the jury. "Gentlemen, I have never heard such a load of old 'horse-s**t in my life." There was a snigger of laughter in the court.

Hank jumped up to object.

Judge Forster calmed him with his hand and was most adamant. "Mr Stanton, I have warned you before. Firstly, I shall have no profanity in my court. Secondly, your job is to ask questions to challenge testimony and elicit the facts. Thirdly, you are not in this court to express your opinion, in trying to influence the jury. Is that absolutely clear? Now, ask your questions of the witness."

The Prosecutor showed no chagrin, nor did he apologise to the Judge, or to the court.

"I put it to you, Mr Lawson, that the last part of your testimony is pure fabrication. Isn't the truth that you lured Mr Corrigan, up the valley, out of sight of his men and the army, so that you could murder him at will?"

Hank objected, but Judge Forster overruled him this time. "I think the witness should answer the question."

John chose his words carefully. "Mr Stanton, I have told you the truth. I walked unarmed to meet Mr Corrigan. Maybe I was naive in thinking he had ditched all his weapons, with those of his men, further down the canyon. Luckily, for me, my wife was more alert and also a good shot. The proof was his gun lying next to his body."

The Prosecutor also voiced his next question in a probing way. "How does the court know that you didn't race down the canyon, find the weapon, race back and place it by the body, before calling for the cavalry detachment?"

"You don't know that," said John. "I put it to you that we didn't have the time and we would have needed considerable luck to have discovered a weapon with Mr Corrigan's initials carved into the butt."

Irwin Stanton realised he was unlikely to get John to incriminate himself or the other defendants, easily. "No further questions."

"You may step down," directed the Judge. "Mr Warren, please call your next witness."

Hank called on Linda to take the stand. Her testimony was not as fluent as John's had been. However, she held her own, impressively, showing a considerable, inner-strength, to fend off the Prosecution Counsel, especially as English was only a recently acquired language. Paco did likewise. As the three defendants had shown such consistency in their stories, Irwin Stanton was not able to break them.

It was close to the end of the second day of the trial. Augustus Forster decided to adjourn for the day. "I shall ask both counsels to give their closing statements in the morning. Following that, I shall give my closing summary and address the jury. May I remind all members of the jury, you are not to discuss this trial with one another nor with any third parties. Your turn will come when I direct you after my final statement tomorrow. Any transgression will result in instant dismissal from the jury, a fine for contempt of court and the loss of all payment for undertaking jury service. I trust that is abundantly clear."

He brought down the gavel to end the day's proceedings.

Hank met up with the defendants back at the cell. Linda and Paco had no experience of trials and were anxious.

Paco broke the question. "How do you think we are doing, my friend? Do you think that the jury believes us?"

Hank was his usual smiling self. "I think you acquitted yourselves impeccably." His beam broadened at Linda and she responded with a beautiful smile of her own. "Linda, you backed up John's testimony, wonderfully well. Paco, you did likewise." Paco also smiled as Hank continued.

"The judge was very fair and, even when he rebuked me, he was even-handed. He has kept the court under a tight rein and maintained an excellent balance. He is trying hard to establish the facts and to stick to them. He is also not allowing bias and prejudiced opinions to come to the fore. The proven facts are in our favour; the ownership of the land and the New Mexico Territory seal against an unregistered and poorly drawn-up set of deeds. The weakest fact is the lack of third-party witnesses to the shooting of Corrigan. The fact that his gun was monogrammed is a big plus, but it doesn't prove self-defence, especially as it wasn't fired."

Hank permitted himself a little laugh. "Linda, I am not suggesting you should have let Corrigan shoot John first." Linda looked horrified, while John and Paco both grinned a little. "I am just saying, if I were a prosecution lawyer, that is the only seed of doubt, I should raise with the jury."

Linda put the question they were all considering. "Hank, who do you think the jury is going to believe?"

"We have all been watching them as the trial progressed. I think that they were most taken by John's faultless testimony and the way he responded to the Prosecutor's cross-examination. The polite, honest and quiet answers, seemed to be very well received. The answer to the Prosecutor's surmise, about Corrigan's gun, was crucial. But, John's counter, not that this was false, but that time to retrieve the weapon, luck in finding it among the pile of discarded guns and having Corrigan's initials, were all too much of a coincidence to be plausible."

Juanita arrived with food and drinks for them all. The cantina had been shut while the trial was on. She and her family wanted to be in court and the number of customers would have been very low, anyway. She was allowed to kiss Paco, sit with him and cuddle. The deputies were relaxed with this group of prisoners and more watchful of reaction, outside of the Marshal' office, in the city.

When Hank and Juanita departed, the trio settled down for the night, as best as they could, given the circumstances.

Chapter Twenty-Two

The dawn broke for the last day of the trial. It was already hot and sultry. Linda, Paco and John were quiet but apprehensive. John held Linda's hand firmly. His love for her was confirmed but it also betrayed his anxiety. Paco maintained an impassive, steely bearing, in the true tradition of the Mescalero, he was.

Juanita arrived with a breakfast for the prisoners and the guards. It was a wonderful break to the tedium of the wait. The shadows, around her eyes, showed she had not slept well. Nonetheless, she managed to give Paco a beautiful smile and a loving kiss, with a long embrace. They ate, sparsely and slowly. No one had any real appetite but they needed to eat and drink something, in preparation for the day.

The court proceedings began at 10:00 am. The Judge called on the Prosecutor to deliver his closing statement. Irwin Stanton delivered the facts as he perceived them. He did not mention the conflict of the deeds. He only stated that Mr Corrigan believed he had a right to this land. The court listened, intently, to the part in which Corrigan had walked, alone, up the valley, to meet the three defendants.

"At that point, we have only the words of the three defendants, to ascertain what really occurred. Gentlemen of the jury, you must decide the balance of the truth because Mr Corrigan is not able to present his side of the story. Did the defendant, Mr Lawson, really walk down the valley, unarmed, to meet him? Had Mr Corrigan secreted his weapon upon him? Did he produce it to fire upon Mr Lawson as he walked back up the valley? Was Mrs Lawson so quick, capable and accurate, with that heavy Spencer rifle, that she could down him before he could fire?"

Linda was incensed. Nobody had challenged the Prosecutor during his statement, which would have been Hank's prerogative. She jumped to her feet and shouted.

"Take me outside with you, in the street, give me the rifle and I'll show you how good, quick and accurate a shot I am!"

There was laughter, and a relief of tension in the court, as everyone responded to the feisty response of this small, beautiful girl.

Judge Forster banged his gavel. "Mrs Lawson. Sit down. As this is the first time you have offended the court, I shall only warn you, along with everyone else, about contempt. Any more interruptions and I shall not be so lenient." He was trying hard not to smile, himself. "Carry on, Mr Stanton."

The Prosecutor continued. "Perhaps, the jury might like to consider an alternative scenario. Having separated Mr Corrigan from his bodyguard, the defendants lured him to his place of execution and he was killed by either of the two men. He was unarmed, they raced down the canyon to retrieve his firearm, before calling the troopers through and concocting this story. Maybe, they thought, you'd show more pity or mercy if the defendant was a woman."

Hank jumped to his feet, but he managed to keep his temper under control. "I must object most vehemently."

Augustus Forster was even more forceful. "Sustained! I shall remind the Prosecuting Counsel that it is his role to lay out the facts in his closing statement. It is not his role to surmise on possibilities nor on unproven motives, when he doesn't have the facts to support them. I warn the jury, you are to disregard the final remarks of the Prosecutor. They are purely, suggestive opinions." He gave them a hard stare to reinforce his point.

Irwin Stanton chose his final remarks more carefully. "I should like the jury to consider what motive Mr Corrigan had, in trying to kill Mr Lawson, as it is claimed. Even if he had succeeded, how would he have escaped?"

Hank objected again. "It is not for any of us to determine Mr Corrigan's state of mind at that precise moment."

There was a pregnant pause. The Judge replied in an even-handed way. "While I agree that it is not up to us to question the balance of Mr Corrigan's mind, it is an intriguing point. My ruling is that I wish everyone to consider, only, the facts as we have them. Mr Stanton, have you concluded your closing statement?"

"I have, thank you."

"I shall now call on the Defence Counsel to give his closing statement."

Hank stuck to the facts in reiterating the story. His final words were these. "Whatever motivation the jury ascribes to Mr Corrigan's actions or his state of mind, the verdict of the court must be made on the basis of the known facts."

"Thank you, Counsel," said the Judge. "I should like to point out that your final remark is the prerogative of my role, not that of the defence. I shall now sum up. The facts of this case are largely undisputed. Those that are challenged are as follows. It is up to the jury to weigh up the balance of evidence. Did Mr Corrigan's men come under incoming fire, in the box canyon? If so, how come there were no casualties, even of a minor nature? Was it Mrs Lawson who fired the fatal shot? Did she do this to protect her husband? Did Mr Corrigan hide his weapon? Is it likely that the three defendants conspired to shoot Mr Corrigan where there were no other witnesses?" He paused for breath and a sip of water.

"If so, and he was unarmed, was it realistic that they could have retrieved a monogrammed weapon from a pile of discarded armaments, prior to calling the troopers up the valley? However clever the defendants are, do you consider this version of events too contrived to be realistic? Conversely, having seen the deeds of ownership, do you think that the defendants had every right to defend it from usurpers? After all, that is one of the bases of American law. Gentlemen of the jury, please retire to consider your verdicts. I should like you to return a unanimous result."

The jury departed.

The waiting appeared interminable. The tension in the court was becomingly more and more unbearable. The defendants were becoming increasingly nervous. Hank's smile was now a constant frown. Augustus Forster was getting irritated. Only Irwin Stanton was relaxed, in the belief that his actions had exacerbated any doubts, lingering in the minds of the jury.

The Judge ordered the jury back into the court.

"Have you reached any unanimous verdicts on the indictments in front of you?"

"No," was the reply.

Augustus Forster was infuriated. "Well, have you reached a majority verdict on any of the counts?"

The foreman hesitated, then looked along the line of the jury. "We have majority verdicts for them all."

"And what is the scoring?" enquired the Judge.

"It is 10-2 on every count," said the foreman.

"I shall accept that." Augustus was exasperated with this long-drawn out process. "On the charge of murder against Mr Lawson, how do you find the defendant?"

"Not guilty."

"On the charge of murder against Mrs Lawson, how do you find the defendant?"

"Not guilty."

"On the charge of murder against Mr Faraones, how do you find the defendant?"

"Not guilty."

There was a cheer from the court, although it was not universal.

The judge brought down his gavel to restore order.

He turned to the defendants. "You have been found not guilty and, Lady and you Gentlemen, you are to be released from custody, with immediate effect."

Turning to the jury, he said. "I am surprised at the length of time it took you to come to a decision and, albeit, only a majority one. I can only think that some of you," he stared intently at them, "were swayed by the Prosecution Counsel's gift of eloquence and you didn't focus on the facts. Nevertheless, I must thank you for your deliberations. To be paid for your services, please come to my office, immediately the trial is adjourned." He brought down the gavel for the last time.

John grabbed Linda and kissed and hugged her closely. Juanita ran from the court to do the same with Paco. There were embraces for Hank and Luis as well. The acquitted trio thanked Tom Holland and his deputies for their courtesy and fairness. They didn't forget to praise Augustus Forster for his open and fair handling of the case. They even acknowledged, how professionally, Irwin Stanton had conducted the prosecution.

Hank suggested that they decamped to Luis' home to get cleaned up. Juanita had to return to the cantina which would now be packed. The celebratory meal could come when all the friends could get together, later.

John was thinking about friends and family. "We must telegraph the outcome to my father, mother, company, agents, Bank of Santa Fe and, not least, Sergeant Jackson, Privates Freeman and Woodstock."

Hank concurred, adding his army contacts back east, who also needed to know the impact of their changes to Fort Bayard.

While Paco and his sister went back with Luis, to get cleaned and change clothing, John and Hank went to Telegraph Office to despatch their messages.

The city was back to normal with the trial over. There was a surrealistic air of anti-climax, almost disappointment. Corrigan had not been a model citizen nor a well-liked man. There was no animosity towards those who had been acquitted. The wiser heads, amongst Corrigan's men, realised they had been spared. They had suffered the ignominy of losing their weapons, but not the ultimate fate of losing their lives. These sentiments overcame any hot-headed feelings of revenge.

The friends were able to get cleaned up and rested before everyone convened at the cantina at the express request of Senor Zapatero.

He spoke to the group, addressing his opening remarks to Linda and John, in particular. "Congratulations on winning the case. This will mean so much to the different cultures of people in Silver City. We know that you will be anxious to get back, to see your baby daughter and the rest of your wider family. However, first, you will need to eat, drink and rest properly."

Paco was the one to answer. "We want to thank all of you for your support. I hope this is going to enable us all to have more settled lives and less trouble."

There was a murmur of agreement from the assembled guests, followed by celebratory drinks of various sorts.

John invited Senor and Senora Zapatero to come to visit them when they could get cover for the cantina. Before they could reply, Paco stepped in.

"Senor, may I have the honour of asking for your daughter's hand? If both you and she agree, could we double your visit with a Mescalero wedding?"

Juanita took the answer out of her parent's mouth. "Oh, Papa, Mama, that would be wonderful." She gave Paco a huge kiss, saying, "Yes please; thank you."

The wind had rather been taken out of her parents' sails. But, it was clear, from their beaming smiles, they were delighted. This called for another round of drinks and a toast to the happy couple. Linda put her arms around Juanita, kissed her, and said, "Sister, welcome to the Ndee and the Faraones family."

It was a heady mixture of excitement and exhaustion that night. Nobody slept brilliantly. However, John, Linda and Paco were anxious to return home for all the various, happy reasons. They had organised everything by mid-morning. Despite what had occurred, there was no complacency on the way back. They took their usual precautions, arriving safely on the second evening.

Epilogue

The repercussions of the trial were profound. Several cases were brought before Judge Forster, in which people reclaimed lands or holdings, wrongly acquired by Corrigan. Many of these were mining rights. The professionalism of the army improved. George's and Hank's dispositions, back east, had not been wasted. The troubles with the Apache, continued for some years but these were mostly confined to the south and west of the territory. The Lawson Ranch continued to develop and prosper.

George and Ann returned from the east, soon after the trial. They were incredibly pleased to be in time for the wedding of Juanita and Paco, especially as they had not experienced Linda and John's nuptials.

As time went on, the Lawson Line was sold to a multi-national shipping organisation. The ranch remained a separate entity in which generations of Lawson's and Faraones thrived. The families were to see the highs and lows of human life, joy and tragedy. Those are the stories of their descendants.

John lived until 1935, when he was 86. His headstone has the engraving of a white cougar. Linda became the matriarch of the family and died, aged 93 in 1944. They are buried alongside one another at the top of the canyon. Paco and Juanita also had long happy lives, their graves alongside their sister and brother-in-law.

Today, the Lawson Ranch is an integral part of the Gila Mountain National Park. It is still a working ranch, but now very much a tourist attraction with activities for the visitors. There is a museum, dedicated to the history of the Mescalero people. The horses form a major part of the appeal. People can ride the trails and be given guided tours of the fauna and flora of the area. Several Lawsons and Faraones still run the ranch and are proud of their heritage.

John's plea to the Ndee, not to sacrifice their lives in a futile gesture of honour, have borne fruit. There remains a great legacy and history for the Mescalero people.

CPSIA information can be obtained
at www.ICGtesting.com
Printed in the USA
LVHW022107260422
717291LV00010B/379